Kingdoms of Parvery Collection

First book

THE SURVIVOR

by

Rowena Redman

Illustrated by Ginevra Giammatteo

To request permissions, contact the author through her website:
www.redmanbooks.com
ISBN 9798848706659

First paperback edition August 2022

Edited by Rachel Redman
Cover art, illustrations and layout by Ginevra Giammatteo

THE SURVIVOR

Author Notes

As I child I was read to well past the normal age of being read to. To this day reading a book, any book is a struggle for me as I am dyslexic. However, my love of books is as deeply ingrained in my character as my dyslexic traits. My parents taught me never to allow my dyslexia to hold me back and to be proud. My parent knew more about dyslexia than most as they publish and sell special needs books for a living. They always helped me as such my mother would read me the childhood classics. I grew up listening to Peter Rabbit, Heidi and Anne of Green Gables. As I grew older my parents bought me audiobooks, I would listen to Catherine Fisher's oracle series and Series of unfortunate Events on cassette tape then CDs as the later books came out. Audiobooks were something of a miracle for me as I learn best by listening. As I listen books truly came alive for me.

I still did and do read and am also a huge re-read because each time I read a book I often discover new facets of understanding. Jonathan Stroud's Bartimaeus trilogy is probably the book I have read more times than any other with Harry Potter making a close second. Birthday and Christmas gifts were always the full audio collection of Jane Austen or Little Women. Now I have an audible membership and my library grows monthly. Audiobooks have allowed me as an adult to enjoy complex reads that I never would as been able to grasp and enjoy as actual books. Such as George R.R Martin's Song of Ice and Fire and the Expanse series. I will never stop reading or buying actual books but just like Shakespeare's plays are meant to be performed for me books are meant to be listened to.

My love of making up stories is another practice that dates back to my childhood but it was not till many years later that I began to write down some of the stories in my head. My passion for storytelling took me to Bolton University where I studied creative writing. There I learn the technique and discipline required for my craft. However, they were not truly put to use until the idea for Kingdoms for Parvery came to me. I have filled notebooks, drawn sketches, invented names and places, built a whole world and most important written daily to complete this work. This first book has been redrafted, edited and checked multiple times and I am in the process of doing the same for the other books that will follow in this collection.

I can't remember the precise moment in the last three years that I decided this book has to be published but so much work and time has gone into it that I couldn't leave it just sitting on my hard drive. The book has blossomed into so much more than I could have hoped for when I first began designing its structure. It's a work I am incredibly proud of and look forward to continuing. I hope your readers will love it too and be eager for more or at least respect the attempt even if it isn't your cup of tea. My final remark to you would be reader a quote by William Faulkner.

"Get it down. Take chances. It may be bad, but it's the only way you can do anything really good."

I dedicate this book to my editor, supporter, first reader and mother. Without you, this book would not be possible. I would also like to thank my Illustrator Ginevra for helping me create such beautiful artwork for the book.

CHAPTER 1

The inky blue-black sky began to lighten into a cold bright blue. It touched the wooden thatched houses and lit the empty-stalled market. Its pale glare woke sleeping animals and snuck into vegetable gardens plucked completely bare. The light seemed to reach everywhere but the dark, thick forest. The pines and cedars that engulfed the Kingdom of Twickerth could grow to over 60 feet; these trees were both prized and uprooted, as wood was the industry of the kingdom. However, the cutters were careful with their felling, the tree must be allowed to re-grow less the wood and work disappear. 'The tree may be cut but the forest must remain' was the common saying. This wood would soon be felled again but for now these tall trees provided a line of cover surrounding their target, the village of Twickgrove.

"Dawn has come and soon they will all awake." The speaker was tall, with a bald head and dark skin. He was dressed in simple black cloth and black leather with no armour other than a mail vest and crude pot helm. It was no different for most of the company of men he had joined, poorly fitted out for the work ahead, unlike the leaders. The company had been created by five leaders and these men were known as the five heads. The purpose of the company was simple: they were swords for hire, usually hired for distasteful work.

The dark-skinned man had been granted the rank of second commander, which meant only the commanders and leaders were above him, but it also placed him in the front line. Just to the left of him were the five leaders of the company, who were in front only because of their rank and not because they would be in the thick of the fight. The leaders were a mixture of men; short, tall, white, dark, fat and thin, but all had an air of menace. Their garb was similar, black and simple, but the five heads also wore finer pieces of armour and even fine pieces of jewellery; this was their method of keeping their wealth close to their person. The dark man was new to the company, so had no such wealth to display. He had needed work and they had been recruiting fighters who weren't afraid of blood, and he had very little fear in his life at all. The conscription had gone well; an additional 20 or so men had been gathered to the company ranks. Each new recruit had been further tested in skill of arms and general intelligence. The results of this test determined their place and rank. As a son of a knight the dark man had gained rank but not respect. None of the new recruits were trusted, they would have to show their commitment first.

"A pointless statement," one of the nearby leaders barked back, responding to the dark-skinned man's words. This man was tall, with a square jaw and small sharp eyes and looked like a leader to the young, dark man.

"Perhaps, but it has poetry, Finish, that you can't deny." Finish was not the leader's true name but that was the only name he used. That was the way of the company, only nicknames were used, and each man guarded his true name as closely as he guarded his life. The nicknames were given to each new man by the other members of the company once they had drawn their first blood and earned it.

The dark man did not have a name yet, nor did the other newcomers, but the coming battle would create them, or kill them.

The leader, Finish, spat over the side of his horse.

"Pretty words hold no more weight than ugly ones," he spoke in a snarl.

"They will wake, but this will be their last sunrise." A nearby commander spoke in a greedy voice. His hair was long and matted, which had earned him the uninventive name of Tangle. Finish turned to look at the commander and tilted his head. This action instantly caused commander Tangle to salute and walk on. The dark man had read the same message in that unusual gaze, this was a conversation for the five heads alone. The leaders continued to discuss matters in low voices, ignoring the men and the men respectfully ignored the leaders in return.

"Waiting is thirsty work," a skinny man to the dark man's right said. He then pulled out a large flask and offered it round the men closest to him. The dark man didn't know the skinny man's nickname, if he had one yet, so he chose to refuse the drink but didn't discourage the others from accepting the offered flask. One man drunk repeatedly, swigging deeply at the liquid. The men around him laughed at his behaviour.

"Enough," Finish's voice rang out loud and clear. Silence fell instantly, the authority audible. "Soused men will die fast, we need our wits about us, our sober wits." Finish turned to another commander nearby. "Wisdom, make sure the lines are in perfect formation, no mistakes. We won't get a second chance at this." Commander Wisdom set off, riding his black and white patched horse, splattering mud on those behind him. Wisdom the dark man knew had been here sometime, the leaders had sent him ahead to gather knowledge of their target. His report had been very detailed, including that he had often spent his time here wet through. Their journey, too, had been slow and wet, the rain had plagued them since arriving in this land. A bad sign some men muttered, the dark skin man didn't care for talk of signs though and soon stopped the muttering.

All ten of the commanders were wandering the lines now, checking each man in turn. In total there were around ninety of them, the dark skin man had counted. The commanders looked to one another, nodded, and then saluted to the leaders. The company was ready.

"We should have gone already; throat slitting is nights' work," the fourth leader spoke out in a nervous spew. He was short and full of anger and for unknown reasons bore the nickname Frost.

"You lost this debate already, killing breeds chaos and we will embrace that chaos. We have the numbers and caution is not our purpose here." Finish spoke clearly and, not for the first time, the dark man wondered what their purpose was here. To deal death to all who lived and breathed in the village, that was all he had been told. It was all any of them seemed to know. He was intelligent enough to know it would be dangerous to ask more, the company did not trust him yet. He knew for a fact that the more seasoned members and leaders of the company had taken bets on which of the new recruits would be killed and which would run. For some reason he was a favourite for running by many of them, he couldn't fathom why. The dark man was not frightened or weak willed, he had long ago learned who he was. He was not a knight like the other men of his family, he didn't get to carry that honour. He carried death, that was what they said, and if he carried death why not deal it.

They waited until the sun was high in the sky and the morning was well underway before moving.

"We need the people out of their homes where we can reach them," the first leader had insisted. "Raiding house to house is too slow." So once the market was open and the village was fully awake, they fell upon its people. The cobbles of the village ran red with the

thick blood and the sound of screams echoed from every house and street. Some of the villages fought back, some were armed, some found crude weapons and others used their fists. It made no difference, in the end they died just the same. The company losses were few, but there were losses, as predicted, not that the commanders cared unless they lost their bets. When the work was done Finish arrived to finish those who were still dying. The dark-skinned man did not baulk, just as he knew he wouldn't, he stood and watched as Finish did his work. Then he felt something grab his ankle and raised his sword. He looked down on a fallen man clutching a young child, probably his son. The boy was already dead, his head a red ruin, but the man had slow-bleeding wounds. One shallow wound to the gut, two deep gashes along his legs and a small shallow cut to his head. But it was the look in his eyes, a deaden hollow look that held the dark man's attention.

"Mercy, please, show mercy, please," the father cried out, pleading. The dark man crouched down to look at him.

"Leave him, I will come to him shortly if he doesn't do me the favour of dying first," Finish barked at the dark man. The dark man said nothing. He put his sword away and instead pulled his knife and slid it right into the man's heart.

"That's all the mercy I have," he said, not sure if he meant the words as an offering or an apology. When he stood up Finish was standing over him.

"There you go, that's your name earned, 'Mercy' it is."

"Mercy," the dark man repeated, "seems fitting."

"Just don't make a habit of it." The dark man, now named Mercy, nodded to Finish in acceptance.

The men moved off in separate directions after this, Mercy without aim, Finish to find more dying. Mercy was heading south towards the border line which was marked by a small band of trees and a thin wooden fence. He wasn't sure why he was moving this way, there were barely any bodies or buildings here to check. Still his feet moved until he reached the fence, he stopped there a moment knowing he couldn't linger long. They would need to be gone soon, they could not waste time, still he lingered. At first, he didn't know what he was looking at, but something in the trees ahead caught his attention and held it. As he stared, he spotted movement. It was slow and darting, a flickering in and out of the trees, someone was out there. He stared a while longer and made out that the fleeing figure was woman. The women had her back to him, her long light brown hair lay down her back, and she hid for a moment behind each tree before daring to move on. She was slow moving and that was clever, or he would have noticed her sooner. He knew he ought to call out or follow her, their orders had been clear, no one was to be left alive. But what did one woman matter. She was injured, he was fairly certain of that, something about the way she was moving. How far could she get, the villages of this kingdom were not close together and she had no supplies. She would not make it far. Mercy turned away and left, letting her continue her pointless escape.

When he returned to the village there appeared to be a loud argument happening.

"I told you, she'd be out in the streets." The first man was unknown to Mercy, fair and confident and young.

"We can't know that. We will have to search." The second man was the commander Tangle and he spoke in a rough, barking voice.

"And how do you suggest we search for some unknown woman?" the first, confident man asked. Mercy had a sinking feeling, so he left the arguing men and entered the house which seemed to be the centre of the debate. The small wooden home consisted of two rooms. The main room was set up as the cooking and eating space with a large inbuilt fire stove. Above this there was a raised platform built around the stone chimney which held the sleeping quarters. The other room was smaller, designed for sitting and resting. In this room lay the bodies of two men. One was another new company recruit Mercy recognised and the other was a clearly villager from his clothes. Next to the bodies were two wooden axes each engraved with a name, Kenneth Shepard and Kurten Shepard, Mercy read. Family heirlooms he guessed. It was clear the man had put up a fight, but he had had no experience fighting with axes. There was blood spray over all the chairs, a knitting and embroidery basket, small carved tables and a stand that held the only book in the room. The open pages held only a few drops of blood, but it was the ornate writing that intrigued him. He approached closer to read. It was a family book containing the names and details of all the relatives; the open pages held two names: Myra Rivers and Myrbeth Shepard. Mercy couldn't say what it was about the family home that interested him, perhaps it was because it had been so long since he had been welcomed into a home. He pocketed the book without further analysing the compulsion.

He moved back into the cooking room where the signs were of the house being hurriedly abandoned. A second door was wide open, and something was burning on the stove rack. It was clear a woman had lived in the house, too, and with these clues it wasn't hard to guess the sequence of events. The company had converged to fight the man, while the women escaped, and this caused the argument. He went back out of the house to tell what he knew; it was possible it wasn't the same women he saw but it seemed likely. However, when he got outside the argument was over and the men were being rounded up.

"We have lingered here too long; we need to depart now," commander Wisdom was yelling, and the other commanders were rousing the men that were looting the houses. So he shrugged and moved out with the others. What difference would one woman make after all?

CHAPTER 2

King Trevard Bardeves dressed in the colours of the season, gold and a deep brown-orange, in his royal chambers. He looked forward to the harvest festival feast every year, it was symbolic of the harmony of the nine kingdoms. How each of the kingdoms survived through the sharing of resources; this unity meant a great deal to King Trevard. He was the ruler of the smallest of the nine kingdoms, Hollthen, and he took his kingship very seriously. The queen entered from her private dressing room wearing a complementary dress of a gold fabric. She seemed sad, her light blue eyes were red and her face was pale and blotchy.

"My dear, why have you been crying?" Trevard asked.

"My bleeding has come again." Her voice was soft and reflected her heavy sadness. Her husband moved closer to her side and took her hands.

"I thought this anguish had passed now, we have our son, Citria."

"I know, I thought it would pass, too. We waited so many years for him, but I still have hopes for more. I thought now that I have borne one child, I would continue to do so but every month I fail once more," Citria's eyes filled with fresh tears.

"This is not a failure; you have provided an heir. Of course, I hope for more children and I'm sure we will have them but if not then we must learn to be contented and just love the son we have," Trevard wiped away his wife's tears. She nodded.

"Yes, you are right. It's just, growing up as part of a big family, I dreamed that one day I would have a big family of my own."

"I understand. Perhaps my experience as part of a smaller family guides my own feelings. My parents were only blessed with Tunora and myself."

"Just you and your sister," she nodded again. "My sisters just make this whole experience harder, they both have two children apiece. Rachel is younger than me and hasn't been married nearly as long and Barilsa writes she is soon to deliver her third." The moisture brimmed in her eyes again.

"Citria you must stop this. When you feel this way just hold Frederick close and know we are a family." Trevard was not very good at knowing what to say at times like this, he struggled with emotional connections, but he hoped this was helpful.

"Yes, we are a family, but it doesn't feel complete yet," she answered. Trevard decided to respect her feelings and stopped debating the point. Instead, he led her to collect their son and attend the feast.

The harvest festival feast was an honoured tradition throughout the Land of Parvery. As the weather grew colder and the nights grew darker all the crops grown in the land had ripened. Once collected all the food was shared between the nine lands of the country. To mark this annual day of joy and celebration all provisions were shared. Wagons of each kingdom's bounty went between all nine kingdoms as signs of fidelity and hope for the year to come. Each king hosted a large feast where all were welcome to honour the occasion. It was a chance for commoners, lords, ladies, paupers and royalty to all share bread together. Hollthen was not a farming kingdom by trade, though they did have a few small fields for corn and wheat. Some of the populace kept livestock but the main source of food was fish and other seafood. The king and queen hosted their feast in the large courtyard of the castle. As the sun set the white stone castle was reflected in shadow form. The three towers appeared taller and thinner whereas the main heart of the castle covered the whole width of the courtyard. The servants lit huge torch baskets making the shadows flicker and giving the illusion that the castle was moving. There were many grand tables serving food to all the people and more tables for seating. King Trevard was circling and talking to his guests, while Queen Citria remained at the royal table, holding their eight-month-old son, Prince Frederick.

The courtyard was packed and busy with happy guests. Noise and the smell of food filled the cool evening air, when suddenly a dappled horse was ridden into their midst. The horse was huffing and breathing heavily, its breath visible in the cool night air. Upon its back were two passengers, a man and a woman. The man's tall frame was shivering slightly, whereas the woman was slumped over the horse's neck wrapped in a thick fur-lined cloak that was so big it swamped her completely.

"We need assistance! Help, please!" the man yelled. People rushed towards them; the man was holding the women on the horse but surrendered her limp form when a guard reached him. It wasn't until they held her flat between two men that the bundle that she held close to her chest became visible.

"There is a child," one of the guards yelled. The queen had given her son to her nursemaid and rushed forward with her husband to handle the disturbance.

"Hand the child to me," she insisted. A third guard gently lifted the baby from the woman and handed it to the queen. The woman tried to lift and stretch her arms, but she was too weak to move;

she let out a just audible thin cry. The queen touched the woman's hand. "We will take good care of you both." The woman made an effort to try and speak but her throat was too dry, and she coughed hoarsely before she could manage a word.

"Myrbeth," her plea was desperate despite her weak voice. As a fellow mother Citria understood, it was crucial to her that her baby survived. "Myrbeth", the woman repeated, her voice growing fainter. She had no care for her own life only the baby's.

"Is that's your daughter's name?" The women gave a small nod, and the queen heard an unspoken plea. "We will keep her safe." The court physician had worked his way through the crowd of people and was now at the queen's side.

"Take them to my rooms," he ordered.

"Will they survive, Alexander?" asked Trevard.

"I will try my hardest to ensure they do, your Grace," the physician promised. At this the king nodded and left his men and his wife at the castle steps. The king turned to the man, who was shivering without his cloak.

"I'm ashamed to admit I don't know your name?"

"Yolis, Sire." Trevard called to a nearby servant.

"Howard, could you take Yolis to the long hall? Give him food, hot spiced wine and ensure a fire is lit. I will come and see you, Yolis, in a short time, after you have recovered."

Trevard stayed at the feast for a while longer trying to restore order and calm. It wasn't very successful though; all anyone could discuss was the one topic; what had happened to the riders and where did they come from? Finally, Trevard excused himself to find answers to those questions.

"Yolis, I hope you feel revived?" As the king entered, he thought again that Yolis's face looked very familiar, but he couldn't place him which was unusual.

"Yes, Sire, I'm most grateful."

"All are welcome under my roof. I need to ask how you came to be here, Yolis?"

"I came to deliver the reports, your Highness." He pulled a satchel from around his body and handed it to the king. Trevard recognised it straight away, it was leather and stamped with the royal crest of the Kingdom of Walsea. The identity of the man became clear.

"You are a scribe of King Emil; you regularly deliver the monthly reports from Walsea to my secretary or head scribe."

"Yes, your Highness, I apologise for my lateness, but the woman slowed me down considerably."

"So, you don't know her?"

"No, Sire."

"Then how did you come upon her?" The king asked. Yolis took a small sip of his wine before starting his tale.

"I left Walsea Palace in the early hours of the morning as I do every month, just me and Windwhistle, that's my horse. We were travelling up the Orchard Road when I saw the woman. She was in such a state, hair all matted, dirt over her face and arms, there was blood, too, but that had long dried. She also had badly blistered feet. We get vagrants from time to time trying to steal fruit from the trees, but she didn't seem to be trying to do that. In truth what really caught my attention was the babe, it was squalling and squirming. I have never heard such screeching and screaming, I defy any man to walk past that. When I moved closer to see if they were alright the women begged me to help, she said she needed to get to Hollthen urgently. They were so pitiful, and I was already going that way." he paused, seeming afraid that maybe that hadn't been the best decision.

"It was very good of you to offer such assistance, there are many who wouldn't have." Trevard reassured him. "So, you brought them to us, but forgive me, I don't see why you were delayed?"

"The baby, the little girl. We had started out and the mother was grateful for the chance to rest on the horse, exhausted she was, I think she had been walking a long time. The little girl just wouldn't stop crying though. We didn't get far before we had to stop. The mother hadn't been able to feed the poor babe, you see, that was why she was crying so much, she was hungry. I gave the mother what food I had but she only took the water, said she felt too sick for food. She drunk all my water just like that, I had to refill it in the river but after that she felt strong enough to feed the baby. I had to stop and wait; I didn't want to pry."

"I quite understand," Trevard agreed.

"The baby calmed after that and both her and the mother slept. I travelled at a slower speed, being careful not to disturb them. The mother woke up just as we rode into Hollthen and she was panicked, she was frantic, saying the babe had slept too long. She started screaming at me, so I rode as fast as I could, but it was dark and I didn't want Windwhistle to break a shoe." He sounded apologetic again.

"You have performed a great service," Trevard spoke in his most sincere voice. "I am most impressed, Yolis, and the mother and her child are greatly indebted to you. I will be recommending to King Emil that he award you with a commendation of some kind."

"Thank you, your Grace." Yolis stood with surprised gratitude.

"I will arrange for you to have guest quarters for the night; your horse is being well cared for," the king rose also.

"Thank you, your Grace. Might I ask, how are they?"

"I plan to check on them now, I will let you know. I notice you only referred to the woman as 'the woman', you don't know her name?" Shock crossed Yolis's face.

"I never thought to ask, Sire. Was that wrong?"

"No, no I just wanted to be sure," the king shook Yolis's hand and then departed for the physician's workroom. As soon as he entered the corridor, he knew something was wrong. Two distressed servants were standing in the corridor, as was his wife, Trevard could guess the cause.

"Citria," he called, "which of them have we lost?"

"The mother," she answered, falling into her husband's, arms. It was a while before Trevard spoke again.

"How is the child?" he asked, Citria dried her eyes.

"She is awake now but not doing well. Did you discover where they came from?" the queen asked.

"Not precisely, but I will investigate. She asked specifically to come here, to our castle. She wanted our protection, the least we can do is to honour that."

The following morning three of the king's best knights and a small complement of guards set out with Yolis as guide to discover all that they could. The king's men did not return for several days. They discovered that a whole village in the neighbouring kingdom of Twickerth had been massacred. They told of men, women, and children; whole families lay dead. As the village was located in another kingdom there was little that they could do, especially since the king was not eager for word of the attack to be spread. King Trevard was horrified by the news and was determined to offer any possible assistance. However, before he could set out to Twickerth there was one matter he felt he had to deal with first. The baby had survived, thanks to the diligent care of his physician. The child had no family and anyone who knew her was now dead. So, who should care for the baby was now Trevard's decision. He could turn her over to King Ivan, as she was his subject. But her mother had chosen to travel no small distance to present herself and her child at his court instead. Trevard would never know why she had entrusted herself and her child to him, but he had to honour her unspoken request. He must decide her daughter's fate to the best of his ability. He went to the nursery to give the queen the news. She was sitting in her chair holding the baby girl in one arm and their son gently balanced on her knee. Frederick was curiously playing with the baby's feet. For a moment, the image warmed him and took a little of the awfulness out of the tragedy. He sighed and forced himself to enter the room.

"We should discuss things," Trevard gestured to the door, respecting the sanctity of the nursery. Citria gave the children to Yvaine, her nursemaid, and Trevard and his wife left and went to their private chambers. There he told her all that his men had discovered.

"How could someone commit such – ?" Citria couldn't even bring herself to finish the sentence. They both took a moment of silence before Trevard continued.

"Citria, we need to settle the child's future," he began.

"What do you mean, her future? Myrbeth is staying with us, I gave her mother my word we would keep her safe," she said, raising her voice to express her indignation and sincerity.

"I knew you would say that," he sighed, "but I need you to understand that I am trying to consider her welfare as well," he spoke calmly.

"What do you mean?" his wife asked again.

"Someone committed this atrocity for a reason, though why I cannot imagine. What I'm certain of is that they had a reason to want every person in that village dead, including Myrbeth." He took a seat at their private table and gestured for her to do the same. "I intend to travel to Twickerth myself and offer King Ivan my assistance. If we intend to raise the child, then I owe him the respect of telling him about her survival. Not just that, her story will become known as she could not be thought of as our own natural child. She would have to be our ward and questions would be asked about her. That will put her at risk her whole life, at risk to men who might come for her." He paused again and waited for his wife to speak.

"What are you suggesting we do for her instead?" her voice was thick and her words faltering.

"We could hide her." Citria began to object but Trevard continued. "No, let me finish, I know it would be very difficult for you. I see you are already attached to her. I don't blame you, but this could be what is best for her. If I quietly find a family from one of our villages to adopt her as their daughter, then no one would need to know the truth about her. It would be easier for her to be hidden. She would remain safe and happy without this hanging over her for the rest of her life." They were quiet again for a long time as she considered everything he had said. She twisted her lip then seemed to think of an important point.

"If we do that then she will never know what her mother did for her," she said, her voice full of conviction.

"True," he sighed, "but that could still be better, safer, for her. Not to mention there is no history of a commoner becoming a ward. This, in addition to her past, would always make her the object of curiosity. Letting her blend in might be kinder." Trevard could see his wife's mind revolving and guessed there would be little point to continue. Citria shook her head.

"I see the mercy and care in this, Trevard, I do, and I love you for it, but it won't be just her mother that will be forgotten. If we hush her away, then everything about this could be hushed up, too. All those people, that whole village that lost their lives would be forgotten before long. That shouldn't happen, but if we raise Myrbeth then she will be a symbol that brings a small bit of light to this dark tragedy." The king sighed; he wasn't certain that his wife was right, but he could see she wouldn't be dissuaded from her choice.

"Well, I guess the next decision we need to make is how to announce her to the world, but not until I return," Trevard said, smiling but still uncertain what would come of this and what this would mean for the survivor, Myrbeth.

CHAPTER 3

Fifteen years passed and much changed in Hollthen. The prince and the ward grew into children side by side, the dead of Twickgrove were honoured and the village renamed to honour the lord and his family that had also been slaughtered. A memorial was built but otherwise the people were forgotten. A great change had taken place in Hollthen castle as Queen Citria had been lost. For many years the king and queen struggled to have any further children until finally she did succeed in producing a second son seven years after the first. However, it cost her life, Citria died only hours after birthing and naming her second boy. The kingdom went into mourning and baby Edmund was handed into the charge of young Myrbeth. She became both mother and sister, devoting all her heart to raising the son of the woman who had raised her. The queen had always been an involved mother with her children and Myrbeth emulated her, devoting all her time to the baby. As Edmund grew, she also became his tutor to stay needed.

"The Doctrine of Kings was formed over six hundred years ago, what was its purpose?" Myrbeth sat opposite Edmund in a stuffy room on a morning early in the year. This was the way they always

began their days, studying the history of the land, the kingdom's resources, basic language, writing and mathematics, cartography and topography and finally court etiquette.

"The Doctrine laid out the duties, territories and tenements of the nine kingdoms," Edmund responded in a bored voice.

"You can do better than that," Myrbeth rebuked him with smile.

"Fine. When the first settlers landed on Parvery there were three kings ruling over varied sections of land and some small wild clan-like hamlets. The new settlers were lost and in need of a home. After many negotiations it was agreed the land would be shared. The land was further divided, and kings were elected to rule over nine kingdoms and their resources."

"Good, much better. What was the Doctrine?"

"It was a collection of documents that outlined the basic trade rights and responsibilities of a king to his people and fellow monarchs. It contained the laws, traditions and rights for all and is the foundation for all the Kingdoms of Parvery. It is how we measure the passing years; the Doctrine was signed in D001 over six hundred years ago as it is now the year D612." He said all this in a droning voice, Myrbeth spoke in an indulgent tone in return.

"I know this seems dull, Edmund, but this was how our history was born. It is vitally important that you know this, especially as you are a prince. You must study it to understand and once you understand you can apply it in your future position."

"I know, but it's years before that will happen," he complained.

"It will happen sooner than you think. Frederick had the same lessons when he was your age."

"And you as well?" Edmund asked.

"I'm not going to hold a high office, so the queen, your mother, taught me separately. I know most of the same knowledge though, and after, well - I continued to learn from books in the library," she fell silent, reflecting. Myrbeth missed the queen very much. She was the closest thing to a mother she had ever known. The relationship she had now with Edmund as his guardian gave her grief clarity. She was loved by guardians who raised her as their own, now she had the chance to do the same with Edmund. She returned to the present and the classroom. She could see Edmund's attention had also lapsed too, so she suggested a new activity.

"Do you want to go for a ride now?" asked Myrbeth, smiling, riding was her favourite thing to do, but it wasn't Edmund's. He frowned and asked.

"Can't we go find and Father instead?" She smiled back and shook her head.

"Not until later, Edmund, he is hearing the people's matters in council today with Frederick, we'll have dinner with them later. But if you don't want to go riding, then we should get back to your lessons." He groaned and held up his hands in surrender before heading for the stables alongside a laughing Myrbeth.

The fisherman stood with his cap in his hand before King Trevard and Prince Frederick. The king gestured towards the carved chair in front of them. The king and prince sat on similar chairs opposite, in this chamber there were no thrones, crowns and no raised platform or any other dividers between the persons present. The council hall was a large empty stone chamber. Alongside the west wall there was a row of occupied desks, each with a scribe taking details of the people in attendance and notes on the council itself. There was also a large table with food and drink for all to partake in as the sessions often ran long. The people all gathered in rows in the lower half of the chamber, some sat and some stood. But each person waited their turn to approach the king. The fisherman took the seat and began explaining his issue.

"Greetings, sir, how can we assist you?"

"Your Majesties, thank you for seeing me. It's my boat that's the trouble, your Grace. My fishing boat, it's not large, only big enough for me and the five lads, but it's been in the family for generations. Only now the wear is getting so bad, that I can't take it out. I have to take it out, but it ain't safe truly. The cost to fix it all proper though is too much." He twisted his cap then held out his hands awkwardly as though looking to accept something offered. Frederick couldn't understand what he expected. Frederick had been attending the councils for nearly two years now, but he still found the problems difficult to puzzle out.

He had begun his education when he was five. Every day he and Myrbeth had taken the basic lessons from old master Birde, until he retired. Then the king had taken over Frederick's education personally, showing him all the intricacies of ruling a kingdom. Myrbeth had continued in the classroom, first with the queen, then to teach Edmund. Even after two years Frederick still had much to learn. He had never thought being a king would involve so much work and be so complicated. A ruler seemed to have to attend to everything, from councils with both lords and his people. He had to check regularly with all the king's men, from his knights to scribes, to the secretaries that took village censuses, to guards. A king had to know everything about his kingdom, his father also told him. The king seemed happy and proud of the progress Frederick was making but the prince wasn't so sure. Just like now with the fisherman's boat problem. His father liked Frederick to answer before he spoke the king's decision, but Frederick didn't have the answer. Still, he knew that sympathy was important, so he framed his face appropriately, preparing for a statement of support. King Trevard had looked at his son briefly then away again, he nodded and spoke evenly.

"We will ensure that your boat is repaired by the best craftsmen, and we will carry the cost. We also will lend you a boat until the work is completed, that way you won't lose a day on the water. I will arrange it all with our Master of Ships." He smiled and stood up to shake the man's hand. The fisherman seemed as surprised as Frederick. He rung the king's hand repeatedly, thanking him over and over. Trevard acknowledged his gratitude and asked that the fisherman leave all his details with one of the scribes before taking his leave. One of the king's servants made a gesture asking if they should call the next person up. Trevard shook his head and held up his hand asking to call a short break. He turned to his son.

"How would you have answered?" Trevard asked.

"I wasn't sure," Frederick replied, playing for time. "Is it an affordable expense?" He asked his father. Trevard smiled as if Frederick had given exactly the answer he expected.

"It is a question of avoiding an expense that none of us can afford. With so many kingdoms and so few resources, every source of food is important. Every day the fisherman cannot go out, food becomes scarcer, families go hungry. The fishermen know this so are likely to keep going out regardless of risk. He came to us because he knows every trip risks the lives of him and his men. A king needs to show that he puts a value on people's lives and one of the ways we can do that is by protecting their livelihoods." Frederick nodded his understanding.

"The people hear that you protected the fisherman and his catch, and they see a king who cares. It's a simple cost that means a great deal," Frederick sighed. "Will I ever get the right answers?" he complained, and his father laughed.

"Of course. I was the same when my father began to train me. You may have been born a prince and future king, but it still takes work to learn your trade. Just like the blacksmith or the builder who take years of practice to learn their trade, so must we. With practice, Frederick, you'll find the answers," Trevard explained gently to his son with an indulgent smile.

For the rest of the council Frederick listened and concentrated. He had felt encouraged by his father, but he was still cautious. There was neighbour dispute over a goat, a woman wishing to present her new child to the king, and finally a physician that had travelled far to collect rare medicinal herbs. Hollthen had a warm, moist climate which enabled a number of rare plants, with all sorts of properties, to flourish. In addition to selling and trading these plants throughout the kingdoms, certain individuals were given permission and taxed for gathering them. Hollthen was also home to the Medical Academy where young acolytes were trained in the healing arts. Trevard didn't ask again for his son's thoughts because he could see his focus and didn't wish to disturb it. When the council was complete and there were no more supplicants, another servant approached the king.

"Your Highness, we need to go over the final preparations for tomorrow's memorial." The servant held out a parchment list. The king sighed and closed his eyes for a moment.

"Every year I hope it will get easier. I can still picture your mother so clearly and feel her absence very deeply." His face looked grave as he looked over the parchment's pages. He nodded twice. "All is in order, Modwin, thank you." He handed the list back to his secretary. "I hope Myrbeth has been able to keep Edmund distracted." Trevard finished.

"He is getting too old for that to work; he knows that no one blames him. He is old enough to understand that just because she died giving birth to him doesn't make him responsible," Frederick said.

"I worry that it is harder for him, never having known her." Frederick paused, uncertain about trying to teach his father something but decided it was worth it.

"It's not Myrbeth he needs to be with, you should include him more. I know he won't be king, but it couldn't hurt him to learn all that you are teaching me. He will probably still be a lord, or one of my advisors. He may be young, but he is eager and needs to know you." He kept his voice even. Frederick felt strongly about this yet didn't want his father to feel disrespected.

"You're not wrong, I have come to suspect the same. There would be an additional benefit, Myrbeth and you are now of marriageable age. Myrbeth's match will no doubt take her to a new home to build a family of her own in time. Perhaps it would be better that Edmund is no longer solely in her charge. They could both use a little independence from one another," he stated, still looking grave and thoughtful. "There are things I must attend to," he said, suddenly leaving. Frederick sensed the dismissal and didn't follow.

The anniversary of the queen's death left them all reflective. Frederick moved through the castle aimlessly. He could remember his mother's beautiful long waves of hair, not quite blonde not quite red and deep green eyes that he had inherited. Edmund had his father's sea-blue eyes. She had been tall, taller than some of the men even, but her height had only enhanced her beauty not detracted from it. People had always remarked on her beauty. Frederick also remembered how gentle she had been. The way she would hum softly and how she had loved to make him laugh. Frederick felt sorry that his brother had never known all these traits. He often told his brother everything he could remember. When Edmund had been younger stories of his mother had been his favourite bedtime stories, but it wasn't the same. Frederick didn't pay much attention to where he was walking until he realised his footsteps had led him out to the royal stables. He looked up and saw Edmund dismounting from his chestnut mare which he had dubbed Flare. Myrbeth had already dismounted her old grey horse Perrotta, which she had named after the first queen of Hollthen. She was murmuring and stroking the horse's coat in a repetitive, soothing pattern. She had learned this gentleness from his mother. Though their appearances were quite different Myrbeth reminded him strongly of her. Losing her at such a young age had only made them closer. Frederick approached the pair, feeling better because of their presence.

"Pleasant ride?" he asked, Myrbeth turned and smiled warmly at him.

"I suppose so, but it was muddy from the rain," Edmund answered in a slightly petulant manner. Frederick smiled knowing his brothers' disposition, so he ventured to suggest another activity.

"How about a round of sparing?"

"I'll grab the swords," Edmund replied with a huge smile. He was just about to run off when Myrbeth spoke.

"He needs to get back to his studies," she complained, but Frederick pulled a disapproving, comical smirk and she relented giving Edmund a smile and a shake of the head. He ran off leaving them alone for a while.

"I suppose it's for the best, the books don't hold his attention for long. For today a break might do him good," she admitted wistfully. She turned to lead her horse back into the stable. "Thanks, Griff," she said, handing the horse over to the stable hand. "I might have made his study schedule too complicated; he just isn't responding well," she said with a puzzled look.

"Actually, I convinced father to include him in the councils and train him alongside me," he told her, not sure whether to be repentant or not.

"Oh, well, that will be beneficial, and he will certainly enjoy that more. I suppose he ought to be closer to you both and he will learn much." She paused for a moment, "he is still so young, though, I hope the king won't expect too much from him."

"I'm sure he won't." They continued to walk toward the practice yard slowly side by side. "How are you?" she asked, taking Frederick's arm and abruptly changing the subject.

"I keep thinking of her, but I don't mind that. At least I have memories of her."

"Yes, we were blessed to know her." Myrbeth knew she was even more blessed since the queen had chosen to raise her despite her common birth.

The next day was bright, warm, and full of sunshine. It was early in the season for such weather, and it was ill-suited to the atmosphere of the kingdom itself. There was a small part of Myrbeth that felt that this was exactly the sort of day the queen would have appreciated, however, even this thought couldn't lift her spirits. The people of Parvery often sent the ashes of their dead out to sea, so there was no grave site to visit. Citria's portrait hung in the royal gallery and, in addition, the king had planted a rare, white blossom tree near the shoreline in her honour as a memorial. It was here that the family would gather. There was to be a feast later that evening, but this was a private gathering. They were joined by Citria's youngest sister, Lady Delilah Prester and her only brother, King Edrick Prester. Her other sisters, Citria had three, were arriving later and would attend the feast. But it was Edrick to whom she had been closest and Lady Delilah, who had been most attached to their home and had never left, that came to honour her particularly. The sun shone brightly, the birds sung, and the waves crashed onto the beach just a short way off as the family met and greeted one another.

"Aunt Delilah, Uncle Edrick," Edmund cried out, running towards the newcomers.

"Ah, young Edmund, I swear you look more like me every time I see you," King Edrick stated, embracing his nephew. Delilah tutted but said nothing. "You will be as tall as me someday, I'm sure." The boy smiled up at him with clear affection. "Citria would be so proud of you, proud of both of you," he said, greeting Frederick next. Edrick and Trevard inclined their heads respectfully first before they too embraced. "And Lady Myrbeth, more beautiful than ever, I see," Edrick took her hand and twirled her, smiling. Myrbeth was not truly a lady, but there were some who afforded her the title as a way of showing respect. Yet strangely it always made her feel a little uncomfortable.

Once the small group reached the memorial tree, they were silent. The branches were covered with buds but only a few of the blossoms had begun to open. The sun radiated a warm glow over the mourners. In the early years after her loss, the family had tried sharing memories and speaking of better times but, even though Trevard never spoke out against this, it was clear he was uncomfortable with it. His grief was still so present in him and often made him withdrawn. They brought candles and lit them under the tree and spoke a traditional poem of memorial. Afterwards the family took to thinking of Citria privately for a time. The party broke up after an hour or so, Lady Delilah noticed Edmund's attention span waning so took him for a walk along the beach. Myrbeth chose to leave after about half an hour more, she started to cry and knew it would be better for King Trevard if she left. She respectfully asked to be dismissed so she could go for a ride, the king didn't answer. King Edrick however said he would join her and led her away. Myrbeth looked back occasionally, uncertain, but Trevard still didn't react. It was about an hour later when Frederick came to meet them.

"Father is still out there," Frederick said, as he trotted towards the pair.

"I know, it's worrying but he will come back in his own time," King Edrick reassured them.

The feast was held in the Long Hall, so named for its nine long tables. It was sparsely decorated and was housed in the main stone heart of the castle. The benches were packed with knights, notable lords and other nobles. That night the long top table at the head of the hall was packed with family and royalty. Myrbeth could not be seated amongst them as technically she was neither. However, she did not need to be seated at the table to hear all that Queen Barilsa Prester was saying.

"Rachel did so want to attend but I told her there was no use travelling such a distance so close to her lying-in. I was there just a month ago and she was so big I'm sure she is likely to have twins again. I asked her what she was hoping for, but she said that she didn't mind since she already has two of each. You know she had her heart set on naming that last girl after Citria, but I told her it was not the done thing."

"I don't think there would have been any harm in it," Edrick stated strongly.

"It would set a dangerous precedent," Barilsa exaggerated, continuing almost instantly, "after all, with all the noble and royal families linked, if we started naming our children after one another they would be all named the same four names after a few years."

"Citria named her children after me," Edrick said, with both force and annoyance in his voice. Edrick and Barilsa never got along.

"But not precisely, not identically, she gave it some variation. So did Rachel in the end, hence baby Cara. I wonder what she will name this one."

"Well, I'm proud of those boys and proud to be their namesake." Edrick said, hoping to end the conversation but Barilsa liked to get the last word.

"I'm not surprised, they are good princes. I was highly disappointed that Citria never had a girl for she always promised it would be named Barbara, or some such name, in my honour." Edrick shook his head in defeat, certain that Citria had never made such a promise. Trevard ignored all of this, he knew it was Barilsa's way to be forward, interfering and outspoken.

"It's times like this I'm glad I never bothered with the fuss of babies," Lady Delilah added loftily.

"Such an odd decision, it is nothing to parade and be proud of," Barilsa said, letting her disapproval show. "Though I suppose Edrick and Parnella will be grateful now their babies have begun arriving. Extra help is always of use," she spoke in such a commanding tone that the table fell quiet under Barilsa's judgement.

Myrbeth left the feast not long after this. She had been seated at the table with Queen Barilsa's children. They had little respect or interest in her. After a few hours of sarcastic jokes and comments, she would have preferred being deliberately ignored, as she often was by visiting royals. She exited to the castle garden for some peace. She was alone for only a short while before Frederick joined her. He had spotted her leaving the hall and ducked away too as soon as he could.

"It's awful in there isn't it?" She was slightly startled by his sudden appearance but pleased to see him. "I hate these formal ceremonies, it's like we are presenting our grief for everyone to see," he said.

"I know, it just feels like a show, or like this is the only time we are allowed to miss her." Myrbeth's voice trailed off because she had felt as if she wasn't allowed to miss her at all. Fifteen years on and people were still confounded by her status as a royal ward. Their opinions varied but very few allowed for feelings that would accompany a true familial connection. After all she was not family, and she was never allowed to forget that.

CHAPTER 4

Weeks passed and the natural pace of the kingdom returned. King Trevard still felt the weight of it. At age 42, grief was his constant companion to replace the partner he had lost. It was a relief when his guests left and he could be alone with it again. The king would never allow himself to forget his duties, but he would shut himself in his parlour or chambers preferring solitude. It was on one such morning that his secretary, Modwin, interrupted him.

"Deeply sorry to disturb you, your Grace," he said, showing that he knew his king's habits. "I'm afraid we need to address the matter of invitations to the Royal Ball." A Royal Ball was a tradition that took place when a prince or princess came of age at sixteen. A ball was hosted as a forum for the royal children from the other kingdoms to mingle casually. The purpose was that the host of the ball would choose a possible candidate for a future marriage match.

"Ah yes, it has come round so quickly," the king nodded his acceptance of the disruption.

"Since the ball is in Frederick's honour, I believe a simple stately style would be best, to show masculinity and class. I have a few options that I believe will suit," Modwin showed the king three pieces of thick parchment which looked identical. Trevard gave a sigh thinking about how much better Citria would have been at this.

"I think the middle one is fine," he stated making a decision for the sake of it. Modwin nodded, not questioning further.

"Now there is the matter of the black or the gold ink?" Modwin asked.

"Black I think, gold seems too gaudy, but all this should be checked with Prince Frederick." Modwin nodded again.

"Just right, I will have the invitations written and sent out as soon as they are completed."

"Hold off for a day, I have a small matter I wish to settle before the preparations can begin."

"Sire?" his sectary seemed caught off guard at this delay.

"The matter of Lady Myrbeth's participation should be decided first." Modwin simply nodded a third time to indicate his understanding and then took his leave.

Trevard arranged for the evening meal to be served in his private dinning chamber to afford privacy for the important discussion. This was a small room just off the long hall. It was plain and bare apart from the carved round table, perfectly set for the four family members. The table was inlaid with the design of a four-pointed star. The king sat at the north point, Frederick at the south, Myrbeth at the west point and Edmund at the east. Trevard as always began the day's discussion.

"Your ball is coming up, Frederick, and there will be lots of decisions to make before the night. You will be familiar with almost all the attendees, I know, but still, it would be wise to re-educate yourself with all the families and their connections. Matching is no simple business; it can never hurt to study the suitability of an alliance." Frederick had turned sixteen two weeks before his mother's memorial. Having his birthday so close to such a melancholy event was difficult for them all. Frederick often chose not to celebrate, unable fully to enjoy the landmark. The ball had been delayed specifically for this reason. Frederick looked glum, so Myrbeth decided to rescue him.

"I could assist Frederick with the celebration details, I know I have not attended a ball before, but I'm certain I could make sure things are appropriate." Myrbeth's heritage meant that she could not attend such an event. Royal balls were designed for royals and nobles to find partners. Frederick had already attended a few balls but since Myrbeth was born a commoner it was not expected she would be invited. Though she knew this, even accepted it, she dearly wanted to experience a ball at least once.

"I do wish you to assist him, Myrbeth, especially since this ball will be held in both your honours," King Trevard revealed his surprise with a gentle grin on his face. His announcement had the desired effect, everyone stopped eating, astonished. Myrbeth spoke first.

"Both of us?" she asked, in a disbelieving tremor.

"That's brilliant," Frederick exclaimed, reaching left to clasp Myrbeth's hand.

"Both of us," Myrbeth repeated. "I don't see how," she was caught completely off guard.

"I know you are not technically of age for several months, but I think it best," Trevard spoke. In actuality her true birthday was not known. It was estimated that she had only been a few weeks old when she was brought to Hollthen, but her date of birth was a mystery, like so much else about her.

"So - so you mean for me to be there as a guest to support Frederick?" she spoke carefully, as if trying to get her bearings.

"No, I mean for you both to host the ball." His previous words had suggested as much but perhaps too subtly.

"But how? I'm not a princess. I can't hope for a royal match." She was filled with horror and nerves. Though her surrogate family had always treated her as an equal Myrbeth had also always been aware of her place. She was a commoner and a guest and must behave as such. She was grateful for all that had been provided for her. But she must never grow proud or spoiled.

"A crown prince would not be suitable," Trevard registered her shock and spoke in the hopes of making things clearer to her. "But I think a younger prince, or the son of a lord perhaps, would be possible." The feelings flooding Myrbeth only increased. She had always wondered what future she could hope for in her delicate position. Her discomfort over the possibilities had never been strong enough for her to dare to ask the king about the subject though. Now he had told her his plans she could hardly speak.

"I think you could have any number of princes dying to be your match," Frederick stated, grinning, but there was an edge to his voice. Trevard sensed the turmoil of emotions he had unleashed in Myrbeth, so he spoke to her freely.

"Citria and I met at Barilsa's Royal Ball. We danced frequently and by the time the night was over we were in love." Trevard struggled expressing emotions, he felt his words didn't do justice to all he wanted to convey. Nevertheless, he continued. "We were betrothed shortly after and never held balls of our own which is uncommon, but our love was special. A Royal Ball is a significant tradition that began with the founding of the nine kingdoms. It gives us a special environment to consider this most important choice." He paused. He was lecturing, getting lost in history that wasn't relevant to the point he wanted to make now. "Frederick is not the only one who has a choice before them and yours is much greater," he said beginning again. "You have lived a different life then you ought to have and you cannot go back to the life you might have led. You may not be royalty, but you are my beloved ward. Myrbeth, you deserve a future and Citria and I have always tried our hardest to give you the best future we could offer you. It is a way to honour all those that were lost in that terrible event. You deserve no less.." Myrbeth fought hard not to cry. Her emotions still so strong that Frederick took her hand again. She did return the gesture, but she just gave it a squeeze and quickly let it go. Instead, she took Trevard's hand in both hers and kissed it.

"Thank you, Father, Sire." She very rarely called the king 'Father', Myrbeth was too humble, too careful. Trevard supposed he was the same in not adopting overfamiliarity but suddenly in this touching moment it felt wrong. Citria had had a different, closer, relationship with her. Myrbeth was freer with his sons, too. Perhaps it was time Trevard worked harder to lift himself from his grief and better express himself to those around him. Myrbeth especially. However, for now he did little more than touch her cheek and assure her all would be arranged.

The invitations were re-designed in a style to reflect both hosts but still kept simple. They were sent out across the land to all the noble households. Invitations usually never received a response. It was such an ingrained tradition that there was never any need to confirm attendance. There was the occasional reply stating some illness or injury that would prevent a few attendances but normally all the invited guests arrived on the day without giving previous confirmation. So, when a flood of letters was delivered to the king, he was astonished and baffled as to what they might contain. Each letter was slightly different but all centred around a similar theme. The senders were outraged that Myrbeth should be hosting a Royal Ball. The kings, queens and lords were furious that someone of common blood was being allowed to take part in such an important ritual. Furthermore, they wished to state that their children would not be attending, in protest. The responses were filled with prejudiced remarks and scathing indictments, their words stuck in his head hours after reading them: 'besmirchment of our greatest tradition,'; 'lowly common stock'; 'a nothing girl that should expect to amount to nothing'; 'no right to claim such a match'. It was awful to read but he knew it wouldn't compare to how it would feel to tell Myrbeth. The thought of delivering such disappointment made him feel sick. Finally, in a reckless fit, Trevard left his Kingdom. He needed some clarity so chose to travel to Merchden, King Edrick's Kingdom, for advice.

"Well, this a fine mess," Edrick remarked, once all had been explained to him. Trevard and Edrick were seated in his parlour in Merchden castle. They had feasted with the family but were alone now and it was in this privacy that Trevard had explained the reason for his unexpected visit.

"I cannot believe the reactions, their words," Trevard held up his hands in horror and exasperation. "No one has ever expressed such opinions against Myrbeth before." He marvelled at the responses still fresh in his mind.

"Well, it is not done or appropriate. It is each king's right to act as they see fit within their own territory. No one would wish to offer you insult to your face or suggest to you how to rule Hollthen. Now, I suppose, they thought it necessary to speak out. I was aware of some disapproval over you welcoming Myrbeth into your home but given our connection most would have more tact than to speak disrespectfully to me as well. I have heard nothing like this," Edrick explained in an apologetic voice. "If there were a match to be made from my own household all this could have been spared." He finished in frustration sipping at his wine.

A household match would of course be impossible. Edrick had no brothers; he did have a son, but he was only an infant. Edrick was closer in age in truth. It was an interesting notion Trevard thought, even though Edrick had been born ten years before Myrbeth. However, Edrick had married 8 years ago now, had two young children and his wife and queen was expecting their third child. Trevard almost wondered whether he should have considered matching Myrbeth to Edrick sooner, such age differences were not unheard of. It hardly mattered now, though, and Edrick was still speaking so he focused on his friend and brother-king again. "But I will speak to my lords to see if they cannot be reasoned with." Trevard just nodded, still pondering how fond Edrick was of Myrbeth.

"I think there will be little use to it, but I thank you," Trevard could see no solution and spoke dejectedly. "I raised her hopes, Edrick, hopes that she didn't have before. I could tell when I first spoke to her of the ball, she had never expected to be afforded such an honour or opportunity to match. Now, I must dash those hopes completely." His voice held a note of despondency.

"Are no princes or young lords to attend?" Edrick asked, equally shocked over the matter.

"Not many, some are still intending to accompany their sisters, since they still hope to make a match with Frederick. King Emil is sending his sons but only because of their close friendship with Frederick."

"Could their attendance yield anything?" Trevard shook his head in answer.

"They already know Myrbeth quite well and I have never detected any preference in their manner," Trevard sighed.

"What about Rachel's boys or Barilsa's?" Edrick inquired in a tentative tone as if feared he knew the answer.

"Rachel's husband has made it clear they will not be attending, but they were a little young for Myrbeth. Barilsa's letter was by far the worst. She stated plainly that if I had expressed my plans to her, she would have spoken about the impossibility of Myrbeth ever making a match. She had the nerve to suggest that Myrbeth be made nursemaid to Frederick's children as Delilah is to yours and that she should be grateful for such a position. But Delilah chose her position, Barilsa does not seem to think Myrbeth should have that right." Trevard's fury was clear. Edrick shook and hung his head in disappointment. "Your family seems to have a very different opinion of Myrbeth to yourself. They do not share your concern for her, why do you think that is?" Trevard asked with genuine curiosity, as if Edrick's answer could provide a solution. Trevard could tell he was considering his answer.

"Perhaps because I was so much younger than my sisters. I, in a way, grew up next to Myrbeth. I got to know her first as a child and now, later, as a young woman, so I don't judge her by what she was born but by who she is." Trevard nodded in agreement.

"I suppose what you say is true. There was a time I thought of sending her away when she first came to us. I convinced myself it was for her benefit, but perhaps I saw some of the impropriety." He quickly stopped himself unable to continue on that line of thought. "I never meant it to be unfeeling, but Citria wouldn't hear of it. She adored Myrbeth instantly. I wish your sister was here. She would have known what to do, what would be for the best. I'm sure she had plans for Myrbeth's future, though we never discussed it." They were both quiet for a while until Trevard broke the silence. "I'm unsure how to proceed now."

"There is nothing much to be done," Edrick replied firmly, "the damage has already happened so I would go ahead with the ball as planned."

"Still allowing Myrbeth to host?" Trevard clarified.

"Absolutely, there may even be hope in it, for one of those who do attend may still fall for her. She does have many charms, despite her common birth," he offered.

"I wish I shared your optimism," Trevard stated gravely and accepting that the ball must go ahead.

The visit was short as King Trevard had much to attend to at home. On his way home he tried to steel himself for what he knew he must do. Trevard wasted no more time and called Myrbeth to his parlour directly upon his return. The worst part of telling Myrbeth was that she held in her pain and tears. She stood stately and straight-backed, facing the truth with a grace that he had not expected. Trevard wished he could find the right words to comfort her. Again, he felt that he had handled their relationship incorrectly, things between them were too stately, too distant. Myrbeth left after only a short discussion and Trevard decided it was best not to follow her. Instead, he next called in his son. Frederick's outrage at the news was predictable; his emotions often ran away with him. Frederick would need a wife with a steady nature and a clever mind to help guide him but now was not the time to suggest this.

"What, they think themselves above her? That they can do better than her? Myrbeth is the one who deserves better, who is better. Hang them all, she will have a happy future despite their vindictiveness," he almost spat out. Having finished his rant, he took several steps towards the door, "I must go to her."

"Anger is not what she needs right now, son. She needs to able to resign herself, she must find the strength to be at the ball regardless of this malice. Of course, I said I would alter the plans if she did not wish to move forward with hosting after all, but she said she still wanted to be there for you, to celebrate with you. I think right now it is best we give her some time." But Frederick didn't heed his father's words, instead he left to find Myrbeth.

He found her sitting in the window seat of her chambers, with clear tear tracks on her red cheeks. She was not crying now though. Frederick came in and sat close to her, taking her hand.

"You wouldn't want to be matched with any man who could not respect you and anyone who doesn't respect you cannot truly call themselves a man," Frederick had however heeded his father's advice about his anger; he stayed calm. His empathetic pain was clear as he kissed her hand lightly.

"It isn't that," she spoke in a shaky voice, "I never had much hope of a match coming from this. I know too well what people think of me. Even with the king's blessing I didn't expect anything to happen"

"What, you knew but you never said anything? You seemed so excited."

"You and your father have too much kindness in your hearts to notice how other nobles treat me. They were always careful not to cause an incident by being too directly hostile, but their views were clear. I'm used to comments and looks, now they have just voiced it out loud to others," she sighed, disappointment and sadness filling her. "I have dreamed of attending a ball since I was a little girl. Your mother, the queen, would tell me of how the king and she fell in love at such a ball. I used to love listening to her describe it all, it was my favourite story. I dreamed one day I would be able to attend a ball. As I grew older it became clear it would not be possible. Now I finally get to host my own ball but it will be nothing like I dreamed. I always knew I would not be distinguished like your mother. All I wanted was to wear a beautiful dress and dance, to have one night where I could at least feel like a princess. Now I feel like a fool, I'm so ashamed." A fresh tear rolled down her cheek.

"They are the fools, and they should be ashamed, not you," Frederick said softly, still holding her hand. "Wear your dress, come to your ball and show them all you are more beautiful and special than any princess." He kissed her hand again and wiped away the tears.

"Even if I do make a match, he won't be half the man you are," she said, and Frederick beamed. The pair embraced and held on to one another, feeling both joy and sadness.

CHAPTER 5

The long hall was simply decorated with glass preserved garlands of blossom and holly and twisted ribbons strung around the pillars. The bright colours glimmered in the light of hundreds of candles. The feast was set to be generous and was displayed across several tables. There were large roast joints, platters of glazed fruits, lemon dressed fish and other meats and sweets. Fires were lit in the generous, grated fireplaces along one side of the room. There were also large boughs hung from the ceilings, a mixture of silver birches and yew trees from which were hung more ribbons. Outside the castle small braziers were lit to lead the guests inside.

Princesses often chose to make a grand entrance by arriving after the guests had congregated so they were noticed by all. However, this was not to be the case here, Myrbeth wanted as little attention drawn to herself as possible. She and Frederick planned to enter the hall together to greet everyone. However, Frederick arrived first, an hour early. He was dressed in his gold and deep blue tunic, with a small plain gold crown nestled on his dark curls. He moved about checking the arrangements were all in order when the servants' clapping caught his attention. Myrbeth had arrived wearing a spectacular peach gown decorated with silver leaves and long draped sleeves. She had woven small white blossoms into her golden-brown hair, she looked magnificent. Frederick couldn't imagine that any of the other girls would possibly be as beautiful.

"You're perfectly exquisite," he exclaimed, heading over to kiss her hand. She smiled, she might have blushed, but Frederick often complimented her like this.

"I took the blossoms from your mother's tree, I thought it seemed right to have some part of her with us tonight."

"Yes, she would have wanted to be here. She would have been so happy and proud of you," Frederick smiled with a slightly sad edge.

"And you, you look very handsome," she echoed. For a moment Myrbeth was truly joyful and she let herself believe that perhaps the rest of the night would not be so bad after all. How very wrong she was.

The illusion was shattered as soon as the guests began to arrive. Frederick and Myrbeth waited by the entrance arch to the hall. The princesses and ladies greeted Frederick with warm flirtatious smiles which wasn't surprising. Frederick was indeed very handsome with his dark curls, slim and lightly muscled frame and deep green eyes. However, the glares they gave Myrbeth were cold and full of a malice she hadn't previously known. She tried to remain positive and not let it affect the night. The princes' snubbing her was just expected. Even those she knew and who had visited the castle regularly before, seemed now awkward in her presence. They gave tentative greetings and then quickly moved into the crowd, looking around with nervous glances. She felt many unfriendly eyes upon her and, while this wasn't completely unfamiliar, it still made her feel highly uncomfortable. However, since she couldn't leave, she stood her ground, was respectful and tried not to act anxiously.

As was traditional, Frederick and Myrbeth opened the ball with the first dance. She had hoped to know a moment of safety in his arms but when they moved into position to begin the guests stood around them in stony silence. Usually, the opening dance was greeted with applause and often other couples would join the dance after a short interval but this time no one did. Instead, they just stood, silent and glaring. This reaction surprised her completely, mostly because it was universal.

"Just keep your eyes on me," Frederick said. It was clear he was also disturbed by the resentment, but he was focused on her. Myrbeth honestly tried to see only him. She concentrated on the way Frederick held her close, the feel of his strong hands, the look in his eyes as he looked back at her. For a moment this worked and she was happy. Then the music ended and the moment passed. Frederick sighed, a grimace passed his face and he took one long last look at her. Then he let her go without another glance. He moved to the fringes of the crowd and asked his cousin Princess Eunice Haughton, Queen Barilsa's eldest daughter, to dance.

Myrbeth viewed the whole crowd around her full of dread, who else would dance with her? To her surprise and relief Prince Halph Yenton of Walsea approached and give a very small stiff bow before asking her to dance. She smiled and curtsied in return. As they began to dance, she could tell by his rigid and uncomfortable manner that he was reluctant to enjoy the moment. Myrbeth guessed he had done this to honour his friendship with Frederick, not out of kindness to her. He stoodfar from her and made many awkward glances around the room. Next his twin, Prince Judan, took his turn but he acted in much the same manner. The twins were previously kind and amusing individuals. It was true that they hadn't been as friendly to her as Frederick or even Edmund, but they had always been pleasant. Myrbeth felt certain that their change in attitude was

because of the other guests pressuring them to act with hostility towards her. She tried to be grateful for the little generosity they had shown but the rejection was hurtful. After the musicians halted for the third time Myrbeth fully expected to receive no more requests. But she was surprised again when a young crown princeling came forward. Prince Osles Navara from Sedgebarrow, a fourteen-year-old full of excitement over his first ball and heedless of the atmosphere, took up two dances. He was full of lots of chatter, all about the ball and the traditions surrounding it. Myrbeth lost herself in his cheery conversation and quite forgot to be nervous until Prince Osles bowed and asked a new partner to dance. Myrbeth was left standing with all her feelings of foolishness and rejection returning. She moved away to collect some food to hide her embarrassment at being snubbed in this manner.

Frederick was dancing with a princess in a silver puffy dress that she didn't recognise and there were a few other pairs of dancers gliding alongside them. Most of the guests were gathered at the tables with food and drink, talking and muttering in mutinous tones. Whilst at one of the large feasting tables choosing what to eat, she heard a small gaggle of princesses who passed by, commenting on her.

"So simple and plain, nothing to fuss over."

"If she was beautiful maybe someone would want to take her."

"Modest, ugly, even, and common. Decidedly common." They laughed casually without any feeling. Myrbeth put down her food, no longer able to eat. She looked around the room and felt alone and unwelcome. She knew almost none of the guests since she wasn't invited to royal events. Whenever Trevard went on a royal progress or visited the other kingdoms, she was left at home with Edmund. She had never thought much about it. It made sense for the king to take Frederick, but she wondered now what would have happened if she had been taken on such visits. She found herself wondering if more royal children should have been paying visits to Hollthen. She knew Frederick's cousins and the Yenton twins because of their close connection to her family but the rest were strangers to her. She had studied the royal lines and knew the names of princes and princesses going back generations. Their actual persons were foreign to her though. She could not match names scrawled on pieces of parchment to the displeased faces around her. She watched the dancers for a while, uncertain of what to do now, until she was approached by someone.

"Quentin Rook, son of Lord Rook of the village of Balvain," he bowed, introducing himself in traditional fashion. She didn't know the boy or his father, but the name of the village did ring a faint bell. "Would you care to dance?" the boy asked. Myrbeth smiled in acceptance and was led back to the dance area. At first the pair were silent as they revolved around the floor. She got the sense that her partner wanted to say something but seemed hesitant. So, she tried to make polite conversation to put him at ease. Towards the song's end, they passed near a group of princes who chose to loudly comment.

"I wouldn't dance with her if she begged me." The humiliation of the night stung her hard and she felt a strong desire to leave the event entirely welling up inside her. She thought she might fain some illness and leave but that seemed a childish thing to do. When the music came to a close Myrbeth distanced herself, still debating excusing herself but Quentin Rook tightened his grip on her and finally spoke.

"I wanted to meet you because I'm fascinated by you," was his very odd comment.

"I'm not certain I understand," Myrbeth said slowly.

"Well, your life story. You are the only survivor from the old attack on my village." She felt an icy lump descend into the pit of her stomach. She realised why the name of the village had sounded familiar; it was where she had been born. She hadn't recognised the name at first because after the attack the village had been renamed Balvain in honour of the previous lord. He and his family had also died in the massacre. Her village had had a different name, Twickgrove, which was the name on the memorial. She had visited that memorial twice. Once when it was first erected, but she had still been a baby, so she didn't remember it. The second time the queen had taken her personally when she was six because she had wanted to see the place she would have grown up. She had become hysterical, crying constantly. Then she had stayed quiet the whole way home. The king and queen had decided she was too young to be exposed to such tragedy and had never taken her again. The memorial and the name of her birth village had been burned into her brain ever since.

"I can't wait to tell my mother and father I met you," the boy Quentin gushed, bringing her back to herself. He was clearly unaware of his partner's reaction and emotions. "Do you remember much about it?" he asked. She shook her head, unable to speak.

"Still, it must amaze people when you tell them," he continued. "What do you think it was like?" Thankfully she was spared having to answer this by the ending of the song. Myrbeth pulled away from him and his ghoulish fascination. It was all too much. She left the ball, stumbling away in her haste and horror. She let her tears fall thick and fast, her dream night thoroughly ruined.

Frederick saw Myrbeth leave and ached to go after. He was still on the dance floor, moving stiffly now his attention was elsewhere. He was watching her, torn with indecision. He had only danced with half of the girls in attendance and as host duty insisted that he stay with his guests. But his heart stung with all the injustice they had heaped on Myrbeth and he wanted to damn the lot of them. His debate lasted only a moment until he was interrupted.

"Is she alright?" his current partner asked. Strangely her concern brought him to himself and he compromised.

"Will you excuse me for just a moment, Princess Gisella?" She curtsied and stepped back with an understanding look. Frederick summoned over a guard who was at the fringes of the festivities.

"Kelbury, could you see that a message is sent to my father at once?" The guard nodded. "Tell him that all is not well with the Lady Myrbeth and that he should go see her." The guard nodded again. Frederick resumed his duties on the dance floor, though he was even more distracted and despondent then he had been previously.

Trevard was in his parlour reading a letter from one of his lords. Lord March had written to inform the king that he was seriously ill and didn't expect to live long. Since the lord had no children, the king would need to think about appointing someone new to act as his agent and governor. There was a knock on the door and his secretary interrupted with the message from Frederick. Trevard abandoned the letter and left to find Myrbeth, an ominous dread filling him. He regretted all that had come to pass but couldn't see what he could have done differently. Trevard reached her room only to find it empty. Her gown was laid out on the bed so she must have been there but there was no sign of her now. Where would she go? Trevard checked the library, stables and Citria's tree before he called the guards to search the castle formally. By this time the ball was coming to a close and the guests were beginning to retire to their quarters. All the attendees of the ball would spend the night at Hollthen castle before leaving tomorrow for their homes. It was not safe to travel at night.

Trevard wanted to put off telling Frederick that she was missing for as long as possible, but he was afraid the frenzied activity of the guards might attract his attention. As more and more of the guards reported that Myrbeth couldn't be found, he knew he had no choice and made his way to the emptying hall. Frederick's reaction surprised Trevard deeply. He had expected his son to rage and storm into the night, intent on finding her. However, he fell back into a chair and looked at his father with a mask of confusion and sadness. After a while he asked.

"Why would she leave us?" then lapsed back into silence. Trevard had no answer for him and, worse, he couldn't answer the even more terrifying question that Frederick had not asked. Would she come back?

CHAPTER 6

That night it rained heavily, forcing all to take shelter indoors. In an old fallen down barn, with nothing more than wet straw and a few rusted troughs, hid Myrbeth. At first after leaving the ball, she had felt like she couldn't breathe. She had always known there was a divide between her two lives; her life of privilege in the castle and the life she would have had as a commoner, but tonight the divide seemed to have come crashing down on her. She removed her dress, nearly ripping it from herself and the blossom flowers fell from her hair onto the floor, broken apart and dishevelled. She began to sob in earnest seeing them as a symbol of herself. She had never felt so disconnected from everything she knew and uncomfortable in her own skin. The nobles had set out to punish her tonight, to push her back into what they viewed as her place.

But what was her place? She had never really lived that life, the life of a commoner. She had been so little at the time of the attack she had no memories from then. It was not even known exactly how long she had lived with her parents, or how old she was precisely;

when her birthday was or what her full name was. She had never known that life, she was raised a royal by a king and queen in a castle with servants and princely brothers. She was a quasi-royal, but she was never allowed to be one. She knew nothing of the life she might have lived. She knew nothing of her parents, either, what professions her parents had had, the daily tasks that they would have done or what would have been expected of her. She felt a yearning, and not for the first time, to understand that life that she had lost.

A sudden reckless impulse filled her in her despair and she acted without thought. She re-dressed in the warm simple clothes that she often wore for riding, a blue dress and cloak without embroidery and her riding boots. She left her chambers and moved quickly through the castle. With the ball still going on most of the guards and servants were busy on the lower floors, leaving the upper part of the castle empty. Myrbeth and Frederick had spent lots of time exploring as children. They had learned a lot of the castle secrets, including a couple of ways to sneak out unnoticed. Myrbeth travelled to the south tower, which was the shortest of the castle's three towers. The south and north towers were defensive in nature and held little more than armouries and guard rooms. They were also old and drafty due to several arrow-slit windows that had no glass cover, but these only existed at the top of the towers. At the base of the south tower were square glass windows which a small thin person could slip through. Which is exactly what Myrbeth did. It was tight, she had been much smaller the last time she had tried this as a child, but she did just fit.

The drop was short, and she was able to land in a crouch without too much trouble. She had fallen on the grass not far from the practice yard. She ran, afraid to be noticed, into the shadows made from the lit castle and deep dark of the night. The castle was ringed by a stone outer wall but Myrbeth moved along it with purposeful steps.

She easily found her destination, even in the dark the large protrusion of the guard's stables was clearly visible. The stables were not lit but still the horses huffed and brayed in the dark, sensing her presence, so she moved quickly. There was a rotted old stall towards the back with a loose plank of wood that could be lifted. Again, Myrbeth struggled but managed to crawl through the gap out into the cobbled streets of the outer village. From here she could move more freely, but still with caution so as not to be noticed. The outer capital village was made up of buildings that belonged to the crown. It was a mixture of modest houses rented to servants who had family and chose not to live in the castle quarters, and large estate houses. The estates were often occupied by family members of nobles, the second and third sons of lords now dead or their daughters who had married wealth but not position. The people here might know Myrbeth as they were often invited to the castle, so she kept her hood up and hoped not to be seen.

She knew the village well and its multiple gates; the River Gate, the Docks Gate, the Floria Gate and the Holly Gate. She chose the Holly Gate that led to the market square of the royal village. As she walked the dusty, pebbled Holly Road, she could see the dark outline of the next village far in the distance. It was only a few miles she knew but still it looked very far in the night. She took a few more steps, then rain began to fall. The deluge of rain began quickly and Myrbeth hid in an old barn, panic rising. She had put very little thought into her desire to leave the castle. Now here she was freezing, damp and hungry. The intelligent thing would have been to turn around; she hadn't gone far from the castle; it would be easy to return. But now she had taken some action she couldn't bring herself to go back. What if she never again found the courage to venture into the world that had been taken from her? Of course, it wasn't exactly the same as the village she had been born in but nowhere was, that village was gone. Still, she hoped she could find some small glimpse of it and that thought was enough for her to hold onto until morning.

The sun rose in a stormy sky, the rain had stopped though the clouds above still loomed ominously. Myrbeth emerged from her hiding spot determined to head for her destination. She turned her damp cloak around and set off. She hadn't been able to travel far in the dark last night, but the walk made her feel less cold and tired. As the morning passed the village of Royal Holly came clearly into view. Much like the kingdom of Hollthen itself, this village was named for the holly bushes that grew only in this region of Parvery. Due to its proximity to the castle and the royal capital the village had become a thriving market town. It was full of all sorts of permanent shops in addition to market stalls that people regularly set up to sell goods. Myrbeth's home village had also been a market town once upon a time. She hoped in going to this similar place she would learn what life was like for the everyday people in a market village.

Myrbeth knew the structure of the village from maps that she had to study as part of her education. There was a large, cobbled square where all the stalls were set up for trade; there were seven streets that led from the square, which was why the square was dubbed Seven Sales. She would start in the square she decided and see where her discoveries took her. When she drew close to the village, she started to meet people also making their way to market. Myrbeth walked quietly among them, listening.

"And we must be sure to find that white cheese your father has a liking for," one woman said to her daughter, who had basket-laden arms. A small group of boys pushed past her.

"If we pool it, we can probably get six meat pies," one of the boys yelled, coins in his hands and others made appreciative noises.

"We must hurry, dear; the best catch goes quick," another woman called to her husband, who was hobbling behind. Myrbeth followed the people until suddenly she was being carried on a tide of bodies over the wide bridge and into the thick of the market stalls arranged all around the square. It was loud and busy in the square with everyone moving in their own direction. The stall holders were yelling, hawking their goods to the crowd. People were haggling over prices and the general buzz of chatter was overwhelming. She had never known anything like it. She stood still for a while trying to take in the whole picture, until someone bumped into her.

"Watch it, little miss," the young girl yelled, running back into the fray.

"Buyers should keep moving so as not to block the flow," a nearby salesman shouted at her disapprovingly. So, she began to move amongst the stalls aimlessly.

The smell of raw fish, cooked meat and the sweet tang of fruit filled her nostrils and Myrbeth realised how hungry she was. She hadn't eaten anything in nearly a whole day. She had a few coins with her which she used to buy two bread rolls, a small fruit tart and some cheese. She ate as she moved. However, once her initial daze was over, she noticed the strange looks she was getting. People were staring at her as she walked by, shooting puzzled looks at her through the crowd and some even pointed her out to other shoppers. The feeling of being unwelcome returned quickly, she didn't feel like crying this time though, she was just tired. She moved out of the crowd and sat on the plinth of a nearby statue. The statue was of King Titus who had commissioned the square to be built, that was over four hundred and fifty years ago. She finished the remnants of her meal, but this only seemed to increase the attention she was getting. She tried to decide her next move, looking at the openings of each of the seven paths in turn. She didn't know where she should go from here.

She slipped into a gloomy reflection on her place in the world. Myrbeth felt defeated and decided she should go back to the castle. Yet she didn't make any movement, she just continued to brood. This lasted several minutes before she noticed movement far off on the Holly Road, the main and only road that travelled from the capital into the square. She watched until the outlines became clear; four knights of Hollthen and half a dozen guards were approaching. Myrbeth moved quickly off the plinth and into the crowd, sure that they were looking for her. She began pushing her way through the foot traffic around the square. She realised now she had never had any true intention of returning to the castle, she was too ashamed. Ashamed of all that had happened at the ball, ashamed for running away, ashamed of not discovering anything, ashamed of not knowing what she wanted to discover. Most of all she was ashamed of her own person.

Myrbeth didn't know exactly where she was going but the guards were getting closer to the square, and she didn't want to be found. A street opened up behind her and to the left, so she carried on, pushing her way through the complaining crowd and took it without hesitation. She needed somewhere to hide, perhaps she could find another deserted barn or something similar. A short way down the street she came to a second small bridge and realised she must be traveling on Bright Bridge Road which crossed back over the Bright Water canal. She should have felt reassured by this but then she remembered that the map she studied was very basic, only showing the overall structure of the village. She still had no idea where she was headed. Which is why she was astonished when she saw the garden. It was made up of neat, organised beds, each one teeming with bushes, plants and flowers of all shapes, sizes and colours. There were pebbled paths in between the planted beds design for walking between the growing vegetation.

Myrbeth would have loved to explore the plant life, to read each careful little label but there wasn't time. In the distance she could see the guards fanning out in the square, checking the crowd. She walked around a bed of several spikey plants with an orange tube-like flower and then a patch of bushy plants with green leaves. She came on a grove of hawthorn trees, and she saw, on the other side of the garden, a large glass and brick structure. She moved towards this at speed. The building was a large shop with a greenhouse for growing certain plants needing a warmer climate. She entered the shop which contained dried botanical specimens, some hanging and some bound with twine. There were jars of all sizes containing various samples and there were other ground samples in small display pots. The shop had a strong odour of herbs, earth and fragrant floral scents. There were three people in the shop. A young man was talking to the elderly lady who seemed to be in charge and an elderly man was moving between the samples muttering to himself. It was an apothecary shop, Myrbeth realised.

"I will be right with you, dear," the old woman called, before returning to the young boy. "I made up some special tea mix, willow bark and butterbur with a sprig of peppermint. One cup a day should take care of your father headaches." Myrbeth wandered through the open spaces trying not to touch anything. Would she be safe here? She wasn't sure and how would she explain to the women what she wanted. Myrbeth could feel the eyes of the old women on her and a new frightening thought came to her, had she been recognised? It was possible, she supposed, the people were always welcome at the castle, the king liked to make every accommodation for them, and it wasn't as if Myrbeth was kept shut away. It was quite possible they knew just who she was.

"Look here, Lady Grouse, you have guardsmen coming this way," the old man spoke, interrupting her thoughts. He was right at the back of the shop looking out of a window through the trees. Panic filled Myrbeth as the elderly man and lady exchanged a look then turned to look at her.

"What could they want?" asked the young boy.

"Be quiet, Anthon," Lady Grouse said, as she swiftly moved past him straight towards Myrbeth. "Follow me, dear," she said, her voice quiet but insistent. Myrbeth was sure the lady didn't want trouble from the guards and intended to hand Myrbeth straight over to them. To her surprise the lady instead led her to a back room filled with plant cuttings and a few saplings. "Stay here," she directed, before going back into her shop. Myrbeth was astonished and more than a little confused. She went to the door to listen but the door was too thick for her to hear much. She didn't have to stay hidden for long though, the old lady soon came back for her.

"They're gone now, dear, why don't you come back in?" Myrbeth did just as she asked, very abashed.

"I can't believe it. It really is her, the lady, the king's ward," the young boy gaped at her, making her blush.

"Honestly, Anthon, I know your father taught you manners," the elderly man stated, giving a slight half bow. "Best close up for a while, Ophelia."

"Yes, I'll put some tea on," the old lady nodded.

"Oh, that's not necessary, I shouldn't trouble you further. I will be on my way, thank you," Myrbeth said meekly, feeling quite shy. She didn't understand why these people had helped her; she was grateful, but still she felt she never should have imposed on them.

"Oh, my dear, it was no trouble, but you can't be going now. Why you will walk right into them, stay awhile, I'm sure they won't come back." Myrbeth thought and decided that she was right. It also would be rude, perhaps, to just leave after these people had helped her.

"Alright," she replied, feeling shy still. The old lady smiled and locked the main door to the shop and then led the way to another back room. This room was spacious and housed a large table and several comfortable, carved chairs. Myrbeth took a seat and the young man sat down opposite, staring at her.

"Ridiculous boy," the lady scolded, "come, be of use and help an old lady make the tea." The boy got up sulkily and went to help while the old man sat himself down in his chair. Suddenly it dawned on Myrbeth that this was the opportunity she had been looking for, to explore the common life she had been so curious about.

CHAPTER 7

They were all quiet for a time and Myrbeth took the opportunity to take a better look at her new companions. The old man was tall, with bright white hair and deep brown eyes. His lined face had a small nose in the middle which seemed oddly out of place. His hands were calloused and he had more than a few small cuts on his fingers. He walked with a stick which he had propped against the table next to him. This stick particularly caught her attention because it was beautifully carved with thick swirling lines that crisscrossed, forming many different patterns and shapes. It was impressive and the old man clearly took good care of it, polishing and cleaning the stick often.

The old women placed a plate of cake squares down on the table. She was only slightly shorter than the old man, but she walked with a bent back that made her seem smaller. She had grey hair instead of white, which she had braided down her back. She had little hands with long thin fingers and dirty nails. She smelled strongly like her shop. She was slightly plump and her thick dress seemed tight on her frame. Her face had soft features which made her seem kind.

The boy lay four cups on the table for the tea. He was younger than she, Myrbeth thought, by a year or perhaps two. His face was smooth and round but with largeish features. Big ears, a fat nose, oddly shaped eyes and a prominent chin. His hair was brown, flat and shaggy. In contrast to this his clothes were smart and neat, and his hands showed no sign of hard work. She wondered whether the boy had a trade or a job? Or if he was in school still. Then tea was brewed and everyone was taking a seat. Myrbeth felt daunted but if she could talk to these people who lived the life that might have been hers once upon a time, she could learn much.

Yet she didn't know where to begin or what to ask. She was saved the difficulty of navigating this conversation however.

"Well, my dear, how can we help?" the old lady asked, once she had sat down at the head of the table.

"Help?" Myrbeth asked, surprised by her phrasing. Was she here for help? It wasn't the way she thought of it but now she heard the word she realised it was right, she was in search of help.

"Forgive us, my lady, but you are out here for a reason," the old man said, staring down at her. Even though she knew he was right she didn't know how to put her desire into words.

"But I don't understand. She is from the castle, why were the guards searching for her?" the boy interrupted.

"They were just worried about me. I didn't say I was leaving," Myrbeth said in a quiet voice.

"Why?" the boy asked, not reading how uncomfortable Myrbeth was.

"There you go again, displaying no manners," the old man tutted. "But perhaps we are all being a little rude. We should introduce ourselves first. I'm Jeremiah Cole, my Lady, and this lad is Anthon Fields," Jeremiah spoke in a clear, respectful voice.

"I can speak for myself," the boy named Anthon complained. "I'm Anthon," he repeated.

"And I am Ophelia Grouse, this is my shop and garden. You're most welcome here, Lady Myrbeth, my dear."

"Not Lady Grouse?" Myrbeth asked, remembering how Jeremiah had addressed her before. Jeremiah and Lady Grouse shared a laugh.

"It's strictly honorary, I'm not of noble birth, much like yourself," Lady Grouse explained. "You see I married the third son of the old lord of Royal Holly. So, everyone started to call me 'my Lady', even though we never lived in the manor house and Bartholomew took a working man's job." Myrbeth listened to the little tale with rapt attention.

"Really, how interesting," she murmured.

"Well, my father is the schoolteacher, and he is grooming me to teach after him," Anthon interrupted, clearly eager to talk to Myrbeth. His voice was quick and held a note of pride.

"Wow, the teacher, he must be a valued and important man," Myrbeth said.

"Of course, we both are," he replied.

"Master Fields is very important, naturally, but in this village we all look out for one another. Isn't that right, Jeremiah?" Jeremiah nodded at Lady Grouse.

"Too true, Lady Grouse, too true, but we wouldn't want to carry on," Jeremiah said. They all nodded, though Anthon was frowning.

Lady Grouse poured a second round of tea and offered the cake to Myrbeth.

"Ginger loaf, dear?"

"I haven't heard of that," Myrbeth inspected the cake, it smelled sweet and sharp.

"Oh, it's lovely, made with a lot of natural ingredients, cinnamon, nutmeg, cloves and ginger of course. I make it myself, from my own recipe." Myrbeth tried a small bit. The taste was sweet, moist and flavourful, she instantly liked it.

"It is lovely, thank you," she hesitated, taking another bite of the loaf cake. Everyone was quiet for a moment which made her feel more awkward. They seemed to be waiting for her to say something, but she didn't feel able to express the true heart of the matter. "I wouldn't mind hearing more about your husband?" she ventured tentatively, wanting to keep the conversation going.

"If you like, my dear," Lady Grouse took a sip of her tea before continuing with her story. "When we were married his father gave Bartholomew a good bit of money. He was a clever man who enjoyed having a purpose which is why he chose to work. He used the money to purchase a couple of good horses and a large, sturdy cart."

"What did he use it for?" Myrbeth asked, not understanding what his job could have been.

"He was a sort of entrepreneur. Every day he rode those horses down to the docks to collect the morning catch from the fisherfolk and bring it back here to market. You see, the fishermen couldn't leave their boats untended, and they had plenty of other busy work. It used to be if you wanted fish you had to travel to the docks to buy them, but most people couldn't travel that far, so the fish didn't sell much. My Bartholomew struck a deal with the fishermen that meant he could sell their catch at market, and they'd all see a profit. He died 10 years ago, so now my son-in-law does the route, and I opened this shop to support all my girls. I have seven daughters; most are grown now with babies of their own, but when I lost my husband, my youngest girls were still living with me. I've always known about plants, my grandfather taught me that everything that grows here has it use, he trained at the Healers Academy you see."

"He was a healer?" Myrbeth asked.

"A king's physician actually, to King Hasence, King Trevard's grandfather, and then King Terence after him until my grandfather became blind with age. His eyes no longer worked but his mind was still sharp, so he passed on his knowledge to me. I use that knowledge to provide for my family and heal my neighbours. See, we all pitch in, that's the way a village works."

"Yes, indeed," Jeremiah agreed. Myrbeth turned to face him wondering if this was true for all villages.

"Yes, indeed." Anthon interrupted again. There was another pause in the conversation, so Myrbeth thought over all that Lady Grouse had said as she drunk her tea.

"But I don't understand, forgive me, I don't wish to be rude, but if people were sick wouldn't they go see a healer, instead of coming to your shop?"

"We work together, in fact. Healer training takes a long time and physician training even longer. Since there is only one academy in Parvery all its graduates must spread across all the Kingdoms. Royal Holly only has one town healer and the court physician is much too busy and important. Healer Fry doesn't cultivate his own garden, so he sends all his patients to me to provide the specific treatments."

"Are you really interested in all this?" Anthon asked.

"Yes, I really am. I find it all fascinating," Myrbeth didn't want to explain why these details of ordinary common life interested her so much. Especially since she didn't fully understand it herself. After all, it wasn't likely that her parents had run an apothecary, healing was an industry of Hollthen not the Kingdom of Twickerth. Though she supposed it was possible her father could have been a healer who trained at the academy. She would never know, but it was possible.

"Well, you would find everything I'm studying fascinating then. I have to learn so much to become a teacher, it's a very important profession," he said in a puffed-up tone. "Not to mention studying how to actively engage students. I study mathematics, engineering, history, topography, resources and so much more. It's very hard work." Anthon explained. This was a new thought for Myrbeth.

"Wow, I never imagined a teacher would need to know so much. Does the school really teach such a variety of subjects?" She asked, it was almost as much as she was trying to teach Edmund. she wondered if she made her lessons engaging enough for Edmund. Perhaps they needed to be more active and interesting.

"Only for the higher students," Jeremiah answered, which surprised Myrbeth because he had said very little this whole time. "Most of us leave school early to focus on a trade."

"Well, that make sense. What is your trade?" Myrbeth asked.

"Jeremiah is a carpenter," Anthon interjected, but he fell silent with a glance from Jeremiah.

"A carpenter, how interesting," Myrbeth replied, but Jeremiah just nodded with a slight smile.

"Jeremiah has always loved carving. I remember every day in school he used to bring a small bit of wood to whittle into a different design," Lady Grouse said. Her attempt to coax Jeremiah worked, he began to speak more freely.

"I've loved the holly trees that grow in these parts since I was a young boy," he began to explain. "That's why I learned to carve. I make all sorts, from utensils to chairs to weapons. I taught my son too, now that I'm old and my hands have begun to seize. He has more of a talent for it than I ever did. I help him mind the store, but I don't do much of the craft work now. I don't mind though; his little wife gave him a baby boy last year, so I make sure he has time for them." After this long speech Jeremiah fell suddenly silent and took a second a slice of ginger loaf.

Her father could have been a carpenter, Myrbeth thought. After all wood was Twickerth's main industry. She wondered if her parents had had a school to go to? What they would have studied, how they met and so much more. Anthon again interrupted her ruminative thinking.

"Why would all this matter to you? I mean you live a castle, surely that's more interesting than anything we can tell you." Myrbeth understood that to him her life must seem like a dream, but she had come out here expecting to find her dream life where she was accepted. She sighed, she had to admit even though these people were kind and welcoming, she hadn't found what she had hoped for. She didn't know how to answer Anthon's question at first, but she looked up from the table to see Lady Grouse and Jeremiah smiling and shaking their heads at one another.

"Use that big brain you have, Anthon. The lady was curious about our lives for a reason. Forgive me, my Lady, but we are familiar with your story," Jeremiah said.

"Yes, we understand, dear. You want to discover a little about your common roots," Lady Grouse spoke reassuringly, patting her hand briefly. Anthon looked apologetic over his brash comment. Myrbeth hadn't been sure what she had expected to find by coming but she believed she had gained some friends if nothing else, she was sure she could confide in them.

"I did want to know about you, you're right, of course," Myrbeth choked out. "I want to know what my life would have been like, with my parents in my village. But coming out here I realised I don't truly belong amongst you," she hung her head and spoke to the table unable to meet their eyes again. "Perhaps I did once, when I was just a baby happy with my family but not now. I lost a whole life that day as did so many others. I suppose what I was really looking for was a home," she explained in a quiet gloomy tone.

"I'm sure it's very difficult dear, living without them," Lady Grouse offered soothingly. It was difficult, but Myrbeth didn't dwell on it often which now seemed strange to her. It was hard, perhaps too hard, to think of often.

"It would be bad, I suppose. I am sorry about what I said about the castle, I just thought you must be happy there." Myrbeth looked up and replied,

"You don't have to apologise, Anthon. You said nothing wrong, I am happy there most of the time. The problem is I don't truly belong in the castle either."

"Now, whatever do you mean by that?" Jeremiah asked, his voice was loud and rough but not unkind, but for the first time the old man seemed confused.

"I'm not welcome there, not truly, not by all the other royal families. They just think I'm common, ugly and beneath them."

"Ugly!?" Anthon shouted out. "No one who has seen you could think you ugly, surely. Why you're about the prettiest girl I have ever seen." Myrbeth smiled and blushed. His attention reminded her a little of Frederick, but it felt much more comfortable when Frederick complimented her. Frederick also was much less forward, but she was sure Anthon was just being polite.

"Does it matter what the other noble families think?" Jeremiah asked, ignoring Anthon's comment.

"I have to agree," Lady Grouse nodded. "Those people didn't choose you; those people aren't your family, dear. Didn't you ever wonder why your mother brought you here to King Trevard and Queen Citria?" Myrbeth's eyes shot up and fixed on the woman opposite her, intensely interested.

"I never knew why she chose to bring me to Hollthen. My mother died shortly after she brought me to the castle. The king and queen never got a chance to speak to her."

"Maybe she didn't get to explain, but to us; their people, the reason is crystal clear, dear," Lady Grouse said. "King Trevard and Queen Citria have a certain reputation. They care for their people. They often come among us and invited us to events and councils. They hear us, they are true advocates for the people and as such they are trusted by the people. This faith resonates through all the kingdom," Lady Grouse spoke, finally putting into words a truth Myrbeth had long known deep down. "They provide for and protect all people, that is the king's reputation. So, your mother trusted that they would do the same for you," she finished.

"Do you think any of those other rulers would have done the same? No, they care too much for titles and crowns. Believing in their superiority, forgetting they were once like us," Jeremiah added in a frank tone.

"I know what the king and queen did for me. I'm grateful, more grateful than you can imagine, but what have I done for them?" Myrbeth's voice was edging towards a hysterical note, so she took a deep breath or two and tried to keep her emotions in check. She needed to express all that she felt without getting lost in the depth of her sensations.

"What do you mean?" asked Anthon. Myrbeth was silent for a long while before she answered.

"I cause them shame; I degrade them," she rushed on, finally confessing her deepest fears. "I can never change who I am and who I am will always cost them." She had to stop or she might cry. She forced herself to take another sip of her now slightly cold tea and a third bite of the cake.

"You see only cost, but did you ever think what they gained in you?" Jeremiah said. "You don't shame anyone. Those nobles should be ashamed."

"Yes dear, you meant so much to the queen, she loved you. Prince Frederick often mentions you and Prince Edmund isn't so shy when you are around. You make him feel safe just like his mother would have, and the king must have been proud of you to show you off by throwing that ball." The ball, she thought in horror.

"It was a disaster; I just shame him. No one wants me," she confessed, repeating herself.

"Then they're mad," Anthon said, decidedly nodding his head for emphasis.

"Being chosen is a tough thing sometimes," Jeremiah added, nodding too. "But you don't want scores of suitors, just one, the right one. Like my Marlena, we had nearly fifty years together and she was the only women for me."

"Yes dear, he will find you, I'm sure as Bartholomew found me."

"Indeed, just like the king and queen. They chose to keep you; my Lady, and I don't doubt they would still want you to come home."

Home, Anthon's choice of word echoed in Myrbeth's mind and she recognised the truth, the castle was her home. She realised that, while she did belong to two worlds in a way, where she mostly belonged was with her family. She deeply missed the king, Frederick and Edmund, they were the only family she had known. Whatever life she might have lived with her parents was lost to her, but her family wasn't. It was home and she longed to return to it. The others around the table smiled at her and she smiled back. Myrbeth knew it was time to go.

"I think I must leave now; I hope you understand, I must go back home." They all smiled at her and stood to bow goodbye. Myrbeth curtseyed in return but then hesitated not moving to leave.

"You can always visit us, dear," Lady Grouse smiled at her.

"Anytime you like," Anthon grinned widely, and Jeremiah just nodded.

"Yes, I will," Myrbeth promised. Then she got to her feet and headed back out into the rain to go home.

Finding a guard was simple, there were two in the square still searching for her. It took a moment for the young guard, named Delbard, to recognise her. She supposed she must look a mess. The wet, bedraggled girl with tangles in her damp hair and mud on her hands didn't match with the always carefully dressed and trimmed King's ward. The ride back home was much faster than walking and they reached the castle walls just as night began to fall. She felt very nervous as they made their way up the steps. She felt a new shame over her flight, embarrassed that she had done it at all. She wasn't sure what reception she would receive from her family. Would they be angry? Inside the walls of her home her cold, wet state took hold and she started to shiver. As they walked Myrbeth worried over where she was being taken when a housemaid spotted her.

"Oh, my Lady," she exclaimed in a high girly voice. "Thank heavens, you are home, but look at you, you're soaked through. I'll have a bath drawn for you at once and some food brought."

"I was taking her straight to the king," the guard, Delbard, explained.

"No, no, she can't see the king like this, not to mention she is likely to catch cold. Come on, my Lady." The housemaid led her away, settling the matter.

"Thank you, Hisbara," Myrbeth said meekly. Hisbara took charge and directed Myrbeth to the servant's hall. She quickly and loudly gave orders and the other servants reacted, rushing to their tasks. Myrbeth stayed quietly and patiently, watching them prepare water and food for her.

"Let's go to your chambers, my Lady, Madge will have the water ready in no time." They took the servant's stairs to the third floor of the castle that housed the sleeping quarters. At the corridor leading to Myrbeth's room she was surprised to find an out-of-breath Frederick. Word of her return must have circulated and he had come to find her. When his bright green eyes found her the worry in his face vanished and his lips broke into a radiant smile. He began to run to her and she guessed he had run through the whole castle to her side. She ran to meet him, crashing into his arms and holding on tightly. She couldn't stop the tears from falling again, she blubbered out how sorry she was. Frederick spoke soothingly, reassuring her that he was just happy she was home. He even kissed and stroked her hair, the touch felt so wonderful to her. After a short time, they were interrupted by the maid, Marge, bringing the water.

"Forgive me, my Lady," she giggled.

"Well, take it to the bath," Hisbara ordered, in a disapproving tone. Myrbeth and Frederick separated, embarrassed. Myrbeth excused herself and he urged her to go rest and recover, promising to bring Edmund to see her a little later.

The bath was warm and welcome. She soaked in it for some time letting the heat permeate her whole body. She thought over the events of the day, astonished at how much had happened, how much had changed. The warmth felt cleansing somehow. She dawdled, taking time over each task, soaping her body and hair excessively, just wanting to linger in the heat and clarity. Later when Frederick, Edmund and the king came to see her they found her warmly dressed and wrapped up in her covers, fast asleep, peacefully.

CHAPTER 8

The king summoned Myrbeth to him the next morning. She was nervous at first but he smiled, a smile warmer than his usual smile and she was soothed by it.

"It's actually a lovely day outside, I thought we could walk along the beach?" he offered, she nodded and followed him outside. The rainfall had stopped and there were barely any clouds in the sky, instead the sun was shining. It was still slightly cold but as the king had said, it was a nice day. Myrbeth took the opportunity of inquiring after the other nobles.

"Have the guests from the ball all gone home then?" she asked, despite her new confidence she still didn't wish to see any of the nobles.

"Yes, they have left," King Trevard frowned. "I wanted you to know some were justly ashamed of the way they treated you."

"I'm surprised they said so, but I am glad to hear that. Do they know what I did?" she asked, in an embarrassed voice.

"No, they had no need to know."

"Thank you. I wondered; how did you know just where to find me?"

"I assure you I didn't. I sent a small collection of guards to every corner of Hollthen to search for you." Her guilt over the situation only doubled.

"Why did you choose Royal Holly specifically? What drew you there?" Trevard asked. Myrbeth took a deep breath before giving the account of her movements that she knew she owed the king. Trevard listened without interruption while she tried her best to explain her actions of the previous day. Once she had finished Trevard didn't speak, Myrbeth feared he might be angry and decided she should ask an important question before he chose to express his displeasure.

"I hope that I can go and visit some of the villagers occasionally from now on? They seemed keen to know me and I would like that, too." The king considered the request for a short time.

"Yes, I think that would be a good thing. Though I ask one favour of you. I would like you to take Frederick with you one day. It would do him good also to become more familiar with the people and their lives. It will help him in years to come when he must rule over them." Myrbeth gladly gave her word.

"Yes, of course." Then she lapsed back into silence, still expecting the king to be displeased.

"I can easily understand your curiosity," he sighed. "Perhaps if I had acted differently, you would have shared your wishes openly." This was not what she had expected at all.

"Oh no," Myrbeth gushed, hastening to acquit the king of any blame, but he silenced her with a gesture. He smiled widely to put her at ease then spoke freely.

"Ever since I was young, I have always had an active mind," he began, "I spent my youth wrapped in my own thoughts. Even with friends I was always thinking, theorising. It is a talent that serves me well now I am king, and I use it to better the lives of my people. When Citria was alive she could recall me to the real world and keep me grounded. She would make sure I didn't miss what was around me, but I fear since we lost her," he paused but forced himself to restart, "since her death I have too often surrendered to my old taciturn disposition. It separated me from my sons and from yourself in ways I never should have allowed." His remorse was clear and each word seemed to be a struggle to speak.

"It wasn't you," Myrbeth said in a rush of feelings, compelled to speak, "the ball was just so terrible and the attitude of the guests. I just felt so rejected, as though I didn't belong amongst you at all. I thought I was burdening you all, disgracing you. I suppose I let them convince me that I belonged among the common people. So, I went out to meet them, I have also always felt conflicted about not knowing about my previous life. I was curious, of course, but I felt as if I wasn't permitted to know about my common roots. If I want to hold my status as your ward, I had to leave my past behind me." Myrbeth stopped to take a breath and Trevard interrupted her.

"Permitted?" He echoed.

"Oh, not by you. I didn't mean I didn't have your permission, it's the other noble families," she explained quickly.

"This isn't the first incident, is it?" Myrbeth just shook her head. Trevard closed his eyes for a moment before speaking again.

"I understand how difficult that must have been for you and why it drove you to explore the village. However, this is what I was referring to. If I had better encouraged the same open confidence you had with Citria between ourselves, then, perhaps, you might have shared your thoughts and all that was happening to you. Shared your worries that you didn't belong anywhere." They were silent for a while. Myrbeth stared at her feet, but the king looked out at the ocean for a time before asking. "Of course, it is only natural to wonder about your previous life, about your parents. Did you find some of the answers you were looking for?"

"No. I learnt a lot, but it's just possibilities of how they might have lived. In a way I left with more questions but fewer doubts." A new question came to her. "How is so little known about them? I don't understand, didn't people come forward, weren't there records of their lives?" The words tripped from her mouth; her curiosity no longer contained. She was caught up with the desire to know more. Queen Citria had told Myrbeth who she was, what had happened in that village. The queen had told her the little she knew about Myrbeth's mother which is how she knew they had the same eye and hair colour. She had also told her all that was known about the attack, the knowledge had never been kept from her. Yet so much was not known.

"We have never really spoken much about what happened to your family, have we?" he said, and she nodded. It was always the queen who had told her about her old life. Sometimes she and Frederick had discussed it, but he didn't mention it often. She remembered the awful day when Edmund had become old enough to understand that Myrbeth was not his true sister. He had been four, nearly five, and Myrbeth hadn't had the heart to tell him the full story. Instead, Frederick and the king had explained the details, but Edmund had never asked her about it. The king gestured toward a nearby bench and together they sat. "After your mother brought you to us, I set out to Twickerth, the Kingdom where you were born. King Ivan received me, and I explained all that I knew and that I had come to offer my assistance. He was not pleased. I think he saw my presence as interfering, but he told me all he had learned about the attack on the village and took me to see the location. It is a sight I will never forget. The bodies were still being cleared and there was blood staining everything. You cannot imagine, though I don't doubt your mind has often dwelt on it. The culprits were never traced. I'm afraid I can tell you nothing about them, for King Ivan would not allow me or my men to assist in the search," he sighed. Myrbeth had never liked to think on those unpunished, evil men, it would be fruitless and far too painful. She was grateful when the king didn't continue on this particular line of thought.

"However, he did allow me to assist in caring for the villagers' remains. I don't think he saw it as work fit for a king and was happy to pass it on. I've never been greatly impressed with King Ivan's compassion, though I ought not to speak ill of a fellow king." He paused, shook his head and returned to the matter at hand. "As per custom, the bodies were burnt and their ashes buried beneath the memorial you visited. I was granted access to the king's census of his people, to the villagers' homes and to the possessions of those who had been killed." For the first time he looked at Myrbeth. There was pain and consolation in his eyes. She sensed that what the king was about to convey he feared would not bring her comfort. She braced herself.

"Many of the bodies could not be identified. Most were not found in their homes but in the streets or at the market. The census was not of much assistance. You see, it only listed the names of the adult villagers, their professions, whether they were married and what number of children they had. The children's given names were not listed. It simply stated how many male or female children belonged to each family line. I suppose census and records are not kept for such a purpose but still it seemed incomplete at best. I had hoped, through my work, I would be able to identify your parents but, as you know, I was unsuccessful. You see, your mother did not live long enough to tell us her name, only yours. Searching through the records there were three married couples who had one daughter but there was no way to tell which couple you might have belonged to." His voice grew grave and slightly higher than normal as he continued. "I cannot even be certain that you were your mother's only child. We assumed it because she fought so hard to keep you alive, and found peace when you were safe, that you were her only child. She had rescued you and willingly gave her life to do so. That might not be the case though, perhaps you were the only child she could save. Perhaps there were others that she couldn't get to. Others that she had to leave behind to protect you." Myrbeth had never imagined that she could have lost more than just her parents that day but what the king said was possible. She could have had brothers or sisters who might have died as well. The awfulness of these new thoughts consumed her momentarily.

"What about a family book?"

"Only a few common families keep them but none we did find referenced a 'Myrbeth'. Now you understand why nothing is known about your family," Trevard finished before falling silent, sensing her anguish.

Myrbeth fought back tears, staring at her feet. It was a long time before she could gain control of her feelings and felt ready to hear more.

"Didn't anyone who knew them come forward?" she asked, sounding desperate. Trevard took her hands in his and shook his head.

"You must understand, most everyone they knew was dead. Nothing like that attack had ever happened before and the news of the atrocity spread. For a long time afterwards all Parvery lived in fear. Fear they would be next to be slaughtered, feared that those who were responsible would return. No one dared to come forward. For a time, we even feared for you as the only survivor. I'm afraid we will never learn anything more than this, years on people are still too cautious to even discuss it." Myrbeth nodded, finally letting a few tears fall before brushing them away again. Trevard's next words were hesitant, "I'm sure this is all very distressing for you in ways I cannot fully understand. Perhaps you have more questions, but I think that is enough for today. I will be more available to you in the future, you have my word. Let's go back to the castle." He led her back and they parted ways.

Myrbeth spent the day alone in her room. She couldn't fix her mind to any particular task, she picked up books only to put them down again. She even tried to sew, which was normally a task she loved, but even this didn't sooth her. She had expected Frederick to come looking for her but when he didn't, she assumed that the king had insisted that he leave her be. Myrbeth felt the empty information like a living weight inside of her. The other predicament over her status no longer mattered in light of this deeper issue. She supposed it had always been with her, an unknown fog hovering around her; she had been afraid to ask for clarity knowing that she wouldn't find it. The queen would have told her had there been anything known about her family or the attack. She had known the truth but hadn't wanted to face it until now. This information was sharp and painful; however, she knew that she wouldn't have to bear the weight alone. That was the change that made her feel strong enough to face the truth. she may have lost one family but she had gained a different one instead. Her new family would help her finally move forward.

CHAPTER 9

The next morning's breakfast was a quiet, subdued affair. The family always met and breakfasted in the private parlour, just the four of them. At the same seats around the compass table. Normally it was a time of happy chatter but not so today. So many difficult events had taken place since that first fatal discussion about the ball weeks ago. Finally, Edmund was the first to speak, breaking the silence.

"Ser Thaze has promised to teach me to fight with a mace and throwing axe today," he said, in an excited voice.

"Truly? Aren't you a little young for such weapons?" Myrbeth worried.

"Don't expect too much of yourself, the more specialised the weapon the harder it is to master, trust me," Frederick cautioned.

"I hope Sir Danville has been consulted?" Trevard asked, checking that the master of arms knew of these plans.

"Yes, Father," Edmund answered dutifully.

"Why don't you head out early to practice a little before your lesson? Those weapons can be heavy, you might want to warm up first," the king offered, and Edmund ran off happily to do just that.

Then Trevard spoke once more. "Now that we are alone, the three of us have some things to discuss in the wake of recent events. We need a more focused approach moving forward, I think." Myrbeth and Frederick exchanged a confused look. "The ball highlighted that the matter of matching Myrbeth will be more difficult than I had expected. Maybe for now, at least, we shouldn't try to pursue a match for Myrbeth, but we will come back to this in time, you have my word." He gave her a solemn look. "However, Frederick, we should advance on a marriage for you. The next step would be to arrange a formal visit so that you can become closer with any prospective individuals. Therefore, I need to know which princesses were particularly notable to you?"

Frederick felt uncomfortable. He had been dreading this, never before had he found himself so reluctant to fulfil any part of his princely duty, but he wished all talk of marriage could cease. His life was happy the way it was and he disliked the idea of such a change. He didn't answer at first, so his father continued. "Custom dictates we host the princesses here, however if there were a number of possible choices or just one then perhaps sending you to the relevant Kingdom or on a tour of the Kingdoms would be more logical." Trevard had that determined look that his son associated with responsibility and the duty of the crown. So he thought over his many dance partners and made a choice.

"Well, I suppose, there were Princess Penalyn and Princess Gisella," Frederick answered glumly. The king nodded.

"Princess Penalyn Hennen from the Kingdom of Valance and the Princess Gisella Navara from Sedgebarrow." Correcting his son and using their full titles. "There is good potential there, especially with an alliance with Valance, I don't believe there has been a match between our kingdoms for quite some time. Sedgebarrow, huh, my great-great grandfather King Paulos married a Sedgebarrow princess. However, there is nothing wrong with strengthening an alliance that is already strong. Two is a small enough party to host here even with the family attendants. Might I ask why those two in particular?" Trevard enquired. Frederick had been hoping he wouldn't be asked that question.

"They were the only ones who were kind about Myrbeth," he said in a quiet voice. He looked gently into her clear blue eyes. She blushed before speaking.

"I thank you, but this choice shouldn't be about me," she said quietly, still blushing.

"Myrbeth is right of course, this choice should be your own and should not be made lightly," Trevard said in agreement, but Frederick defiantly held Myrbeth's gaze and his ground.

"How could I care for someone, if they cannot care for you?" his voice was a little louder than he intended but it had the desired effect, for neither his father nor Myrbeth argued with him any further.

"Very well, I will have Modwin see to the arrangements," the king concluded the discussion. "I believe I will also invite your Aunt Tunora; it has been too long since we have seen her." Frederick's aunt, his father's sister was married to the king of Sandoz but even though Sandoz was one of their neighbouring kingdoms she did not visit often. Frederick had very mixed feelings about this since his aunt at any time could be abrasive.

"Yes, it would be pleasant to see Queen Tunora again," Myrbeth agreed, with a smile that seemed genuine, but Frederick wasn't sure. After all none of Tunora's five children had attend the ball, even though three were of age and invited.

After breakfast Frederick chose to join Myrbeth on a morning ride.

"Shouldn't you help the king?" Myrbeth asked, as they started out at a gentle trot.

"Father won't mind," he said, hoping it was true. "Where are we heading today?"

"Shall we ride to the river?" Frederick nodded in agreement. The Brightwater canal was the main source of water for Hollthen, but it was a man-made off-shoot of the river that came from Walsea and briefly passed through a small section of Hollthen's coast. It was not until they were on the empty River Road to this natural river they spoke again.

"Will this visit be hard for you?"

"I don't expect so, you said the princesses were kind," Myrbeth answered, seeming unsurprised by the topic.

"Yes, but what about their families?" Frederick persisted.

"The focus will be on you." She seemed to take a moment to think before saying anything further. "The point has been made over my status; I don't think they will continue."

"You don't seem sure?" She gave a warm, wide smile and said she was, but Frederick didn't believe her. She had never hidden anything from him before or lied to him, Frederick didn't like it at all. He knew how sensitive this was for her, but he wanted her to confide in him. So, he tried a different question.

"Myrbeth, why didn't you ever tell me about the nobles' distaste towards you?" She frowned, then smiled before sighing and answering.

"For the same reason I never told the king, these people are your allies and I didn't want to cause any further discord. You just said yourself you couldn't care for someone who couldn't accept me, but as king one day you will have no choice, Frederick, but to work respectfully with the nobles." It was Frederick's turn to frown, but he knew she was right.

"Fair enough, but I still don't like it much," he grumbled.

"I know, but it really wasn't as bad as you are imagining, just a generally cold attitude, most never said anything before. They just can't understand your parents' decision." Frederick nodded, not sure of the right words to express how important Myrbeth's presence was in his life.

"You really think you won't get hurt again then?" he asked.

"I do, and I promise to tell you or the king if any of the guests act unkindly."

"What about Aunt Tunora?" Frederick asked, voicing his earlier suspicions.

"Oh, she is as nice to me as she is to anyone. Truthfully, she told me once that King Rollin was deeply against your parents' decision to make me their ward and that she argued with him, you know how she always has to disagree with her husband. So, she is pleasant to me to make her point." Myrbeth laughed and after a minute Frederick joined in. They rode for quite a while before Myrbeth stopped. "Promise to try to enjoy this visit and not waste time worrying about me."

"It's not a waste of time, but alright I will try. Let's both have fun," Frederick said, grinning, and Myrbeth nodded and gave another laugh.

Queen Tunora's party arrived five days later.

"My dear sister, welcome back to Hollthen," Trevard opened his arms from the castle steps to greet her. Their embrace was brief and stiff. Frederick was standing with Myrbeth and Edmund waiting for their turn to greet their aunt.

"Brother, the castle has changed much, I see." This was not true, yet Queen Tunora always greeted her brother with this remark, it was her way of showing that this was her home no longer. Frederick normally found this attitude amusing, but suddenly he found himself thinking, how difficult it must be to be a princess growing up in one castle only to have to leave it for another. To suddenly be expected to live in a strange kingdom, it must be hard.

"Yes, it probably has, sister. Your number is smaller than I expected," his father said. The queen had only brought her eldest son, Prince Manual Boutiner, the crown prince, and her youngest daughter, Princess Marianne Boutiner. Had father invited all his cousins and perhaps even his kingly uncle too? He had never told Frederick so. He wondered why they hadn't come.

"Yes, Rollin sent the other boys with Sara to Twickerth for a visit. You know her betrothal to Crown Prince Urvant was announced last month."

"Of course. A shame not to see them, but I'm sure we will all meet soon," Trevard smiled, and led his guests to the stairs where they all exchanged hugs. Tunora's remained awkward as did her son's who was a little shy by nature. Princess Marianne though was excited and very affectionate and clung to each of her cousins in turn.

"I'm tired from the road and would like to rest before dinner," Queen Tunora announced, once the greetings were completed.

"Hisbara will show you to the prepared rooms." Tunora followed the servant without another word.

That night dinner was held in the long hall and conversation continued to be difficult.

"I was attempting to remember when you were last here, Tunora?" Trevard began.

"I believe it's been a year or so. I was here for one of the children's birthdays," Tunora answered dryly.

"It was my seventh birthday, two years ago," Edmund supplied.

"We have seen yourself and Frederick, though, uncle. We all enjoy your visits," Marianne said, in a cheery voice, while her brother just nodded. An awkward silence filled the room again. This was one of the reasons Frederick never particularly liked his aunt's visits; it was always like this. He felt the urge to break the silence.

"I'm looking forward to the tournament, aren't you, Manual?" he tried.

"Very much," his cousin replied simply.

"Ah, yes, the show of manly strength. A rather boorish method of seduction if you ask me, but I suppose it's tradition," Tunora smiled, as if enjoying her own private joke. "I'm sure you'll impress." It wasn't entirely clear whether she meant Frederick or her son. They all ate in a focused manner, not speaking.

"Are you excited for your sister's wedding, Marianne?" Myrbeth asked.

"Oh, it won't be for some time. Rollin and King Ivan are still navigating the terms of the alliance," Tunora answered instead. The awkward tension rose, and conversation was abandoned for the rest of the meal. All in all, Frederick decided he couldn't wait for the remainder of the guests to arrive.

It was four days later that the whole family, with Queen Tunora and her children, stood ready in the castle courtyard to receive the other guests. As was traditional for such royal visits each of the princesses arrived with a family escort. Princess Gisella Navara was to arrive with her father, King Jonathan Navara, who was to stay only until the next day in order to participate in the welcoming feast, then he would return home. Princess Penalyn Hennen was to come with her mother, Queen Docca Yenton and her younger sister, Princess Evangelina Hennen, who were to stay throughout the visit. The carriages arrived and the guests emerged. The king's herald stepped forward and announced each of the guests in turn, leaving a short amount of time between names for all to bow or curtsy to the individual just named. The individual then bowed or curtsied in return, this was all done in order of rank and age. It was as if they had never met before.

Frederick looked over the new guests feeling nervous and uncertain about the visit again. Queen Docca and her daughters were copies of one another; short with long curly fair hair, wearing heavily embroidered gowns. The Princess Evangelina was noticeably young and clung tightly to her mother's arm. Princess Penalyn smiled widely and smoothed her gown excessively. King Jonathan escorted his daughter on his arm. King Jonathan showed clear signs of early ageing. He was in the process of turning bald and his now lined skin was beginning to sag. Gisella in contrast was the picture of beautiful youth. She had dark red hair, glossy brown eyes and clear alabaster skin. She did not smile, but glanced around taking the castle in, looking deliberately at everything. As the chief host Frederick moved forward to offer the guests a tour of the castle. His father came forward too, offering his arm to Queen Docca.

"It is most pleasant to see you again, Trevard," she said, in an affectionately warm tone. Frederick knew that his father had known the queen as a child. Her older brother King Emil Yenton had been, and still was, Trevard's best friend.

"And you, Docca," he returned, smiling. The two princesses came to stand either side of Frederick, and Edmund walked beside Princess Evangelina. Manual, with his sister, and King Jonathan escorting Queen Tunora, brought up the rear. Frederick looked back, frowning slightly at the sight of Myrbeth staying behind to direct the flurry of servants collecting luggage. After the tour everyone retired to their chambers to dress for a small private feast in the long hall. Tomorrow evening there would be a large welcoming feast with all the lords and knights of Hollthen in attendance. There would be dancing and music to celebrate the tournament that would open the entertainment for the auspicious royal visit.

The long hall was warm and smelled heavily of roasted meats. Everyone was talking merrily as the food and drinks were served. Frederick, however, was not happy. He was struggling with his companions already. Princess Gisella proved to be unsocial and uninterested. The more he tried to engage her in conversation the less she spoke. He might have made more of an effort if it hadn't been for Princess Penalyn. She was talking constantly; he hadn't remembered her being so gossipy at the ball. It had started during the tour when most of the party had lagged behind. She suddenly babbled out in rush.

"I was surprised to see your aunt here; I had heard the queen never left her castle. Not surprising, after all that she has been through. It's such a sad, tragic affair, her falling in love with that prince and then him dying so suddenly. He took a fever, didn't, he? And then died before they could be married? Such an awful thing for her to go through when she was so young, I cannot imagine it. Then she met King Rollin and they bonded over being disappointed in love. The king had proposed, and the girl had refused him. Refused him, can you believe that? I mean his family were all happy because she was only a lord's daughter, not quite good enough for a crown prince. He lost his head over her though, so tragic. He and your aunt married rather hastily, I don't think either of them wanted to be sad or alone. Well, none of us do, but it soon turned sour." Frederick was astonished. He knew the story, of course, and she seemed to have all the basic facts right, but still it was a shocking thing to say. She wasn't being cruel or even unfeeling, Frederick noted, she was just chattering. He hadn't known what to say but she didn't seem to need any response.

It was the same now, she was chattering away very quickly about whatever thoughts occurred to her. After a short time, he learned to tune her out. He sat bored and forlorn near the top of the table. That is until Penalyn began to talk about Myrbeth.

"She does look lovely in purple, but then she is quite a beauty, I think." Myrbeth was seated at the other end of the table, so couldn't hear what was being said or surely she would have blushed, thought

Frederick. "She has such a fine figure that she can wear anything she likes, I can tell. Me, I'm too short and plump, clothes look so unflattering on me, I have to make all my own dresses. But Myrbeth, she has such a shapely figure, so lovely, that clothes just suit her, no matter what." Frederick found himself smiling and he turned to also admire Myrbeth's figure. Frederick was pleased when the day was finally done. He had completed his duties as a host by showing his guests to their quarters and was now heading to his own rooms a few corridors away. To reach them he walked past Myrbeth's, the door was open so he looked in on her. She was brushing out her plaits with a distracted look in her eyes.

"How did tonight go?" he asked, interrupting her thoughts.

"Shouldn't I be asking you that?" she smiled and turned to face him.

"Alright. Not well," he said, changing his answer.

"Well, it's too early to tell anything," she said, in a relaxed voice, Frederick wished he could share her ease over the situation. He still felt nervous and conflicted, but he knew it would be better tomorrow when he could focus on the fight instead.

"What were you thinking about just now?" he asked.

"I was just wondering if it felt strange to your father and the two queens," she explained.

"Strange?"

"Well, around 25 years ago this was them, meeting potential matches, deciding their futures. Now it's our turn," Myrbeth outlined with a little laugh. Frederick laughed too, thinking what that must have been like.

"It's even stranger to think that in the future it will be our children's turn."

"Yes," was all she said in return. It was only short a time later that Frederick was curled up in bed dreaming pleasant dreams, a shapely figure and brushing of golden brown hair.

CHAPTER 10

The next day Frederick was to open the first day of the tournament. The tournament itself would be full of the lords, knights and guards of Hollthen. There was even a law that allowed boys of common birth to participate, as long as they were over the age of fourteen and could demonstrate a certain level of skill. There would be three types of entertainment; there was a traditional tilt round, a round of sword fights and the last round was a melèe, where varied weapons where permitted. Every weapon had to be blunted or covered, though, the king would never allow his men to be killed in what was essentially a sport or game. This was not the case in every kingdom however, Frederick knew, but he agreed wholly with this. He couldn't imagine truly harming any of the men he knew so well.

Opening day was dedicated just to him. This was because he was not to participate beyond this day since the object of the tournament was to give him an opportunity to connect with the princesses. However, this chance to show off his fighting skills was important, and Frederick couldn't deny he was excited to do something familiar and physical.

"I think you've grown taller again, I'm not sure this all fits properly," Edmund complained, trying to force the straps to fasten. He was acting as Frederick's squire for the first time.

"That piece fits on my arm not my leg!" He picked up another piece of amour from the table "This is a greave, for the leg, see." He bent down and tied the greave to his left leg.

"Right, I should have known that," Edmund looked abashed.

"It's fine, you have never had to think about it before." It was true, as a young prince Edmund didn't yet have his own tailored amour suit and wouldn't receive one until he was fourteen and of fighting age. Edmund had only ever worn protective sparing amour before, and the guards always fitted him with that. "You will learn, why don't you find the other greave and try again." Edmund managed the rest of the pieces with a few more helping prods from Frederick. The crowd had been taking seats while the prince was being prepared and when he come out into the stand that had been erected around the practice yard they applauded loudly. Frederick smiled and waved, the joy and excitement welling in him.

The first day, his day, was also split into different rounds and was to begin simply with a tilt. Frederick rode against Sir Thaze who was a champion tilter. Frederick had never been particularly skilled with a lance and he knew he wouldn't win. Some princes might have insisted on being allowed to win or have picked an easier opponent to have a better chance, but not him. He wasn't afraid of admitting he was out-matched or being defeated in front of the crowd. He saw it as a show of humility and felt it more honest than rigging the fights to make himself seem the expert. He and Sir Thaze shook hands before mounting their horses. They were each handed a lance, a small horn was blown and the tilt began. He managed to hold on for five rounds before Sir Thaze succeeded in unhorsing him. Guards and the royal physician ran out to check on him but Frederick was fine, he got to his feet and bowed to Sir Thaze who bowed in return while the crowd applauded again.

Next, he and the master of arms, Sir Danville, did a demonstration fight which was not too different from practice since they never landed a blow, merely exhibited their skill. They fought with some specialised weapons; Frederick had got the idea from Edmund's training session. They used maces, spears and throwing axes, and finished with target archery with both bow and crossbow.

"Are you ready, young princeling?" Sir Danville asked, in an excited growl.

"Begin sir, I'm ready," he replied, equally excited. They continued these small exchanges as they fought, in loud voices so the crowd could here.

"You should have been quicker, princeling; you might have had me."

"Next time, sir." Then later, Frederick complimented the master of arms. "Good feinting, sir."

"Now try it with your left-hand, princeling." The crowd clapped politely as each fight was concluded and each new weapon brought forth.

Next came a fight between him and his cousin Manual, using blunted swords. They met and shook hands before beginning. Frederick knew he would have no trouble winning this time. He had often trained with Manual so could easily predict his response to each of his own moves. It wasn't that his cousin was a bad fighter, but he lacked confidence and would often allow his opponent to lead the fight. Frederick had a thought, though. As an act of kindness, since his cousin was continuing in the tournament and he was not, he thought that he could give his cousin a boost of confidence if he threw the fight a little. He decided he was going to lose on purpose, but training with Ser Danville for the mock fights had taught him a lot. If he chose the right thrusts to match his cousin's normal choice of parries, then he could give Manual a better chance. His plan ended up working better than he had hoped. As Manual became more assured, his attacks also grew in sophistication to the point where Frederick was starting to struggle. The fight was much closer than Frederick had expected, and there were a few times Frederick's stance faltered. With this Frederick changed his mind, giving his cousin confidence was important but so was being honest. In the end Manual fell down and yielded with Frederick's sword at his throat. Frederick then threw down his sword and pulled Manual to his feet. He clapped him on the back and raised their arms up high as the crowd cheered.

The final spectacle of the day was a team mock battle. Manual and Frederick both picked two knights from the challenger's list to create their teams. Frederick had the first choice and chose Sir Korth, the captain of the guard, who looked deceptively old and was surprisingly strong. Manual chose next, choosing Sir Thaze for obvious reasons, Sir Monkford was Frederick's next pick, for similar reasons of strength and heavy build. Manual concluded with Ser Kelas, a young knight who was rigorous in his daily training. The two teams shook hands and formed up on horse, each choosing the weapon they felt most familiar with. Frederick chose a blunt blade, as did Sir Korth, Manual and Ser Kelas. Ser Thaze chose a broad spear that was lighter but not dissimilar from a lance and Sir Monkford a small throwing sword and mace. The horses and riders stood at opposite sides of the field and waited for the starting horn.

"Got a rousing battle cry, prince?" Sir Monkford asked. Frederick hadn't thought of that. He tried to think of one but all he could come up with was something he had read in a book once.

"Hark, ride onwards, good men," he offered, uncertainly.

"Nope too long," Sir Korth said bluntly.

"Keep it simple," Sir Monkford suggested. Frederick thought again. Now he was sixteen and of age, Frederick rarely felt young anymore but standing between these two seasoned knights readying for battle, he really did feel like a boy playing at war.

"How about just 'charge to victory',"

"That will do nicely," Sir Monkford smiled at him. "Cry it out and pull out your sword, quick before the trumpet." Frederick raised his voice and cried the words, drawing his sword as instructed. The crowd cheered, the trumpet sounded and the six men kicked their horses into a gallop, the sound of their hooves pounding the ground.

Frederick made a beeline for Sir Thaze, determined to prove himself after all. This move quickly confused the field, Manual had been riding straight at his cousin, clearly not expecting to have to tackle a real knight, but when his would be opponent made a fast turn to his left Manual didn't react quickly enough. His horse rode straight between Sir Korth and Sir Monkford, both of whom had fast reactions and struck a blow each. One to Manual's right side and the other to his back. The force sent him off the left side of his horse to the ground and knocked him out of the fight. That left Sir Korth and Sir Monkford to double team Sir Kelas, letting Frederick tackle Sir Thaze alone. Sir Thaze smiled, greeting the prince's challenge, he held his spear steady but at an upward angle and met Frederick's first blow with the throwing sword. The metals met with a clang and Sir Thaze brought round the spear, but Frederick had expected this and lifted his shield to meet it. This pattern was repeated a few times, with Frederick thrusting with his sword and Sir Thaze blocking each blow. Frederick realised he would quickly tire with this; he was already quite worn from the day's exertions, he needed to act, to somehow catch the knight off guard. His thinking distracted him and he nearly missed a thrust from the spear, he caught it at the last second on the very tip of his shield but he felt the blow jarring down his arm. So did his opponent though; he saw Sir Thaze's right arm flinch and lose its grip. Frederick attacked quickly, swinging his sword straight into Sir Thaze's hand, forcing him to drop the spear, now he only had the throwing sword.

A throwing sword was half the length of a long sword and lighter, to offer a greater throwing distance, Frederick knew it wasn't designed for swordplay. Now he didn't have to watch out for two weapons, Frederick made a bold choice and threw away his shield then gripped his blade with both hands. Using all his strength he swung the sword. His blow landed hard on Sir Thaze's short sword, the metals' meeting created a sharp clang and the short sword spun out of the knight's hand, landing point down and quivering. Sir Thaze let out a loud laugh and held up his hands in surrender and the crowd erupted into applause and cheers. Frederick had nearly lost his seat but had used his thighs to cling on to his mount tightly. Once he corrected himself he looked around; Sir Korth and Sir Monkford had evidently taken down Sir Kelas some time ago. Sir Kelas was laying in the sand, dazed and with a dinted helm, and Sir Korth was assisting him on to a litter. While Sir Monkford had moved his horse away from the field and had been watching Frederick's progress. Frederick felt his concentration lift finally and the exhaustion and aches from the day became more apparent. He let out a relaxed sigh, it had been a good day. The three victors formed up again and circled the field, as the crowd cheered them with a last round of applause. Some yelled out congratulations and called out,
"Good fight."
"Well done, Prince Frederick."
"What good sport," Frederick waved to lords, knights and commoners, feeling the warmth of their admiration fill him.

The victory lap ended at the royal seat where the king stood to dub them the champions. Frederick looked to the seats on the left where Myrbeth was sat between Princess Penalyn and Princess Gisella, all three were beaming at him, but it was Myrbeth's features that stood out most clearly for him. Her smile only made her more beautiful. Dusk was beginning to fall and everyone made their way to the castle, but Frederick headed back to the dressing tent where he found his brother.

"You were amazing, Frederick," Edmund exclaimed, grinning.

"Thank you, Edmund, it'll be your turn one day," he smiled back, then he stood still so Edmund could remove his amour. This took much less time than fastening him in had taken but before they were finished his father came to join them.

"I'm very proud of you, son, you did quite well."

"Thank you, Father." A thought occurred to him. "Why don't you compete anymore?" he asked.

"Oh, I never enjoyed swordplay much and after experiencing true battle I chose to give up altogether," Trevard explained in a matter-of-fact tone.

"When was this?" both boys asked, they had never known their father had fought before. Parvery was a peaceful land, and they couldn't imagine what situation could have required a king to take up arms.

"It was a minor skirmish, some foreign invaders, I believe you and Myrbeth were not even three at the time. Tonight is not the night for such a tale though, we need to dress for the feast."

The princes nodded at their father, each secretly vowing to ask again another time. Night had truly fallen when the doors to the long hall were thrown open, the guests stood as King Trevard entered first, escorting Queen Docca and Queen Tunora. Frederick followed with a princess on each arm, then Edmund walked in with Princess Evangelina, and Prince Manual with his sister again, King

Jonathan led Myrbeth this time. They took their seats and the king called for the food to be served. Frederick was very hungry and ate a great deal, but he didn't talk much. He was deeply engaged in imagining what it must be like to be in a real battle.

CHAPTER 11

There was a total of fifteen challengers entered in the lists and the day began with a parade of all the men in their amour. The day was much colder than yesterday and there were dark clouds that seemed to threaten rain. Myrbeth was sat next to Queen Tunora in the stands, and she didn't seem in good spirits.

"Don't they remind you of peacocks," she commented dryly. Myrbeth didn't want to be rude so she didn't answer but instead commented on something else.

"Manual looks fine," she tried.

"Yes, the amour suits him," was Tunora's only response and then she fell silent. Myrbeth didn't know how to respond so she didn't try, she had talked enough yesterday. Princess Penalyn had asked endless questions about everything she could think of; about the knights, Hollthen, the king, Myrbeth herself, and Frederick, of course. She had asked what kind of fighter he was, what interested him, what sort of a king he would make and what sort of a husband he might make. Myrbeth found each question harder than the next to the point where she was struggling not to repeat herself.

As her opposite Princess Gisella had been almost completely silent but Myrbeth was sure she had been listening to every word. Today Frederick sat between the princesses, and he looked just as uncomfortable as she had been.

The silence continued between Myrbeth and Queen Tunora as the jousts began. First was the young guard, Delbard, that had escorted her home. He was set against a burly arrow smith called Bell. Myrbeth had watched enough of these competitions to know that strength was no guarantee of success. Sure enough, the arrow smith's strength lost to the skill of the younger, skinny guard. The day continued and the list grew shorter as more competitors faced each other. Queen Tunora didn't speak again until it was Manual's turn to joust.

"This won't be much of a show, I fear," she said sighing.

"I'm sure they will both do well," Myrbeth spoke positively, Manual's opponent was to be a guard named Poole who she knew to be lazy in his disposition, making him something of an easy target.

"No, Manual isn't all that competent, I'm sure his foe is far superior."

"He did well against Frederick," Myrbeth said, attempting to be supportive.

"Frederick was gentle to him on purpose," Tunora spoke sharply, showing her disapproval at his concession. Myrbeth was sure that she was right, she knew Frederick's fighting style and he hadn't used some his favourite moves. Instead of being disappointed, like Tunora, she saw kindness in his actions and greatly admired Frederick for it.

To most people Tunora seemed a cold woman but Myrbeth had always suspected that that wasn't the case. It was just that she was deeply unhappy and disappointed in life, she supposed such an unfortunate life was a difficult thing to bear. Tunora was proved wrong about the fight. Manual met several of the guards' blows and finally, on the third tilt, succeeded in exploding the guard's lance. The handle of Poole's lance flew backwards and knocked him out. The crowd cheered and some even laughed. The queen gave a quick half smile before saying.

"His father will be pleased; he has always had doubts. Necessary I suppose, a king must be strong. Perhaps Manual would accept tutelage from Frederick, he could use it." Tunora brushed back her black hair excessively seeming to be debating something before continuing. "I was sorry I was not able to bring Landly with me," Tunora said, referring to another of her sons. "His father was quite adamant about it. You would not have wanted him, though; he is quite stupid, and fatter than Manual. I fear he will not make a good match. King Rollin would not even let me bring Reno, though he is much too young for you. He forbade me to make any sort of agreement with Trevard; he likes to control all matters," It took a moment for Myrbeth to work out the meaning behind her words. The queen had not been allowed to bring her sons into her presence. Then it occurred to her how unusual it was that the visiting princesses had not been accompanied by their brothers. She was the reason why. It was the ball all over again; princes not in attendance because their parents couldn't risk that they might become close to her.

The rejection hit her again as she realised she would always be worthless to these people. She was quiet for the rest of day. She looked over at Frederick and saw that she wasn't the only one not enjoying the festivities. During the fight he had seemed happy, but now he just looked glum. A worse thought crossed her mind. She might never be married and that would be disappointing, but a worse fate would be to watch Frederick forced into an unhappy marriage. To watch that jade him as Tunora had become jaded.

That she couldn't bear, it would break her heart entirely.

King Jonathan left early the following morning at the first light of dawn as he had many days journey ahead of him. They all rose early to say goodbye then retired to the long hall for breakfast.

"I think the tournament went well," Princess Penalyn commented, she often seemed to start the conversation. Couple this with her constant need to talk and Myrbeth wondered if there was something about silence that made her uncomfortable.

"Yes, Lord Burchard made an impressive champion," Frederick replied.

"Indeed, you were very impressive too, Prince Manual," Penalyn said, smiling across the table. It was true, Manual had distinguished himself, surprisingly going on to finish in fifth place. The prince gave a shy smile and nodded in acceptance of the compliment.

"I hope you will excuse me, but I'm very fatigued from all this festiveness. I plan to rest today," Queen Tunora sighed.

"Oh, but you will miss seeing the academy," Edmund said, excitedly. Now that the tournament was over the party was to travel out to the Medical Academy for a special tour.

"I have seen it before, Edmund, I assure you I will be much more comfortable here."

"You are welcome to join me at council if you wish, Tunora," King Trevard offered.

"No, thank you, brother, I just wish to rest." Her voice grew a little sharp and the conversation ended, leaving an awkward atmosphere. It was a relief to get outside and start their trek. They were to travel on horseback, so after breakfast was finished, they went to the stables and mounted up.

"How long a ride is it, Frederick?" Penalyn asked once they had exited the castle gate.

"It's a little over 8 miles, so it is a nearly a couple of hours ride, but the way is quite pleasant," he answered.

"Yes, that's very true," Queen Docca agreed. "I remember the route though it's been many years since I have seen the old academy."

"I didn't realise you spent so much time here, Mother," Penalyn said.

"Oh, yes, I spent a lot of my childhood here, and Trevard and Tunora often visited us in Walsea. We were all very close," Queen Docca replied.

"You were close with Aunt Tunora?" Edmund exclaimed, in an incredulous voice.

"What Edmund means is we're surprised she has never mentioned it before," Myrbeth tried to soften his words and gave Edmund a disapproving look, letting him know he was being a little rude.

"Yes, she was almost like a big sister to me. I'm not surprised she doesn't talk about it. That will be because of Jacus, my younger brother, I don't suppose she talks about him either?" Queen Docca turned to ask Prince Manual and Princess Marianne.

"I have never heard of him," Marianne shook her head.

"I have," Manual said in a quiet voice, he looked very uncomfortable. "She used to talk of him to me when I was little. She said I looked like him, but father didn't like it much. She stopped when I was nine, she thinks I have too much of father in me now."

"I suppose as a baby you did share his colouring but there isn't much of a resemblance. These are subjects best not talked of, though," Queen Docca concluded. Prince Manual had light reddish-brown hair with brown eyes he which had inherited from his father, but Myrbeth vaguely remembered that when he was little, he had been fair haired. Myrbeth imagined that Tunora might wish that her fair little baby had been the child of her lost fair-haired lover and how that illusion would have shattered the more Manual grew to look like the husband she was so unhappy with. Again, Myrbeth felt a worried, tense sensation, she remembered the king's words, that matching was a serious business. She hadn't fully appreciated how true those words were.

Hollthen Medical Academy was located in the village of Floria. The road that took them travelled past stone cottages with thatched roofs, past the meadow land where the holly bushes grew until it reached the high fence that surrounded the Academy's gardens and grounds. These gardens were not dissimilar to Lady Grouse's garden, only much larger. The grounds also housed several large glass houses where plants could be grown that needed a warmer environment. The Academy itself consisted of a large outer hexagonal ring of stone buildings which was the main heart of the academy. Then it had one large wide white tower in its centre. The unusual building was quite stunning to behold.

"Wow, it's like a palace," Penalyn said in an awed voice.

"In a very real way it is a palace. It has its own servants and guards, not to mention a whole team of groundkeepers," Frederick answered.

"It's beautiful," Princess Gisella said. Myrbeth had always thought the same. A man wrapped in a yellow robe came out to greet them, Frederick dismounted to meet him.

"Master Woolrich, thank you for welcoming us," Frederick bowed, and the master bowed in return. Frederick then introduced all the members of the party before the master turned and led them toward the large carved doors. He showed them classrooms, preparation rooms, a feasting hall, and various workrooms which were all housed in the grey hexanal building. All while explaining the various levels of learning the academy focused on.

"We take boys as young as twelve to be novices, until such time that they have completed our basic training then they gain the rank of junior and are allowed to choose a speciality of either Healer, Physician or Master."

"What is the difference?" Princess Penalyn asked.

"Well, a Healer is trained in what we call rudimentary medicine and horticulture, meaning that they can treat common maladies and ailments. Physicians are trained to heal wounds and less common illnesses. Masters stay here at the Academy to help train future novices." Myrbeth frowned. She knew that the Academy only taught men and boys; medicine was considered a male profession. Now that she had met Lady Grouse it seemed quite prejudiced.

"Why do they were such funny clothes, mother?" asked young Princess Evangelina.

"The different colour robes show their different ranks," Queen Docca explained.

"What's in the tower?" asked Princess Marianne.

"The tower houses our sleeping quarters."

After they were shown around inside Master Woolrich lead them outside for a tour of the grounds. Here the group stalled a little as Princess Gisella asked several questions about all the different types of plants. The party split into two groups with Frederick, Queen Docca and Princess Evangelina staying to hear the answers to Gisella's many questions. Myrbeth, Edmund, Princess Penalyn, Princess Marianne and Prince Manual explored ahead.

"Come on, Marianne, I will show you the beehives and wildlife garden," Edmund offered to his cousin.

"Of course," Marianne replied excitedly, happy to follow him.

"Be careful not to disturb anyone, creatures included," Myrbeth insisted, as they ran off. She moved to catch up with Penalyn and Manual who were in a grove of rosehip bushes.

"I'm very sorry about your mother." Myrbeth overheard Penalyn saying. "I know what it's like to have a parent that thinks you're not good enough."

"Really?" Manual asked, this was the first time he had spoken since the ride.

"Yes, my father is the same because he only wanted sons. He is never kind to me or my sister, he just loves my older brothers and spends all his time with them. He is forever saying he wishes we were boys too. He will be glad when I'm married and gone." Penalyn sounded gloomy and Myrbeth decided to turn back and find the others, to give them privacy. She thought better of Penalyn now, wondering if her talkative nature was simply because she was ignored at home. She felt truly fortunate to have such loving parents even if they weren't her true parents.

The royal visit was to last two weeks but after a few days it became difficult to think of new activities to interest their guests. Myrbeth could see how this method of courting might work to create matches some of the time, but she could tell that it wasn't proving successful on this visit. Neither princesses nor Frederick seemed particularly interested in each other.

"I was thinking a long walk to explore the countryside might be nice today?" Frederick offered to his guests at breakfast on the fifth day.

"That would be pleasant," Gisella replied, with a rare smile. He had suspected she would like the idea, she seemed to prefer the outdoors to all other things. A few others nodded in assent to the plan.

"I would rather not walk again. I would like to stay and attend to some sewing, but don't worry, Lady Myrbeth can keep me company," Princess Penalyn answered, in an assured voice. Myrbeth would have preferred to be part of the walking party, but she couldn't refuse, so she smiled and pleasantly responded.

"Yes, that sounds very relaxing."

"I will also stay, but shan't sew, I think I will read instead," Queen Tunora's said to no-one's surprise.

"I think I would prefer to stay, too," Prince Manual stated to everyone's surprise. Thus, the day's events were agreed and most of the castle's occupants set off.

Princess Penalyn settled herself in a south facing drawing room with a new dress she was embroidering. Myrbeth found needlework relaxing but today she would rather have been outside. She wasn't unskilled at sewing, however one look at her companion's work and she felt very incompetent.

"Your stitching is perfect and very detailed," Myrbeth complimented.

"Oh, that's just practice, I sew almost every day. In fact, I have been missing it so I'm very glad for the chance to get back to it." Myrbeth smiled as convincingly as she could and then quickly returned to her own work. Princess Penalyn prattled on with gossip from her home and Myrbeth made an effort to seem interested. She often found her attention wavering, though. She would look outside at the lovely weather, get lost in details of the tapestries hanging on the wall and find herself daydreaming. After a short while she noticed Prince Manual, who was sitting a little way off with a book, was not reading at all. He had opened the book in the middle but hadn't once turned the page. The reason soon became clear, he kept sneaking looks at Penalyn, repeatedly staring at her. Suddenly his decision to stay in the castle became clear. She watched him, waiting to see if he would act but nothing happened, so she decided to give a helpful nudge. Princess Penalyn was talking over the details of her ball which was to happen in a couple of weeks after she had returned home.

"I'm so sorry I won't be attending but it sounds lovely," Myrbeth remarked quickly to interrupt her flow. Penalyn had already apologised that she couldn't invite Myrbeth. "You must be going through this, Manual? Perhaps you could help Penalyn with some of the details, I know you have been to several balls."

"Yes, I have been to a lot," he said, flustered at being called on.

"Oh, heavens I always know just how I want things to be. I've had to battle with mother over everything," Penalyn said, and for a moment Myrbeth wondered if that would be the end of the conversation.

"Well, that's clever of you, but I never knew what answer to give. My mother had to pester and pepper me with questions about all the details for my ball. It didn't matter much what I said though, she always picked something different," he added glumly.

"Yes, my father does that, he says I'm making too much of a fuss of things," Penalyn smiled sadly.

"Well, your ball sounds very creative, some of the ones I have been to are just so simple." Manual's compliment made Penalyn glow, and she fluttered her eyes in clear invitation and appreciation. Manual came to sit closer.

"Simple? How so?" Penalyn asked, all her attention focused on Manual who suddenly became unusually talkative.

"I should be leaving I have a matter to arrange myself," Myrbeth said to the inattentive pair. She extracted herself from her needlework and left the room.

It was now early afternoon; it was quite possible that the others would have returned. So, she went in search of them, she was pleased when she found Frederick alone.

"How did the walk go?" she called out to him. Frederick turned, smiling, clearly pleased to see her and waved enthusiastically.

"Better. Gisella seemed to enjoy herself. She was more interested in the scenery than me again. It's good that she was happy, though it made the day less boring," he said, sounding brighter. "How was sewing? Sorry you got trapped."

"It wasn't so bad either. I think Manual is very interested in Princess Penalyn, that's why he stayed behind today. She feels the same, I think."

"So, some good can come from this visit after all," Frederick exclaimed, letting out a small laugh but he soon stopped himself, "but I don't want to be un-gentlemanly ."

"When are you ever un-gentlemanly?" Myrbeth smiled and took his hand, giving it a squeeze, hoping to encourage him to speak his mind.

"I'm trying," he began in a hesitant voice. "Both the princesses are beautiful and pleasant, but I'm just not interested in marrying them. I suppose the upside is they don't seem very interested in me either. But I won't get away with it, I must have a queen. father will insist on it," he ended in a frustrated voice. Myrbeth knew the pressure he must be under and tried to sooth him a little.

"Yes, but it doesn't have to be either these of princesses. You can choose whoever you want. If these two aren't right, then you try again." Frederick sighed.

"I'm not like father, I didn't fall in love at any of the balls I've been to. The girls are all pretty and nice, but I don't want any of them," he admitted. Myrbeth thought for a while.

"It might not be love, but you could still be happy. Choose someone you like, someone who likes what you like. Frederick, choose a friend. Then maybe it will become love someday."

"I suppose that might work," he said, clucking his tongue. She couldn't blame him for being sceptical. "It would be good if Manual finds some happiness."

"If we encourage it, you know how shy Manual can be," Myrbeth replied, smiling happily.

"Yes, let's play matchmakers," he beamed at her, giving her hand a squeeze.

The next day a boating trip was planned. All the young people travelled out to the nearby Brightwater canal which ran through the royal capital into the sea surrounding Hollthen. The boats were small and only designed to hold two people. Frederick instantly took charge of the pairings.

"I can row Princess Gisella, Myrbeth why don't you help Princess Evangelina. Edmund can take Marianne, and Manual, why don't you and Princess Penalyn take the last boat?" He then proceeded to assist Princess Gisella into the first boat without waiting for debate and Myrbeth followed his lead. As the boats glided down the canal Myrbeth and Evangelina fell behind the rest and Frederick's boat took the lead. Despite this, Princess Gisella's loud comments could be easily heard as she trailed her fingers in the water.

"Such a lovely shade of blue, with hints of grey and green. The way the willows dip in their leaves as if they longed to feel the cool depths, too. What a beautiful sunny day, how the light glitters on the water." Myrbeth smiled, noting that she had an interesting sort of mind really. She guessed that the princess was very intelligent but often hid this around company that made her uncomfortable. When they reached the beach, they pulled the boats onto the shore and sat down on the sand for a picnic. Manual sat close to Penalyn at her request.

"Stop grinning at them, Myrbeth," Edmund whined, wanting her attention.

"Just have some sausage," she said, smiling and teasing. Frederick smiled at her too, as Manual offered a plate of figs to Penalyn.

"Now you're grinning," Edmund pointed at his brother. "Why?"

"Just enjoying the day," he answered.

"It is lovely," Gisella mused, now running her fingers through the sand.

"It is, come on Edmund, Evangelina, let's build a sandcastle," Marianna suggested, Myrbeth saw, however, that once the three youngest had settled some distance away to build a castle, that Marianne was also watching Manual and the princess. Apparently, Frederick and Myrbeth were not the only ones who wished to encourage this coupling.

"You must have lovely views in Sedgebarrow, I've never visited farm country, but I hear it's idyllic," Frederick commented to Gisella to disguise the atmosphere.

"Yes, it is such a beautiful place, I could never tire of it. Each season brings new delights and there are so many blooms, so many thousands of types of flowers." She seemed to lapse into her own happy thoughts and spoke no more.

"We have nothing like that in Valance," Penalyn jumped in to carry on the conversation, "it's all just rocks, dirt and dust from the quarry, I wouldn't mind a little change in scenery. What's Sandoz like?" she asked Manual directly.

"Well, it is basically desert and mountains. I'm not sure it's all that pretty," he answered.

"I'm sure it's charming," Penalyn persisted.

"You would be welcome to visit," Manual offered uncertainly.

"You would want me to come?" she asked in a coy voice.

"Of course," he answered quickly, "yes, I would." Both Frederick and Myrbeth felt their matchmaking was becoming a rousing success.

CHAPTER 12

Toward the final days of the visit the king asked to speak to Frederick. He had concerns; the visit didn't seem to be going well.

"Son, I wish to discuss the importance of making a match. I don't wish to seem to repeat myself, but I have seen the great unhappiness that can occur in an ill-suited marriage," he said gravely.

"You mean like Aunt Tunora?" Frederick asked. Trevard sighed.

"That would be one example, but I've believed there isn't much happiness in your Aunt Barilsa's marriage either. Though she would never admit it. Finding a person that complements you can be difficult but will help when your marriage or kingdom faces tough times."

"So, you don't mind then, that I'm not taken with the princesses?" Frederick asked nervously. His father smiled and shook his head.

"You are young, there is plenty of time to find a future queen. I believe I can manage many years yet before I need to step aside. You may even rule a few years without a queen by your side. Though I think that unlikely, ultimately it's important you understand there is no need to rush in." Frederick smiled and King Trevard smiled back. Frederick was relieved at his father's words and felt comfortable enough to tell his father about what was happening.

"Then I guess you won't mind if someone else is considering a match with one of the princesses?"

"Oh, who?" he asked.

"Manual has displayed an interest in Princess Penalyn and vice versa." Far from appearing angry or upset, Trevard laughed.

"Manual and Princess Penalyn, that I had missed. How strange and marvellous. I think that boy could use a positive influence. I've had my concerns about Tunora's children though it is not my place to meddle. What made you suspect the happy couple?"

"Myrbeth noticed it first and we have been working together to encourage things," Frederick admitted, surprised at his father's comments.

"A worthy cause, to bring happiness to others," he smiled. Soon after this he dismissed his son as Frederick had a beach walk with Princess Gisella planned.

Frederick came out of the castle courtyard to find it empty. It appeared she hadn't wanted to wait for him. He knew he ought to catch up with her or go in search of Penalyn but instead he spotted Myrbeth heading towards the castle gate and rushed to her side.

"Where are you headed?" She smiled pleasantly, surprised at his unexpected company.

"Into the village. It's been a few days since I have visited." Since her return from Royal Holly, Myrbeth had made regular visits to her new friends.

"Then I will come with you. You did promise father you would introduce me." Myrbeth gave him a suspicious look.

"Aren't you needed elsewhere?" she asked, raising her eyebrows.

"Apparently not. No one wants my company," he said in a false, sad voice, pulling an equally false tragic face. Myrbeth laughed.

"Well, I always want your company." At that he beamed and held out his arm which she took, and they left the castle together. The walk into the village was passed in happy silence at first.

"So, remind me of all your friends' names?" Frederick asked. Myrbeth had told him about her new friends, and he knew how important they were to her, he wanted to make a good first impression. Myrbeth listed their names and told him other details about them as they walked down the road. The walk was very pleasant; he had missed spending time alone with Myrbeth like this. Once she was finished, they walked in silence for a while, arm in arm and Frederick felt happier and more relaxed than he had in days.

"The princesses seemed to be enjoying their time here," she remarked. "Princess Penalyn especially, I think there will be a wedding from this visit after all," Myrbeth joked.

"Just not the one people might expect," Frederick joked back.

"I think she will be good for Manual, though. He is too shy for his own good, Princess Penalyn will make him happy and encourage him to be bolder. He will need that help when he is king." Frederick was surprised how closely her words echoed his father's.

"Well, isn't that why we have queens, to help us be better kings?" Frederick's smile dropped slightly. "Though I don't know what help I would need."

"You need someone to make you think before you act. You're too reckless sometimes and you let your emotions run off with you," Myrbeth spoke in a playful voice, hoping not to offend him. He smiled in return, not at all offended.

"But that's just what I mean, you already do that for me, and all the rest. There won't be anything left over for a queen to do. You take perfect care of me." He beamed at her, but Myrbeth looked suddenly awkward, so he dropped it.

He switched to discussing the weather which looked as though it might take a turn for the worse. The conversation soon relaxed again and passed the time. The pair soon reached the village. Myrbeth led him straight through the market square, down a long cobbled street and in the direction of a finely carved wooden archway on the right. The archway opened into a vast compound. In front of them was an odd array of wooden artifacts, tables, chairs, statues, cabinets, and other such carved pieces. There was a door open to a workshop and some way behind a lovely log-built house. A young man came out of the workshop, smiling in greeting.

"Hello Samuel, how is your boy?" Myrbeth smiled in return.

"He is growing so big; he is nearly two now and just running around everywhere," the young man replied happily.

"Sounds lovely, is Jeremiah around?" she asked.

"I'm coming, but these old knees do slow a man down." Jeremiah came out from behind a tall clothes chest, he was heavily favouring his stick. "It's good to see you again, little Lady, and your Grace, it's an honour to meet you." The elderly gentlemen directed a bow at Frederick and a smile at Myrbeth.

"I'm equally honoured," Frederick replied.

"Surprised you could get away with all those guests up at the castle," Jeremiah commented. "Is it true one of the princess's hails from Valance?"

"Yes, the Princess Penalyn Hennen," Myrbeth answered.

"Well, that would be a bad match if you don't mind me saying so, your Grace." Frederick was more than a little confused but interested too.

"What makes you say so?" he asked.

"That's stone country, such a marriage would mean greater stone trade. That wouldn't suit here at all. Stone and trees don't mix; we are growing people, I'm a wood person. Always have been, wouldn't want stone stealing away my livelihood'" Jeremiah finished solemnly. Frederick had never thought of his marriage this way, that an alliance between kingdoms could change the balance in Hollthen. Or that the commoners would be so interested and affected. Frederick responded with equal frankness, deciding his people deserved the truth.

"The match won't happen, respectfully, as you say we're not a good fit."

"It's for the best, your Grace," Jeremiah said, in a solemn voice but with a wide smile.

"It seems everyone's mind is on matching at the moment," Myrbeth said, with a forced giggle. It didn't sound like her Frederick thought but he had no chance to ask her if there something wrong. Jeremiah gave a little frown and changed the subject.

"Suppose you're here to check on your order?" he gestured towards the workshop.

"Or because I wish to see you," Myrbeth replied. Jeremiah directed them to one of the work benches. Laid on the table was a small plain dagger and sheath. Around the weapon were pieces of carved holly wood that were made to fit the hilt and sheath.

"Once we got the basic shape, we added the grooves to support the grip, now it's Samuel's turn with carving. Shouldn't take too long, a little over a week I think."

"Well, that should be perfect. Edmund's birthday is still nearly three weeks away."

"We will add a leather strap to fasten it to a belt or boot," Samuel added. "You want a tree design, I remember."

"Yes, a blossom tree, white, if possible," Myrbeth confirmed.

"Yes, we can paint it," Samuel said, while his father nodded his approval. Frederick had been quiet, admiring the work, but now he spoke.

"I haven't been able to think what to get him, but he will love this. It's just right." Myrbeth smiled.

"I remembered when you turned nine, your father bought you a dagger, but I believe the king has got Edmund a book. It's the riddle book he is so fond of, you know he gave it to you some years back. So, I thought I would try to find a knife of some sort. The blacksmith only had ones that were either too simple or too gaudy with jewels. So, I bought a simple one and brought it here for Jeremiah and Samuel to work on." Frederick nodded.

"It will be perfect," he echoed, but he was still unhappy that he hadn't thought of anything. He had been too distracted lately.

"Don't worry, I will help you choose something for him. There is still plenty of time," Myrbeth smiled at him.

"We could do a bow in a similar style. That wouldn't take too much time," Samuel offered, but Frederick shook his head.

"Edmund's not much of an archer," he explained.

"We'll think something, your Grace, we have all sorts," Samuel said, gesturing outside over the expanse of the compound.

"Will you come in? Francine and the lad are out, I'm afraid, but we could put on some tea," Jeremiah looked a Myrbeth expectantly.

"Of course."

"Good, I need to rest these knees for a bit." Jeremiah led the way to the log house. Over tea there was much discussion over possible presents, and it was finally settled that a matching shield would suit. Frederick reasoned that there would even be enough time to take it to a shield painter, the only change he asked was that the crest of Hollthen also be carved into the corners of the shield. They left soon after this, Frederick pleased with his purchase and the first of Myrbeth's new friends.

Myrbeth led Frederick back to the square and along a different road, the large wooden schoolhouse was immediately on the left. Frederick had visited the schoolhouse before, of course; his father had a tradition of hosting the re-opening of the school each year.

The school always closed in the late autumn for several weeks until the cold of winter had passed. It hadn't been that long ago that they had opened the school for this year's crop of students with a large picnic. Then his father had made his speech about the history of Parvery as the traditional first lesson. Frederick couldn't imagine what they were doing here now, though. Myrbeth walked along to a small window at the back and gave a wave. She then went and sat nearby on a bench to wait. She didn't have to wait long until a boy about their age or a little younger came bounding out.

"Hello, Anthon," she called out, smiling in greeting.

"It's been well over a week since you came to see me," he said in a cheery voice, "I've missed you." He sat down close to her. Frederick was taken aback by his overly familiar attitude. No one behaved like this with Myrbeth, except himself, or Edmund maybe; he didn't like it much. The boy smiled over at him then, bowed his head and said, "You must be her princely brother, very nice to meet you, your Grace." Frederick nodded in return, in a slightly stiff manner.

"Will your father be free soon? I was hoping he would have those lesson notes," Myrbeth asked, then, turning to Frederick, she explained. "Anthon's father has been helping me with tutoring Edmund. Honestly when I told the king I would handle his education it was because I couldn't imagine what I would do with my time if Edmund was placed into someone else's care. But it's been much harder than I thought. There is more to teaching then simply stating what you know and then expecting others to know it as well. But Master Fields says with a little planning and structure we might get on better."

"He thinks quite highly of you," Anthon beamed at her. "He says you're a very intelligent lady and caring too." The way he spoke made it clear that he agreed wholeheartedly. Myrbeth blushed and asked her question again.

"Will there be a break soon?"

"Oh yes, in just a little while. Here, I finished it yesterday." Anthon handed over a finely bound book that Frederick recognised as belonging to the castle library. Myrbeth saw Frederick's eyes follow the book as she took it from Anthon.

"Anthon is going to be the schoolmaster someday. So I have been lending him books to improve his knowledge, with the king's permission, of course." Frederick didn't reply since what he had been truly watching was how close Anthon's hand was to hers. "I'm afraid I didn't bring a new book for you. I thought you couldn't possibly have read it yet."

"I found it fascinating," he said by way of explanation. As they discussed the book Frederick just watched them with a very stern glare that went completely unnoticed. He had never felt such gut twisting anger and wasn't at all sure what to make of it. To his relief the schoolmaster soon came out and interrupted the pair.

Frederick was uncharacteristically quiet for the rest of the visit and all the way back through the square and down yet another street. Myrbeth tried to engage him once or twice, but he just nodded or grunted in response. Until he felt more like himself, he wasn't going to allow his emotions to lead him into trouble. He barely noticed where they were walking. He was surprised when they came to a large garden, it reminded him strongly of the garden at the Academy. Myrbeth didn't enter though, instead she walked to a large house on the opposite side of the road, she knocked and waited.

"Where are we?" he asked, but before Myrbeth could answer a graceful elderly woman came to the door.

"Ah, you're here and in good time too. Come in, dear, come in," the women led them into a parlour just to the left, "take a seat and I will be right back." This left Frederick with more questions but when he opened his mouth to ask them Myrbeth shushed him. When the woman did return, she had a bundled-up baby in her arms, which she handed carefully to the eagerly waiting Myrbeth.

"Her mother has just fallen asleep." The woman seemed to notice Frederick for the first time. "Oh, your Grace, forgive me," she bowed. "My latest granddaughter, born four days ago," she offered, gesturing to the baby.

"How lovely," he said, approaching the baby.

"What's her name?" asked Myrbeth.

"Susan, a very simple name," Lady Grouse said, shaking her head with obvious disapproval. "I gave my daughters such lovely names, after flowers, plants and trees. Now they've grown up and I've got five grandchildren. Julianne, Lynette, Beatrix, Kathleen, and now Susan," she shook her head again. They were all silent for a while not sure what to say.

"Willow is doing well, I hope?" Myrbeth asked breaking the silence.

"Yes, she is well, dear," was all the answer that was given.

"She is a lovely baby," Myrbeth tried again.

"True. She is very pretty." There was only a slight pause before she continued. "It won't be long before it's your turn, dear, best be thinking of a few names yourself." Myrbeth gave a very troubled smile and didn't answer. Shortly after, baby Susan began to cry in earnest.

"She must be wanting feeding." Lady Grouse took the baby back into her arms. "I will take her back to her mother." Myrbeth quickly made excuses and she and Frederick took their leave.

They were both quiet as they walked back to the castle. Frederick didn't care for the silence at all. It was the closest they had ever come to anything like a quarrel. Finally, when they reached the castle, he decided he would say what was on his mind since he wasn't accustomed to keeping his thoughts from her.

"That Anthon boy cares for you," he announced. Myrbeth however didn't react, she just continued to stare at her shuffling feet.

"What's wrong?" he asked.

"Oh, it's just what Lady Grouse said back there, about baby names," Myrbeth answered, in a careful voice.

"About Susan being an awful name? I'm sure she didn't mean it." She shook her head,

"About me thinking of names for my own."

"Well, that could be nice but there is plenty of time if you're not sure about it," Frederick shrugged.

"I'm not sure I'm going to need them," she said, with a slight sob.

"Of course, you will," Frederick said, trying to be reassuring but not certain where this had come from.

"I will never have a child if I can't get anyone to marry me." She was still trying to hold back the sobs, but one tear had escaped.

"I'm sure these difficulties since the ball won't last forever."

"It isn't just the ball. Didn't you notice that none of the princes accompanied their sisters on the recent visit? It's because of me, and Princess Penalyn was forbidden from inviting me to her ball," She was crying wholeheartedly now, unable to say anything more. Frederick wanted to say that she was wrong but, now he realised the irregularity of the princes' absence, he could offer no other explanation. It had been not so unorthodox that Myrbeth had never been invited to balls, but now he could see how she was being cruelly excluded, all to prevent her from making a match amongst the nobles. He moved to comfort her but she pulled away. This was unlike her, and Frederick felt awful standing at the castle walls just watching her cry. After a short time Myrbeth dried her eyes and turned back to face him.

"I know there are other paths, but I do love children and want to be married just like any girl," she admitted, then she paused as if unsure whether to go on. However, she steeled herself and carried on. "I don't care for Anthon as he does for me. I haven't discouraged him though. I don't encourage him, either, and he is kind and clever and very sweet," she paused again at the look on Frederick's face, but then forced the rest of the words out in a gush. "I did think that, perhaps, if no one else would have me ..." Frederick interrupted her.

"No, you can't marry him."

"I know you don't think much of him, but he will be the school-master one day, so we would have a good home," she tried to continue explaining.

"It is not that. He is a commoner, Myrbeth." She snorted. "Don't. You know I'm not prejudiced, but you aren't one of them. You belong with us, our family. We are royalty and the people are our subjects. We can't show favouritism or have close ties, it can't be like that. We must know them of course and care, but if you were to marry one of them then you would be lost to us. You know that. It's hard enough to think of some snobbish prince taking you to a far-away kingdom. Having you at a distance would be hard but to keep my distance from you would be impossible." She gave another sob and flung herself at Frederick without a word. He held her tight for a long time. More and more he was being forced to think about what would happen when they both found matches. What it would be like if she married and moved to another Kingdom. How little they would see one another and what it would be like to share her with someone else. Myrbeth's fingers loosened their grip, but he didn't follow suit, not wanting to let go. She was the first to step back.

"I know it isn't fair on the king to worry so much, I should trust him but there is only so much he can do. I cannot stop being afraid that no one will ever love me." This was too much for Frederick because she was loved, he loved her. Overwhelmed by his own emotions he kissed her passionately and impulsively, pulling her back into his arms. The kiss lasted several golden moments before they broke apart. They pair looked at one another with secret and surprised smiles. However, before a word could be spoken, they were interrupted by a pageboy.

"Your Grace, I was sent to fetch you, sir. Your father, the king, re-quests to see you right away." Frederick's dismay was great. He had no desire to leave but he couldn't ignore the summons. He sighed, nodded, and went with the page. If the boy found the prince's walk-ing backwards and not taking his eyes from the Lady Myrbeth until she was quite out of sight at all strange, he didn't comment. Finally, Frederick forced himself to turn his back on the sight of the still retreating speck that was Myrbeth.

CHAPTER 13

Frederick met the king in his parlour trying to remain calm and natural though he felt anything but. His father looked grave and didn't speak at first merely gestured to a chair. Frederick felt jittery and didn't wish to sit but made himself do so.

"What we are about to discuss must be kept an absolute secret," the king said in a very stern voice.

"Of course," Frederick said with ease. Trevard repeated the point.

"I want your word, Son, it will go no further; you will not repeat this to anyone. Especially Myrbeth." Frederick gave his word, somewhat reluctantly now. His father nodded, took a deep breath and began.

"I have received the monthly reports from Pidar, they confirm some strange news. Both the Merchden and Walsea reports have accounts of refugees from distant lands fleeing to Parvery's shores," he said, gesturing to the papers on his desk and the crest stamped satchels resting on a nearby table.

"Fleeing from what?" Frederick asked.

"According to their stories there have been deaths, killings. Whole groups of people found dead, families, villages." He paused and in this pause the gravity of his words sunk into Frederick's mind and heart.

"But that sounds like ...," he interrupted, in a shaky voice.

"Yes, the black knights. I strongly suspect they have returned and are killing again. As you know the people of Pidar are great seamen, their king has plotted the attacks on some vast maps they have." He reached for one of the papers on his desk, a map with a red ink line along several islands ending at Parvery. "It shows that their most likely course is to return to Parvery." A horrible silence followed those words.

"They are coming here? But that would mean ..., Myrbeth," was Frederick's first disjointed utterance.

"Yes, as we have always feared," Trevard said, then followed on to say, "I don't want her told until it is certain." His voice was clearly a command.

"But I'm sure she would want to know," Frederick ventured gently, not wanting to contradict the king.

"I understand the desire to be honest. It is an admirable instinct, but I don't want her worried," the king spoke, and Frederick heard the finality in his voice. So, he raised a different concern instead.

"What will we do? We must be prepared."

"If their numbers are anything close to what I suspect, then all the kings will have to band together in a coalition. No one kingdom can tackle them alone and this threat could affect us all." Frederick could see his father's mind working very hard to puzzle out how this coalition might be formed. So, he took a minute to himself before asking another question.

"Why have they returned?" he asked.

"I can only speculate," the king replied, and Frederick gave an encouraging gesture, he wanted to know what his father thought. "Well, my theories, such as they are, centre around the first attack." Trevard sipped water from a nearby goblet before continuing. "Your

mother and I often speculated about the reason such a horrible incident had taken place. For a while it brought us good fortune, in
the form of a daughter, it was not the case for so many others. At
first people lived in fear that there would be more attacks. We were
afraid that Myrbeth herself might still be in danger, as I believe you
know. But after a year or so of silence and no trace of the culprits, it
became clear that they were gone for the present. This in my mind
left only one possible motive, gold."

"Gold?" Frederick repeated, perplexed.

"Yes, money is the only possible explanation for motive. You see,
Frederick, while it is no doubt true that those men had a taste for
blood or an enjoyment of killing itself, you would have to, to do such
awful deeds, this cannot be their only motivation, or they would
have continued to kill. Their disappearance clearly suggests to me
that they were directed to commit that crime and paid or compen-
sated in some fashion." His disgust was clear, but Frederick felt
confused which must have shown. "They were mercenaries, and the
village massacre was a job." Trevard simplified.

"I understand your theory, Father, but what puzzles me is why?
I mean who would pay for that? Why would they?" he repeated,
completely at a loss to understand such callousness, paying for such
cruelty.

"I've often asked myself that question. There are two possible reasons for paying for such a deed, I have fathomed. The first is that
the town itself was required for some purpose. You will remember it
was transformed after the massacre. This re-purposing might have
benefited some party or other, so they paid to make it possible. The
other possibility, as I see it, is that they themselves, the knights that
is, demanded a ransom. The town was proof of their wicked abili-
ties, and they used that proof to demand payment. In return they
would leave and commit no more murder." Trevard fell into another grave silence and Frederick was quiet too, thinking through his

father's theories.

They were terrible, mostly because they were plausible. After a long while something occurred to Frederick that seemed equally as terrible.

"But that would mean someone of noble birth would have to be involved. Only a lord or a king could pay them a high enough price, no matter what their reason. Such murder couldn't have been cheaply bought, could it?" He spoke, too shocked by the implications to feel outrage yet. His father nodded.

"No, it wouldn't have been cheap, I can only imagine the horrendous cost. I long ago came to the same conclusion. You might have wondered why I have always kept Myrbeth in the safe confines of the castle. I dared not put her at risk from this unknown noble. However, that is how I came to miss the nobles' lack of acceptance of her." He shook his head before returning to his original point. "You understand now why I have not spoken before of this; it is not information that should be treated lightly. You are old enough now to comprehend that such accusations cannot be made against any one individual without proof, of which we have none."

"Surely that implicates King Ivan, as Twickerth was in his kingdom, he must at least have knowledge of it." Frederick rushed to conclude, a desperate urge to protect Myrbeth and catch the culprit making him hasty.

"No, nothing is certain, it could be a rival king or a renegade lord, we cannot throw around blame. To do so would be very dangerous. I have found no proof King Ivan is involved, no proof of anything. We must not assign blame where there could be none." The king was deeply serious, so Frederick nodded his understanding.

"This is part of why you don't want Myrbeth told anything isn't it?"

"Yes, I've sometimes feared she would put the pieces together herself. She is certainly clever enough and has been given plenty of motivation recently to think on all that happened to her. But if she has worked out any of the puzzle pieces she has never said so. On the whole, I believe she doesn't want to consider the matter, for which I can hardly blame her. In fact, our recent discussion made me certain so. I was very careful with my words to her. I don't wish to thrust such awful theories upon her when no good can come of it."

"Yes, I agree she should be protected, but if it is possible that a king is involved doesn't that make turning to them for help highly dangerous?" Frederick logically knew that kings had to work with kings; that unity was the foundation of Parvery and all of its laws. Still, he was certain he couldn't trust any of them anymore.

"You mean for the coalition, yes, I will certainly have to tread carefully. I think, however, no king could risk not taking part. It would seem suspicious, and now the knights have returned no one will want to appear guilty of helping them," Trevard seemed sure.

"I see that, Father, and I agree, but actually I meant turning to them about Myrbeth. I know everyone has refused her as a match, but I also know you haven't given up searching for a match for her. If one of the kings changes their minds now it could be for the wrong reasons. We cannot trust anyone not to try to lay hands on her." While Frederick had other, deeper reasons for not wanting Myrbeth to marry, his concerns were genuine.

"Yes, you make a valid point. Well, I think, for now, it is better to put both your would-be marriages on hold. There has been little success so far and now there are more important things to consider." Frederick was relieved to hear this. Trevard sighed, "and as you say I have still failed in Myrbeth's case to find any sort of hope for a match." At this another wild impulse overtook Frederick and he spoke in haste.

"I want to marry her. I'm her match, Myrbeth belongs here with me." Frederick could see the shock on his father's face, to him this idea was impossible.

"You can't mean that, Son," he said, his voice no longer so firm or authoritative.

"I do, Father, I've never meant anything more. I love her." Trevard fell back in his chair in astonishment.

Clearly, he had not suspected anything between them more than sibling-like affection. But Frederick had often found himself thinking of Myrbeth in other ways.

"Does she feel the same?" Trevard finally asked.

"I believe so. I'm certain she does." This wasn't completely true, but Frederick hoped it was the case. His father did not speak again so Frederick did instead. "I believe I have always loved her, though it is only recently that I have come to realise how much, how completely. I cannot think of another with any sort of desire and I'm jealous of any threat that might separate us. I don't act out of pity because no one else wants her. I act because I could not bear anyone else to have her." He finished his explanation by repeating. "I love her, and she belongs with me." Trevard held up a hand then proceeded to pour himself a small goblet of wine. Frederick knew to wait patiently since his father rarely drank wine except on special occasions. He took a few sips before speaking again.

"A father's job is to promote the happiness of his children. I wish matters were so simple that I could grant the wishes of you and Myrbeth to be together and celebrate." He spoke each word heavily, emphasising their weight. "There are, however, other considerations. You are to be king one day. I love Myrbeth with all my heart and appreciate her for all that she is and all that others believe she is not. She could even be a fair and gracious queen, but a queen has to command the respect of not only those they rule but also of the other royal and noble families. I fear this would be beyond her, through no fault of her own." He took a few more sips of wine before continuing. "Recent events have shown me that, despite our views, our love for Myrbeth, it is not shared. I fear that making her a queen would only anger our fellow rulers who we so rely on for trade and beneficial relations. As a future king you must prize and protect these relationships. I'm sorry, Son, but I cannot grant you permission." Frederick took a deep breath and tried to remain calm. He knew his father would not be moved by an outburst.

"I understand what you say, Father, I do not take my duty lightly. I feel that Myrbeth would only make me a better king. We should support her against ..." Trevard held up his hand to stop his son's speech. His face paled.

"Perhaps I should have predicted the possibility for this," he stopped, "I understand that you are sincere and will not easily lay aside your feelings. How did I not see this might happen? How different things seem now," he mused. "Have you begun anything?" he asked awkwardly.

"Yes," Frederick replied simply, with his mind on their kiss. Trevard sighed.

"If you must proceed I won't order you to stop. However, I ask that you would do so with discretion, great discretion. A scandalous rumour could ruin you both for future matches. In the meantime, I give you my word I will consider what you have asked." Frederick was surprised, usually when his father made up his mind he didn't reconsider. Frederick could tell Trevard's mind was set against them, but he also knew that his father valued his word and meant this promise.

"Thank you, Father." Not long after this Frederick left. He felt torn between his revealed, deep love for Myrbeth and his trust in his father's judgement. He could only hope this would be resolved without conflict.

CHAPTER 14

Myrbeth debated with herself for a long time, it was true the king had not asked to see her as well, but he also wasn't in the habit of excluding her. If she followed Frederick surely the king would not turn her away and she longed to follow Frederick. She was so close to something she had dreamed of more deeply than she had ever admitted to herself. She was nervous to face him. What if the kiss didn't mean what she hoped it meant? Yet she couldn't just stay standing there. She moved her feet, her mind still too full to decide on a destination. The whole time she was walking Myrbeth tried to convince herself she was not going to the parlour. She knew it wasn't the truth, before long she was in the corridor that led to the king's parlour. It was a long corridor; she could see the door but she didn't approach it. She spent several minutes debating her need to see Frederick. Her feelings of confusion clashed against her sense of duty and manners. She shouldn't interrupt them, she knew, but she really needed to see Frederick's face so she might know if he loved her. Finally, she moved towards the door despite her inner conflict. What she heard astonished her beyond belief, she quickly retreated. A few tears slipped down her cheeks but she tried her best to hide them as she quickly run away. Too astonished to stay quietly hidden.

It was sometime later that Frederick entered his chambers and found Myrbeth there waiting for him. They shared a deep look of hesitation for just a moment but as a smile stretched both their lips, their happiness was clear. Frederick quickly moved forward and kissed her again.

"I heard what you asked the king," Myrbeth spoke after they broke apart. "Frederick, do you truly wish to marry me?"

"With all my heart," he said simply, caressing her face.

"You never gave me any sign, I never let myself believe that we could happen." Myrbeth babbled.

"I believe in us, Myrbeth, loving you is so natural I don't even have to think about it. The way I loved you just evolved, which is why I didn't fully realise that I was in love with you, but now that I know I can't not be with you." Myrbeth felt flushed and lightheaded. She wasn't sure she could express her feelings with the same clarity, she had been hiding them for so long.

"I've always known I loved you. I couldn't help it, but I never dreamed that we could be together. I mean you are the crown prince, and I am no one ..." Frederick interrupted her.

"Don't speak like that. I am and will always be yours, no matter what. Even if father doesn't grant permission for us to marry, you will have my heart always," he promised. He took both her hands in his and kissed them.

"Is there even a hope of the king giving his blessing?" Myrbeth asked, with a tremble in her voice. "He already said a crown prince was beyond my status, how could I blame him for refusing me his own son."

"Father agreed to consider our match and I am determined to bring him around. You know he thinks highly of you, truly."

"Of course, I know he loves me, but he has to act in the best interests of the kingdom, after all I wouldn't know the first thing about being a queen."

"I firmly believe that you are what is good for the kingdom, and I think I can convince father of that. There is a lot of logic, as well as love, in the match." Frederick outlined his whole conversation with the king while Myrbeth listened, still feeling anxious. "I'm certain father will change his mind; he did say he wanted to make us happy."

"I am happy, but are you certain this is what you want, that I'm what you want?"

"I'm completely certain, you are my perfect match. How long have you known how you felt?"

"I cannot name precisely when I realised I felt more for you than I should. I remember you climbing into bed with me the night Edmund was born. We were so excited we didn't sleep until dawn and after that it was a year before either of us wanted to sleep alone. I remember how you brought me flowers whenever I got sad for the longest time." She paused as if lost for another minute, but Frederick carried on her thoughts.

"I remember when you started to sew little trees on my vest shirts to keep her with me and you would leave messages about your day in my chambers." She beamed at him and took over.

"I remember at your first tournament when you won you brought me on to your horse to take a victory lap. I remember every gift you ever gave me; you are always so thoughtful."

"What's thoughtful is everything you do. I remember now how much we have always loved each other." As Frederick finished, he wrapped his arms around her, and she took a moment to feel the joy of the situation. Even if they could never marry, Frederick loved her and this could never be taken away. He loved her, not any one of the beautiful high-class princesses he had met, but her. It was miraculous and she marvelled in it for a time.

"We must think of our guests," she spoke, recalling that both she and Frederick had neglected the princesses today. Frederick, knowing she was right, nodded in acceptance. However, as they left the room, he took her hand and didn't let go.

The dinner feast proceeded as usual but Myrbeth could barely focus on what she was eating. Frederick looked equally happy, absorbed in his own thoughts. He sat between the two princesses; Gisella was silent and Penalyn was equally absorbed in Prince Manual.

"I enjoy making sand art."

"Sand art? I don't think I have ever seen that before."

"I'm not surprised, it's a practice of our people. In the mines they melt the sand to make the glass, but not all of it is pure enough so they dye it all sorts of colours and then create pictures with it."

"That sounds very interesting, what do they do with the pictures?"

"It just a pastime for most, but some of the old mine workers do sell their art to make their living," Manual explained.

"You will have to show me sometime."

"I'm not sure, father thinks it's very common and even mother says it's not a fitting interest for a prince." Penalyn tutted.

"I think it could be manly in the right hands." Then Queen Tunora turned to Myrbeth and spoke in a clear voice over everyone else.

"Sara will be pleased over their coupling. It's a silly tradition that the daughters cannot be married before their elder brothers, but who are we to question tradition." Myrbeth didn't know what to say to this, nor did anyone else. She couldn't help but wonder what Queen Tunora would think if she knew about Frederick and herself. Indeed, what would any of the nobles think. She had a pretty shrewd guess.

When no one answered her, Tunora continued, ignoring that she had once again brought all other conversations to a halt. "I will be glad to take our leave in a few days, it has been quite a tiring visit." Myrbeth knew the queen well enough to know that she rarely spoke of her true feelings, but Myrbeth suspected that at the heart of things Tunora, too, would miss the company.

"Yes, the castle will feel quite empty," Myrbeth replied.

"Yes, it will be very quiet and boring," Edmund agreed.

"Home will be boring too, but I suppose it will be nice to hear all about Sara's trip," Marianne agreed, and with this more relaxed conversation resumed. Later that day, the king called a private family audience to announce he would be taking leave of the castle as well.

"I will be taking a short tour of our fellow kingdoms. There are some new developments in trade that I would like to oversee personally. However, I leave things in Frederick's capable hands." His voice was casual, but Myrbeth was more than a little surprised by the suddenness of this trip. Perhaps, she thought, it was even a little suspicious.

"Are you sure, Father? I've never acted as regent before?" Frederick asked in a nervous sounding voice.

"Completely certain. If anything particularly difficult arises you may write, I will keep you informed of my progress. Or you can send word to your Uncle Edrick, but I'm certain nothing of the sort will occur. You have been doing very well of late, I have every faith in you." Frederick seemed to glow with pride.

"I might include Edmund in some of the day-to-day decisions, if you approve?"

"Truly?" Edmund said in an excited tone.

"Yes, perhaps. But you are still young, try not to trouble him too much, Frederick." Trevard answered and Edmund beamed. "You have been excelling in your lessons of late, so perhaps a challenge would do you good." He added, nodding to Myrbeth, crediting her. Myrbeth was pleased with the praise and with Frederick including Edmund, but she still found this all very suspect. Especially given recent events.

The leave-taking day arrived. The process of saying goodbye was just as formal as the arrival had been. King Jonathan had briefly returned to accompany his daughter and did not seem disappointed or surprised to hear a return visit was not planned. Queen Docca seemed slightly more upset with the unsuccessful visit.

"It would been so pleasant to see our families joined as they were once supposed to be," she lamented to Trevard. "Oh well, at least she has still attached a future king," the queen concluded, looking at her daughter and Manual saying their own farewell. There were already plans for the two families to meet again in Sandoz soon. Finally everyone was loaded into their carriages and Frederick let out a long breath as they left the courtyard. The king left with his sister, intending to begin his tour in Sandoz before moving on.

Those who were left behind quickly fell back into a familiar routine, with Frederick becoming heavily involved in the important work of the kingdom once again while Myrbeth and Edmund returned to the classroom. As he had promised, however, Frederick regularly included Edmund in his tasks, which left Myrbeth to her own devices more than she cared for. Which is why she was surprised to receive a request to visit the king's parlour one evening.

"It seems a little strange to see you sitting in that chair," she said, entering the room and seeing Frederick sitting behind the king's desk.

"It feels strange to me, too, but I suppose I will grow into it," he said uncertainly.

"You asked for me?"

"Yes, there was something I wanted your thoughts on." He sorted through a few papers on the desk and beckoned her closer. "The schoolmaster has sent us a request; plans for an additional school room for the purpose of storing books."

"Oh, the library we discussed. I didn't know he was going to move forward so soon," she said, taking the plans from him.

"It's all perfectly possible, still you know the building better than me. I thought you might offer me a little insight." She smiled and then quietly perused the plans for a while.

"I'm not certain," was all she said at first. "The room doesn't look right," she ventured tentatively.

"In what way do you mean?"

"It's too small. There is only room for the books. The children won't have anywhere to read them."

"We can solve that," Frederick smiled at her. They discussed it at length and by the time they had finished the plans looked very different. The next night Frederick asked her to come again. This time he showed her apprentice records from the Physician Academy, and a petition from their fisher folk to expand fishing territories.

"They say the fish numbers are becoming depleted and they must expand into deeper waters," Frederick outlined.

"Well, that's complicated. As they cannot risk infringing another kingdom's fishing rights," Myrbeth said.

"Yes, the answer won't be simple. I'm considering writing to father, but I would prefer not to. I thought together we could puzzle it out." She took a seat next to him and Frederick poured them both a little wine. However, after proposing a few relevant points Myrbeth could tell that he had already considered them.

"Surely this is the sort of thing the king has taught you," she ventured. Frederick looked suddenly awkward. A new thought occurred to Myrbeth. "You are trying to teach me, aren't you?" she asked. He looked slightly guilty and nodded.

"You said that you didn't know how to be a queen. Well, there was a time when I didn't know how to be a king. Father taught me; he always says that we must learn our craft just like any others. Jeremiah was not born knowing how to carve but he learned, so can you," he spoke in a kind reassuring voice. Myrbeth could see the logic in his words but still felt uncertain.

"I suppose, but I never thought I could play this role," she spoke in a quiet voice.

"I know but I want to help prepare you. We can go slowly and I will help you," he took her hand and she smiled.

"I am not sure if the king would approve, he has not given permission." She was still hesitating.

"He won't mind you helping me privately." She supposed this was true.

"Alright then, show me how this is solved." She kissed his cheek and returned to the fishermen's dilemma.

During the day Frederick still kept Edmund by his side as he assisted his people, but each evening he took to inviting Myrbeth to the parlour for a lesson. Myrbeth had expected the king would not be away very long, but Edmund's birthday was fast approaching and they still had no word of his return. She couldn't believe the king would miss such an important day and her suspicions only grew. He was up to something she was sure, but she was afraid to know the truth. Thankfully two days before the planned celebrations, word reached them that King Trevard would be home that evening. She grew more nervous than ever. Finally, Myrbeth decide to confess her fears to Frederick.

"Frederick, the king didn't leave ..." she stopped, uncertain, then began again. "He isn't trying to find matches for us?"

"No, it's just a matter of trade visits," Frederick said in haste.

"It's not that I distrust him. I just would have expected him to take you as well and when he didn't, I thought there must be a reason. Especially since he hadn't mentioned this visit previously. The timing seemed to suggest ...." but Frederick interrupted her.

"I'm sure it's nothing. I had to stay because he made me regent as the next stage in my training. As for the suddenness, I'm sure it just slipped his mind with so much else happening." After this Frederick quickly changed the subject. The king returned late into the night, very tired and worn out. Though he happily greeted both Edmund and Myrbeth he quickly sent her to bed stating he needed to talk to Frederick alone. It was clear the king was keeping secrets, something he had never done before. What else could it possibly be? Despite Frederick's attempts to reassure her Myrbeth was still left with an ominous feeling gnawing at her.

CHAPTER 15

It was different and yet the same. Mercy had never seen this part of Parvery before, yet there was an eerie sense of familiarity everywhere he looked. It was the dead of night when they began to pull their small landing crafts onto the beach of one of the coastal kingdoms. Mercy was in one of the first boats as it was his job to coordinate their numbers as they landed, a familiar task. Here they stood again over fifteen years later, surveying another damned village, familiar again. They were much further out from their destination this time and the view of the village was quite distant. There was no tree coverage, or any coverage at all, surrounding this different village of a different kingdom of Parvery but it still felt familiar. But this lack of cover made their formation even more vital. They would have to travel a little way to reach their goal as a group without attracting attention, familiar. It must be done in the dark and it must be done quietly, familiar. It was all too horribly familiar; he still couldn't believe they had returned to this place. This went against every rule he had learned in the company, to revisit a previous site involved a lot of risk. You get out and never go back, how many times had he heard that. Parvery, of all their sites they could have revisited why this one. Everything in his gut told him this was wrong, that being here was wrong. Times were not so tough that they needed to resort to this and yet he had lost the argument against this action. So, to Parvery they had come once more.

After their first visit the company had left Parvery in all haste to go to a distant land and lay low. The five leaders distributed to each man his share, and many went their separate ways. Only some of the new recruits were given the opportunity to join the Five Heads company. Mercy was one of those few, he had signed a five-year contract without thought; he had nowhere else to go. The core of the company was made up of around thirty men and its five leaders but with the new members they became quite large. Mercy soon regretted his decision though, as fighting broke out between the leaders. Most saw no point in taking new work as they had been richly paid for the Parvery raid. So, the company languished; gambling, drinking, and paying for companionship. Only a small faction was dissatisfied with this idleness, proving much more modest with their own share. As the money dried up, the fighting among members only grew worse and a string of crimes broke out. This destructive spiral might have continued if Finish had not taken definitive action. Finish killed the rest of the leaders and many other members, taking sole control of the remaining company. Before they had been ruled by joint decisions but now they answered to one clearer voice, anyone who dissented was also killed. They began to rebuild under Finish's new steady structure and the company returned to around 30 members. Finish had a strong sense of pride in his work and a dark sense of humour which had caused him to re-name his fighting company the Black Knights.

"It's what the folk of Parvery have named us after our time there. It's an ironic and fitting name for us, don't you think?" He had declared to his men.

Many of them feared Finish. Others, like Mercy, respected him for this brutal choice and hard rule. Finish introduced small taxes to pool the company's money. After a time, he used it to buy a large galley ship he named Freedom's Price. With this they became profitable pirates answering to none but themselves, living on board and taking jobs as they pleased. Life aboard the ship suited them all well. Mercy rose high in the company, gaining the rank of commander. He was thought of by many to be Finish's second in command. In truth Finish needed no assistant in leading and would happily kill Mercy if it served him. Mercy knew this and didn't mind; he was good at taking orders and had never wanted to lead but the pair did work well together. In fact, he had never questioned any of Finish's commands, until word of the planned return to Parvery reached him.

Despite his usually even temper Mercy found himself very incensed and he went to confront his leader and sometimes friend.

"Parvery! Parvery! why would we go there? What could be there for us?" Mercy yelled, as he burst into Finish's cabin. The cabin was large and lavishly furnished to display his wealth and status as the leader. Mercy had never cared for it but he understood the necessary show of power. Finish didn't smile at the interruption but instead clicked his fingers, ordering the two ship women out. They gathered up their clothes and left and Finish re-dressed himself. He was no longer young, and his ferocious appearance had only grown with age. His hair was receding but far from hiding the fact he kept it slicked back. His dark eyes carried a few wrinkles, but they were still sharp in both look and ability. Now, dressed in his usual black clothes he moved from the bed to the writing table. He gestured to the opposite chair before speaking.

"The same thing that always awaits us, gold," he answered, his anger was evident, but he kept his voice even. Despite the circumstances Mercy did not hold back.

"If we live long enough to claim it or aren't arrested instantly. I thought we were done with this sort of risky work." Mercy had made the decision to push things and there was no point backing down now. "You promised us you would protect our interests when you took over, Finish."

"I choose what work we do," Finish responded, his voice was still calm but there was a new layer of ice in his words. Yet he continued to speak freely, much to Mercy's surprise. "You are protecting the men, but I protect them too. We will be fine and Parvery will be every bit as profitable as it was previously." Mercy decided to back down slightly, it wasn't in his nature to question the chain of command. Also, he knew Finish might explain more if he was calmer.

"I'm sorry, I know you are looking out for our interests." Finish was mollified and returned to his jollier, usually even temperament and yet there was still warning in his words.

"I guide the interests of us all," he said.

"What is the job?" Mercy asked.

"The same as before, to cause carnage amongst the villages." Mercy felt his gut churn, but Finish wasn't done speaking. "Truthfully, there is another reason we must return to those shores. There was a mistake that needs correcting."

"Mistake? What mistake?" Mercy said, suddenly vigilant.

"There was a survivor of our first attack." With those words the thing that had nagged Mercy for many years came crashing hard down upon him.

"A survivor? What survivor?" he asked, trying to make his voice sound normal and disinterested.

"A girl, a young common whelp, she survived and apparently has thrived. Her existence wasn't an issue until recently. Now part of our return is to complete the job we were hired for. This girl must die." Finish spoke without emotion.

"Why?" Mercy asked, unable to resist the question again. "I never understood our orders then and nor do I now. Going back just to kill this one woman now makes no sense."

"There was profit in it then as there is now," Finish repeated, he paused to pour them both a little wine. Mercy thought about asking again but he knew Finish only saw things as simply as this. Mercy sighed as Finish pushed a glass towards him, "and it's a girl not a woman," The correction seemed unusual and illogical. Mercy could still remember the figure of the fleeing woman, he even dreamed about it sometimes. She had had light brown hair, was slight of build and was definitely a fully grown woman. He hadn't been close enough to see wrinkles or a developed bosom or any other signs of age, but he was certain in his assessment. If she was a women then, even a young women as he had been a young man, she would be a full grown woman now and he was now a grown man of thirty one years.

"How old is the girl?" he asked carefully, wanting to be certain.

"Fifteen or sixteen, she would have been a babe during the first attack no doubt." This detail only confused Mercy further.

"What did she crawl away unnoticed?" Mercy tried hard to make his voice sound jocular rather than panicked. Could it be that this was a different escapee for whom Mercy was not responsible?

"Her mother apparently squirrelled her away to another kingdom where she now lives under the protection of the king." Finish picked up an apple from his table nearby. He bit into it, clearly not sensing any motive or anxiety behind all of Mercy's questions, so he kept going.

"Is she some king's ill born whelp, then?"

"It is not thought so, but he did instate her as his ward, since the mother did not survive." Finish took another bite, looking down at his mud caked boots, clearly bored. Mercy used his disinterest in the conversation to rethink his memory. He pictured the fleeing figure of the women again, he concentrated hard trying to see a bundle. Did the women have a bundle of cloth in her arms? Could she have held a baby? He had not been close enough to see at the time but how else could it be explained.

"A girl, a baby girl, how can she matter?"

"She was never supposed to live. She is now the king's ward and causing trouble to the natural order of things. Trying to rise above her place." Finish grinned at the notion, showing he had no malice towards the girl he was casually planning to kill.

Mercy had never been so close to confessing the truth than in that moment. He felt he owed Finish that much but something held him back. As Finish took another bite of the apple, Mercy took a deep breath and tried to understand why even now he was still remaining silent. To this day he couldn't really explain why he had let that woman go but it had led to this. A common child in a castle. Still, after all this he had no inclination to see her dead. Did he feel some sort of kinship with the girl? No, that was ridiculous, he had never even met the girl. Never even known she lived. So how could it matter that she was now to die. Still killing her would not be simple. As he thought further it became clear it would take no small amount of skill. This girl's existence needed to be corrected, very well, but not by him. Mercy was no master thief able to sneak into castle walls. Whomever went after her would need to be a sleuth and assassin. While Mercy had no trouble killing, even when he did not care for the task, he had none of the skills required for this job. So confessing his possible involvement in her survival would be of no use. If he confessed, he knew enough of Finish's temperament and code to know he would insist that Mercy finish the work himself. While this was only fair, he would fail. What was the use of confessing if he

156

could not put the mistake right? So, Mercy steeled himself for what must happen.

"I will back you, Finish; I won't fail you; you know this. Still, you must see the risks in returning?"

"There are no risks, I assure you." Mercy was puzzled by his easy confidence.

"No risks? There are always risks," he said.

"Not this time, this job is clean, just like last time. We have a benefactor of sorts." Finish grinned again, throwing the apple core out the ship's window.

"You mean the man paying us?" Mercy asked.

"He pays for more than the job, that's what matters." Finish answered, without explaining anything.

"Who is he, and what is he paying for?" Mercy had never been so curious and wary. He knew they must be being paid, but who was this benefactor? Why could he possibly need the company and the work he was paying for?

"Careful now, I like you, but there are some questions that you shouldn't ask." Finish got to his feet and moved to close the window. Mercy knew Finish would say no more.

"Fair enough, I don't need to know who, I just hope you are right about him," Mercy said, dropping his curiosity. Much to his surprise Finish laughed.

"What is it that you are so afraid of?" he barked out after he was done laughing.

"A double cross," Mercy stated plainly.

"A double cross," Finish repeated the words and laughed again. "Oh, Mercy, you do not understand these men, the way they think. There is no honour in a double cross. We are safe, they will deliver all that was promised, you will see." He threw a second apple to Mercy. "Relax, my friend, all will go well." Mercy didn't share his confidence but chose to say nothing.

He saw himself as partially responsible for this return trip. As such he would take on the duty of assaulting the village. He would take on the dangerous elements, he would place himself in the thick of things and he would shield every man he could.

"I want to take the lead on the attack, Finish." Finish tilted his head and looked at him for a solid minute. Mercy was used to this; this odd gesture was his way of catching men off guard while sizing them up. It unnerved even the toughest of men and had unnerved him once but now he stood still, waiting for judgement.

"Perhaps I might give you the command, but not initially. We have a few simple raids that need to be attended to first on the way to Parvery, for ready coin. We also have a little light recruiting to do, just to bulk up our numbers somewhat. The larger mission, though, once we arrive in Parvery, that you may lead. I also wish you to help choose the men we will send to deal with this troublesome girl. It will have to be men we trust; I will accept no mistakes this time."

"Yes, there must be no more mistakes," Mercy had echoed.

Here he stood now, the wet sand clinging to the damp soft leather of his boots on that familiar shore. His worries had only increased as they put their plans into action. The initial raids on other small island they had found on the way had gone off without a hitch. The company collected a fair amount of coin and its newest members had become seasoned to their ways. Mercy had believed that this was the only reason for the small raids, however once they were completed, he had learned differently. It was a warning to the people of Parvery of their arrival. Mercy would have argued that giving such a warning was beyond foolish, but it was too late to unring the bell they had already rung.   "It's all part of the plan," Finish had simply said,

Mercy understood then, the plan was not his, it was the bene-

factors. The benefactor was issuing orders and Finish was following them, expecting to be well rewarded. Mercy did not trust this
benefactor or his plan, but he had little choice but to follow it to its
conclusion, whatever that conclusion might be.

CHAPTER 16

Trevard was glad to be home, travelling between all nine kingdoms in a such a short time-span had been very tiring. Even more so since his mind had been occupied with worry over this new threat.

"Was the coalition a success?" Frederick asked instantly. Trevard could tell that keeping the secret of his mission had not been easy, so he did not keep his son in suspense.

"In principle," he sighed, "all the kings agree to come together to fight the knights, if these attacks are indeed the Black Knights' work."

"If?" Frederick asked, confused.

"They want to be certain first, they want proof," the king's voice was grave.

"Proof, but does that mean they're waiting for another village to be attacked first?" Frederick cried in astonishment.

"Yes." Trevard said bluntly. "I suppose we will need proof in order to locate them, but it will come at a heavy cost." A cost that made Trevard sick and cold. He had thought he could stop this from ever happening again, but he had been wrong. Now how many would pay the price for his failure.

"So, what do we do now?" Frederick asked.

"We focus on Edmund's celebrations and then we wait. There is nothing else we can do but wait."

The awful news came sooner than expected. Only a few days later the village of Watley, in the Kingdom of Arabat was set upon early one morning. There was no doubt that the Black Knights were the culprits, as they left a sign. A large number of black cloaks were left behind, some hung over the doors of houses, some thrown over bodies, others covered in blood, and some were even set on fire, which caused blazes alerting all those around. This element was new, the first attack in Twickerth had not been so obviously marked, this was clearly done for dramatic effect. It only made the horrific event more tragic. Fast messages were sent throughout the kingdoms reporting the news and requesting aid. Hollthen was at the opposite end of Parvery and so word of the attack reached the Bardeves last. As soon as King Trevard read the message he sprang into action as there was much to do. The first, and most difficult, step was to tell Myrbeth the truth; he now had no choice but to unfold the whole story to her. He couldn't deny he was dreading causing her pain once again. Yet she surprised him with her endurance. She was not angry about being kept in the dark, she didn't even seem overly shocked.

"I always knew they would come back," she spoke softly. "It might sound strange but it's true. They were like the monster under the bed or the shadow in the cupboard. You try to convince yourself that it's not real, that you have nothing to be frightened of. But this monster is real and I am afraid." She walked away from him, clearly not wishing to hear the details of their latest carnage. Trevard respected this but as she left his parlour he heard her repeat, "I am afraid, very afraid."

The castle suddenly became a hive of activity. There was much to prepare and very little time before the coalition needed to congregate in Arabat. The king would need to bring food, medical supplies, his physician and healers, but, most importantly, he would need to bring soldiers. Some of the guardsmen and knights were to stay behind, but most were to leave to fight alongside their king. The following morning at breakfast the family could discuss nothing else.

"Frederick and I must leave this afternoon," Trevard confirmed in a distracted tone, quick action like this always made him worry things would be overlooked.

"You are both to go?" Myrbeth voice was high and mildly agitated. The king had not announced his intention before to take Frederick.

"Yes, Frederick is a good fighter and old enough. Since it was I who put together the coalition I must do my part to hold it together,"

"I'm ready to go, Father." Frederick sat up straight holding his head in a proud and respectful pose.

"I'm sure you will do all that is needed, Frederick," Myrbeth said, trying to be encouraging, but her voice was unnaturally high. The king smiled at her.

"Yes, I have every faith in him. However, I had hoped that you and Edmund might manage the kingdom while we are away, and I have every faith in you too."

"You want both of us?" she asked in surprise.

"I know Frederick has been tutoring you as well as Edmund. I'm sure you will be an effective team."

"I didn't realise you knew," Frederick said, his posture dropping and face looking slightly downcast. He had kept his tutelage of Myrbeth a secret because he thought his father wouldn't have approved, but Trevard smiled now.

"I think you will find there is nothing that happens in my kingdom that I'm not aware of."

"If you truly think I am ready." Edmund coughed loudly, "I mean, we are ready," she corrected herself. Edmund nodded and everyone laughed.

"Yes, I'm sure we will all rise to the occasion."

Edmund hovered around his father and brother for the rest of the morning as they made their preparations and packed. He seemed a little lost and worried but was unwilling to admit it. He and Trevard were alone in the king's chambers but still Edmund barely spoke. Trevard had insisted on packing his clothes for the journey as all the servants were busy on tasks elsewhere.

"Why are they called the Black Knights?" Edmund asked after some time. "I mean, they are not real knights, are they?"

"I don't believe so, no. They are certainly not knights of honour," Trevard replied.

"So why call them that if they are just bad men?" Edmund persisted in his question.

"I'm not sure why. When they first attacked, and I went out to the village, someone told me the Black Knights were responsible. I presume someone chose the name because of their choice of cloth and it just stuck." Trevard wondered why this interested Edmund so much.

"It's not a very good name, the 'crimson killers' works better or the 'bloody knights' at least. Unless did they leave lots of black cloaks?"

"No." Trevard answered sternly. "This deliberately flaunting their work is new," and disgusting, the king couldn't understand this sort of behaviour.

"Well, I think we ought to change the name. The 'bloody men' or 'crimson coalition' perhaps," Trevard put his hand on Edmund, then patted his shoulder.

"Enough, son, enough." The boy nodded and went back to being silent.

The whole castle came out to bid the party farewell. It was known that the men were facing great peril and that some would probably not return so the people came to send them off. Everyone wanted to honour their courage in proudly facing this threat. Some handed out laurels or flowers, others saluted or shook hands, everyone wished them well. Myrbeth and Edmund stood at the forefront of the farewell crowd with King Trevard and Frederick facing them. The men that were to accompany them stood behind in formation. The goodbyes were formal and short, private goodbyes had already been said. Edmund seemed to take it the worst, he was so young and had never seemed more the small boy than now.

"You will come back, won't you? Promise me you will try," he spoke in a faltering, small voice. His father placed a comforting hand on his shoulder again.

"We shall try, I have left sealed instructions in case it becomes necessary to make alternative arrangements and Modwin knows who to contact," the king added. Then he placed his hand upon his other son and turned away. Frederick took a hand of each and held it for a moment before he too turned to leave. A trumpet sounded out to signal it was time to move. As they led the men away Trevard saw Myrbeth enfold Edmund in her arms out of the corner of his eye. He worried deeply what would happen to them if the worse came. Edmund was so young to be orphaned, and, though Frederick was strong, he was not ready yet to be king and Myrbeth would lose a second set of parents. Trevard could say nothing though as he split away from his children. Then Edmund spoke again, just audibly.

"I'm afraid, Myrbeth, I'm very afraid."

"I know. I am as well."

Trevard and Frederick arrived at Arabat greatly tired. Already days had passed since the attack and time to catch the culprits was running short. They had ridden relentlessly knowing that this time the knights could not be allowed to escape. When they reached the capital, it was heaving with people. There was an encampment set up for the soldiers within the village, but the nobles were to be housed in the palace. Queen Barilsa and her children came out to greet her guests.

"King Trevard, you are the last to arrive and I see you have brought Frederick," she offered by way of greeting.

"Yes, Queen Barilsa, we thank you for welcoming us," Trevard replied.

"I see you have brought your lords, too," she continued.

"Yes, you might remember Lord Yarrow, Lord Huntington and Lord Burchard, I'm sure you have met at feasts or tournaments previously."

"You're most welcome to our home," she nodded to each man in turn. "My children, Prince Rydall, Prince Jeffrey, Princess Eunice, Prince Francis and Princess Odette." They each gave a small bow in turn.

"But whoever have you left in charge of your castle?" Barilsa asked in a perplexed tone.

"My other children. Forgive us our impetuousness, but there are matters of importance we must discuss with my fellow rulers" Trevard was stern, having no desire to discuss much of anything with Barilsa, who, no doubt, had a myriad of topics she wanted to give her opinion on.

"Hm, yes," she frowned, but otherwise let it pass for the moment. "We don't have a large palace I'm afraid," she spoke inaccurately. "My servants will show your lords to their rooms, but we won't have room for so many men. An encampment is being set up nearby, my servants can lead these others to a space where they can set up their tents." Trevard had expected as much from what they had seen travelling through the village so didn't object. Despite Barilsa's words, Arabat palace was the second largest in Parvery, reflecting that Arabat was the second richest kingdom. The kingdom was known for fine wool and silks which were used to make cloth that was used across all the nine kingdoms. The rulers of Arabat had built a palace to reflect this wealth and importance. The palace would indeed be stretched to accommodate such numbers but they had the capacity the king was sure, if the royal family were willing to make adjustments to their own comfort. Trevard knew that Barilsa's feelings of intolerance and superiority would not have stretched far. Though he was astonished that this tragedy had humbled her at all.

"I thank you for the hospitality, I must join my fellow kings. Are they in conference in your husband's hall?" Trevard asked.

"No. Some left a short time ago to inspect the village, except for my brother, Edrick, who also only recently arrived. Also, my husband is leading a party to hunt the culprits," she said tersely.

"Then I will find Edrick and we will join the others." He turned back towards his horse. Frederick did likewise but Trevard stopped him. "No, Son, you stay here. There are still somethings I would shield you from." Frederick nodded in obedience. "Get the men settled." With that Trevard left him.

The kings did not return until late in the evening. The feasting hall was full of food, drink, and the noise of men. However shortly after he sat down, Frederick noticed his father wasn't there. Frederick ate a little then went in search of him. He found him in his chambers with a small plate and a heavily pensive expression.

"Was it very awful?" he asked. For a long time his father didn't answer and when he did, he said simply,

"It cannot be described." Frederick had never seen his father like this, it unnerved him, so he tried again.

"The news at table was that the Knight's encampment was found?"

"Yes, that is what is greatly worrying me," Trevard replied, after another long pause.

"Worrying?" Frederick asked.

"I never expected it to be this simple. To catch them on the first attack seemed impossible."

"Why impossible? I mean it's why we came out here, so surely, it's good news."

"I'm not so sure." Trevard got up from his seat and began to pace about the room. "Years ago they left no trace, no clues for us to follow at all. Now, however, there is a positive wealth of evidence. No, this feels as if we were being led straight to them," he outlined, his voice had a thick edge to it.

"You think it might be a trap?" Frederick asked.

"That is certainly a possibility, but I still see another's hand in this. I'm almost certain someone is controlling not only the Knights, but also us. We are being led by some puppeteer, some shadow king."

"But why? For what purpose?"

"I don't know, but that, Son, is what I'm afraid of, very afraid." Trevard confessed reluctantly.

In the early hours before dawn all the men assembled on the ridge over the Knight's camp. Some of the kings argued that, with such little time to prepare, their attack could not be well coordinated, but their protests were shouted down.

"Once the battle begins any sort of plan will fall to pieces, you would know that if you had ever fought in one," King Isaiah cried out. The hubbub of voices objected and agreed in equal measures. King Rollin called,

"We have to seize the moment while we have the upper hand." This was met with cheers.

"I agree we have to act now; we could lose them again if we don't." King Edrick had nodded his accent.

"Yes, surprise is the only way, otherwise we risk more villages." King Ivan concluded to more cheers.

Trevard didn't speak only listened, even when Frederick looked to him to object, he just shook his head. Later he explained. "Whoever we are up against is playing a very clever game, we must tread carefully. Besides the others won't heed any warning, the victory is too close in their minds."

The ambush took place and, just as predicted, the coordination of their attack formation was extremely disorganised. Any attempt to agree on a line up quickly fell apart and was eventually abandoned as the sun rose. Each of the kings organised their own men as they chose and argued for what each thought the best place to make a stand. There were more than two dozen tents below in the gully and no visible signs of movement. The feeling of a trap intensified. Trevard looked to his son, Frederick looked back at his father and said, "Father, I'm afraid, I'm very afraid."

"I know, Son, but all the same we must do our best." Then he put on his helm and Frederick did likewise.

CHAPTER 17

The gully was a long, dry tunnel and little more. It ran deep into the fields outside the capital, not far from the village that had been attacked. Despite the cracked earth there was some scrubby growth, but it was scarce. The terrain was deep, and Frederick worried how the horses would manage such a steep run. He couldn't see who started the charge but suddenly with no warning, discussion or herald they were all rushing down towards the gully.

The sound of over a thousand horses rushing downwards together was overwhelming. He had never pushed a horse to this speed, he had never felt a creature move this fast. The wind, the speed, it should all have been exhilarating but the fear lessened it. All feeling was being replaced by a strange numbness. The sound was too loud not to cause a disturbance, their foe would be roused. The Black Knights, however, had not been prepared for the onslaught, that was clear. They came out of their tents unarmoured and undressed but not totally unarmed. Some were half dressed carrying dirks, others were in full black clothing with swords in hand, some had clothes and axes and more still were naked apart from their steel. As they reached the tents Frederick lost sight of the vast host as his vision concentrated on focusing on just a few people, the people just in sight. Just those that posed an immediate threat to him and his father. First, he was rushed by a burly man with a battle axe. He was dressed in faded leathers, black of course, and had no mail or armoured plate, unlike Frederick. His face was covered with a heavy stubble and his mouth was open in a snarl. His axe was held low, aiming for the legs of Frederick's horse. Frederick knew he had to act or be lost straight from the start. His father's voice came to him then. As they had dressed and prepared for the battle in the early hours of the day his father had given him some last pieces of advice.

"Don't over think things, in the heat of the moment it can be difficult to know what course of action is right but worrying about that can be fatal. Act quickly and trust your training. You can think, but don't hesitate." So Frederick acted. He pulled a knife and threw it. His hand was shaking and his aim was off. He hit the man's muscular upper arm, the wrong arm. But the pain of the injury made him slow just by a second, and it was enough. Frederick threw a second knife, his aim was still poor but more effective, the knife landed in his opponent's throat. The man coughed, spluttered, choking, his eyes grew wide and then he dropped. Frederick's first kill but he couldn't think about that now. He found he was glad he had brought so many weapons. He hadn't been able to decide what he might need so had taken whatever he could carry or conceal about himself. He remembered, strangely, that it had not been that long ago that he had wondered what it would be like to be in a real battle. Now he wished he had never had to find out.

Frederick felt sick but knew there was no time for that either. He took a quick glance around; his father was a short distance to his left. This had been another piece of advice his father had given.

"Stay close to me at all times and I will assist you if you need it. Even if you don't need help make sure you stay close. Keep aware of where I am at all times, and you won't get lost."

"How would I get lost?" Frederick had asked, a little sceptical.

"It is easier than you might imagine," had been his father's only response. Frederick could understand now, the battle was chaos, and it was easy to get lost in the melèe in more ways than one. It was fine though, he assured himself, his father was close by. He also spotted his uncle too, King Edrick, in the distance. His friends, Halph and Judan Yenton were much closer to him, battling a group of four knights. He moved forward to assist them when an arrow flew past him. Two enemies of slight build had placed themselves up the hill and were shooting down on his fellow fighters. Frederick had never been much of an archer and there were too many people between them for Fredrick to reach the archers. Besides, they were boys, young boys, much younger than him but older than Edmund; he didn't want to fight boys. Then a deep cry of pain caught his attention, Halph had taken a blow and fallen; he wasn't getting up.

Frederick had to get to him, but it still wasn't safe to move without getting shot at but staying still would make him a target too. In frustration he picked up the axe from the fallen man and threw it at the archers, it missed naturally. Yet it wasn't a complete waste, the axe scared them into moving their stance. The archers repositioned a few yards over where there was some tree cover and where they could no longer aim at Frederick. His path now clear, he ran to his friends, but too late. Judan was pinned down by three of the men and the fourth was moving towards Halph. Halph was now trying to rise on all fours when the fourth man raised his sword and pushed it down into the gap where pauldron and backplate didn't meet. Halph let out another high-pitched cry, Frederick could see the blood dripping from the blade. The fourth man was repositioning to strike another blow. Frederick moved angrily and recklessly, throwing knives at the fourth man. He only had three knives left but he did get a hit. The second knife landed in the man's boot. It must have missed his foot because he just pulled it out, threw it away and shrugged, moving on.

A new terror filled Frederick, what if Halph was dead? Possessed of these fears, Frederick rushed to reach Judan to fight the three remaining men alongside his friend. The fourth man, the one who had killed Halph, for surely Halph was dead, had moved on to fight someone else. Frederick would find him, he would avenge Halph, but now he must protect his twin brother. He must help Judan, surely that is what Halph would have wanted.

With two fighters' things went much easier. Judan slashed at one and cut a deep wound into his right arm that bled so fast. He bled so much it was unbelievable not to mention slightly sickening. It seemed to gush uncontrollably. This wound caused the man to panic and run madly but Judan stabbed him through the back, killing him instantly. Frederick quickly knocked out another foe with a sharp below to the head and killed another with his sword to his belly. Once this small battle within the battle was done both boys turned to Halph's limp form. They bent down to take a closer look. He was still breathing but each breath came out sharp and shallow.

"We ought to get him help," Frederick said, thinking of all the healers and physicians left back at the castle.

"We can't," Judan looked distressed but calm. "We would never get him out of here." He wasn't wrong Frederick realised, carrying Halph out of the gully would be difficult even without all the fighting and people to avoid. Not to mention they may hurt him more.

"What do we do then?" Frederick asked.

"He must be protected, or he could be trampled."

"Right, so we hold here," Frederick said, getting back to his feet.

"No, I will stay with Halph, he is my brother, but you will be safer if you keep moving, Frederick." Judan urged him onwards, Frederick knew he was right, he must fight on.

He nodded and then paused again, searching for targets that were unengaged. As his eyes searched, he saw more carnage. A bloody king lay dying, his face heavily beaten and his crown askew. Two bodies lay face down on the gully hill, unidentifiable. A lord with whom he had sat at the feast table last night had taken multiple arrows to the chest. He forced himself to remember to look for his father and spotted him fighting next to Lord Huntington. This time far off to his right, Frederick moved in this direction without further thought.

"Little boy, come here little boy, come to me." The man who spoke was to his left and having just killed his previous opponent had done the same search for a new target. He was short, with red hair and dark eyes. He held two long-bladed short swords both marked heavily with blood. He licked them both with a hungry taunting look before advancing on Frederick; it was revolting.

Frederick had not fought like this before, the man was highly skilled, moving the swords with fast precision. He blocked each of Frederick's cuts, thrusting his own sword back and jarring his arm in the process. It quickly became clear that Frederick was over matched. Frederick was barely keeping up, he needed help. He looked back a few feet to where he had left Judan, but no help could come from him as he was already engaged. There was a loud clang that seemed to ring endlessly. The man had bashed the butt of one of his swords into Frederick's helm.

"The least you can do is pay attention while I kill you, little boy." The blow made Frederick slightly dizzy and disorientated, giving his adversary ample opportunity to do as he wanted. Suddenly a sword appeared through his opponent's chest. Frederick looked up to see his father standing behind the redhaired man pulling the sword back out.

"Father," he cried out, relieved and still slightly discombobulated.

"Stay close and I will keep you safe," Trevard said, and Frederick nodded but then regretted it as his head spun again. Trevard steadied him with an arm on his son's shoulder and they moved forward slowly. They had only taken a few steps towards a rare, armoured foe intending to fight him together, when a terrible thing happened. A prince, dressed in plate stamped with the Twickerth crest was beheaded not a foot from them. The armoured foe forgotten, Trevard ran forward to fight the knight who had dealt this death. Frederick found an older knight behind him to tackle, still dizzy and now horror filled.

Frederick fought two more men before he had a chance to breathe again. He looked around surveying the gully which was now littered with bodies and heavily stained with blood. It was everywhere; it was spattered on the tents, mixed in the mud, and splattered all over the Black Knights and royalists alike. Frederick felt that sick feeling rising up again, but he forced himself to remain calm. 'Look for father', he thought, but as he surveyed the field he wasn't there, he wasn't anywhere. Frederick looked right and left but he couldn't find Trevard at all. The panic began to edge in then as he searched the endless faces for the one he knew best, but to no avail. He moved, out of fear, first to his left meeting one foe, he was another young lad. Frederick quickly knocked him to the ground without a second thought, wanting him out of the way. Then he quickly switched directions, ducking between a fighting pair and barrelling down another. He began to notice that many of his comrades were no longer engaged, the Black Knights were losing. Most were dead or incapacitated. The royalists were winning but this brought him no comfort since there was still no sign of his father.

Frederick climbed out of the gully for a better view, his father had the distinctive Hollthen crest on his cloak which should make him easy to spot but it was to no avail. Not only could he not see him, but the archers started firing on him again. He ducked down and slid back into the gully, arrows bouncing off his armour. Once back in the dip he forced himself to begin searching the fallen. There were so many he had never known or didn't recognise. Occasionally, however, there was a face he knew, Lord Yarrow of Royal Holly lay face up, eyes blankly staring. The body of the Twickerth prince was a gruesome headless sight, Frederick now remembered he was named Urvant Pedcott. He also remembered that his cousin Sara had been engaged to him. He saw Sir Rossi from Merchden and Sir Booth from Arabat and other knights and guards who were familiar but whose names wouldn't come to him. Each face brought relief and dismay; they were not his father, but they were people who mattered to someone.

"They are breaking," boomed a voice from the distance but he wasn't sure who spoke. If the statement hadn't been true before it was now. Those left alive were dropping weapons or trying to steal horses to get away.

"Get them to surrender," shouted another voice, this time closer and more familiar, King Emil Yenton was just a few yards ahead. Frederick couldn't resist looking towards him as he thought of the awful news about Halph that awaited the king. King Emil was with King Rollin Boutiner and King Leopold Haughton. They were marshalling a group of soldiers to chase a few Black Knights that had climbed out of the gully and were trying to escape on foot. Frederick searched the faces of the chasing royalists; his father wasn't with them either. The panic increasing, he moved between the crowd of fighters, checking and double checking.

As he searched, another Black Knight tried to attack him, Frederick yelled in fury and fear but met him all the same. Frederick swung his sword repeatedly without aim until the attacker who was already injured collapsed into the bloody mud and didn't rise. Frederick resumed his frantic searching, he was almost running from one person to the next, until he tripped on a twisted root sticking out of the gully wall and fell to his knees. The force of the fall caused his armour to cut into his knees badly and he cried out in pain, fear and frustration. His breathing came fast and his whole body felt heavy and full of aches. He couldn't get back to his feet even if he tried. Frederick knew that he had to move, the battle was not quite over but despair was filling him. All day he had been pushing back his emotions, but he couldn't any longer and they flooded though him. He felt tears brimming in eyes; he knew he shouldn't cry; he was a man now and this was war. He had been prepared and trained for this, yet he had not been ready. How could he be, but he had to be stronger, he had to be. He needed to find his father, he had to get up and find his father. Suddenly a hand appeared on his shoulder and for a moment he thought he was certainly dead but when he turned around the face was of his father. Relief flooded him, he finally got to his feet and threw his arms around him. Trevard held him tightly too.

"It's over, Son, it's over. Just breathe deeply now. You did well, breath, Son."

CHAPTER 18

Most the day had passed when the blood-stained members of the coalition returned to Arabat palace. At the front of the line of royalists came the wounded, some unaided but bloody, others were being supported by friends or were collapsed on horseback. Behind them was a wall of armed men, guarding the few prisoners that had been captured and tied. Lastly the rest of the warriors came on foot leading horses with the dead laden on the creatures' backs. They all collected in the palace courtyard and the inhabitants of the palace came out to meet them. Trevard brought one of the horses straight up to the castle steps, for the body that lay upon it was that of Prince Rydall Haughton of Arabat. Frederick had never seen his aunt so silent as she came down the steps. Queen Barilsa never spoke a word. Instead, she ran her hands through her son's light hair while tears fell down her cheeks. Prince Jeffrey, he second son, was carried past her by his father King Leopold. The prince spoke in a weak voice.

"I tried to help him, mother." He winced in obvious pain and closed his eyes as he was transported to the throne room. Each of the kings had brought their court physicians and a few more healers, knowing they would be needed. While the battle had been taking place, they had set up a makeshift infirmary to treat the wounded men in the throne room. Frederick watched as King Emil and Prince Judan carried in the bloodied Prince Halph, who was still living. Frederick and Sir Thaze were carrying a guard named Voss from Hollthen who was equally bloody.

"Come straight back, Son," Trevard said in a quiet voice as he passed. "There are many who need assistance, and you don't want to linger in the way." Frederick nodded and obeyed, coming in and out of the castle three times. Once all the wounded were inside Frederick decided to check on Halph. He walked over to where Judan was standing. The identical twins both had light blonde hair, though

Halph choose to wear it long and Judan kept his short. They both had brown eyes and small noses, but Judan's jaw was square where Halph had a rounder face. Frederick knew that, unlike their younger twin sisters, Halph and Judan didn't enjoy looking similar and often went out of their way to emphasis their differences. He supposed these scars would be another feature that differentiated them.

"How is he?" Frederick asked.

"The physician says he will live, nothing vital is harmed." Frederick let out a sigh of relief and hugged his friend. As they embraced Frederick saw a sheet being placed over the guard Voss.

The bodies were taken to the feasting hall and respectfully laid out. That evening a ceremony to honour them took place. The hall was filled with candles, the queen, her daughters and the ladies of Arabat carried bunches of scented wildflowers which were placed next to each body. The largest and grandest bouquet was reserved for Prince Rydall, who took pride of place at the top of the hall. No one begrudged him this honour, as similar ceremonies would be held when the dead were returned to their homes. At the foot of each body stood a man bedecked in a beautifully embroidered black cloak. The cloak held an ancient symbol of death, three thin point-ed triangles twisted around each and then encircled by nine rings. Each of these men held a large golden goblet of wine from which the mourners drank to honour each departed man. This honour of be-ing a cup bearer was usually taken up by a close relative. However, in the current circumstances many of the kings, princes, lords and knights had elected to take up the honour for those far from home and family.

Prince Jeffrey, supporting himself heavily on a walking stick, had insisted on holding the cup for his brother. Their father, King Leo-pold, stood at the feet of one of his lord's. His younger son, Prince Francis, who was too young to be involved in the battle, stood at the feet of a Arabat household knight. Frederick had insisted on having the honour for King Jonathan, it felt only right given his recent visit with Princess Gisella. King Trevard stood at the feet of Lord Yarrow and Sir Thaze was standing over the guard, Voss. Frederick looked over at his father, standing solemnly. He could clearly remember his father wearing the same traditional cloak at his mother's funeral. His father had told him years later of the high importance of being a cup bearer despite the weight of the cloak. He had not understood what he had meant until now, the cloak did not weigh much physically but it was not easy to wear. As the mourners began to circle the hall, taking drinks from each proffered cup they hummed the traditional funeral ballad. A mournful song, written for both deep and high voices but without words, only harmonising sounds. At the intervals they all spoke out as one: "May they find peace in victory."

Victory didn't feel at all like Frederick would have thought, or how it felt in the tournaments. It had come at such a high cost.

The next morning Frederick woke late after a difficult night's sleep. His first thought was to visit Prince Halph. However, Frederick didn't know the palace well, as he had only visited a few times and he got lost. The guests were housed in the main, stone belly of the palace, which had five floors. As if this wasn't large enough, a previous king had added a connected three-storey building on the south side and the current king had added a two-storey wide tower topped with a dome. Domes were all over the Arabat palace, including one large, flattened dome on the eastern protrusion of the palace. It was when Frederick somehow found himself inside the curved corridors of the eastern dome that he finally asked a servant for assistance and was led straight to Halph's quarters. He peeked his head around the door.

"Frederick, please come in," Halph spoke from his bed.

"I didn't wish to disturb you, if you were sleeping," Frederick explained, surprised to find him awake at all.

"Sleeping on my side like this is hard, especially with the pain from my back," Halph indicated the deep gash he had sustained just below his shoulder which looked red and irritated. "They say I must stay like this while the treatment seals the wound, but my shoulder doesn't feel as bad now the physicians have reset it."

"That sounds painful," Frederick had not wanted to know the full extent of Halph's injuries and still didn't. Thankfully Halph just grimaced in response and Frederick was able to change the subject.

"I see Judan would not leave your side," Frederick indicated towards a large chair where the sleeping form of Halph's brother was slumped at an odd angle.

"Twins are never apart for long," Halph joked. "Father has been here almost constantly, too. Though he left a while ago to send word to mother that we were safe and hasn't come back. He is making arrangements to head home, though it will be a day or two before I can travel, I imagine. I assume you have also sent word back to

Hollthen?"

"Yes, father sent word to Edmund and Myrbeth last night." Trevard had sent back a guard to the castle as this would be the quickest way of spreading the news. All the visiting kings had no doubt done the same now the danger was past.

"That will be a comfort to them, I guess others will be receiving very different news." They both paused, thinking about that. "What happened to the Black Knights, did we take any prisoners?" Halph asked.

"Yes, we did, the kings are debating their fate now, I believe. That is no doubt where your father is. Some of the kings believe they should be executed immediately, but my father is trying to impress upon them how important it is that we extract what information we can."

"But will we get much information?" However, before Frederick could respond a new figure came through the door.

"Oh, cousin Frederick, I didn't know you were here, otherwise I would have brought you breakfast, too." Princess Eunice said, as she entered with a servant, both carrying trays laden with food.

"That's fine, have the two of you been introduced?" Frederick asked, offering to complete the formality. Technically he was sure that Prince Halph and Princess Eunice must have met several times and thus had been introduced. However, he wasn't certain they had ever spoken, so the formalities seemed appropriate.

"We know each other," Eunice said simply, but Halph was more detailed.

"She was here when I woke up, tending to me. Of course, we have met at a ball or two, but I never had the courage to speak to her before." Halph gazed at her wondrously. Frederick felt like he was intruding and said something just to speak.

"Thanks, Eunice, but I'm not sure I feel like eating," he said.

"Oh, I know, it's all so awful," she said, sniffling. "I used to say that he wasn't a very good brother, Rydall, that mother spoiled him. But it was only because he wasn't sweet like Francis, or funny and protective like Jeffrey, but he wasn't bad, not really. Of course, it doesn't matter, now he is gone," she said, beginning to cry. Halph shot Frederick a reproachful look and took Eunice's hand in both of his, the feeling of intrusion only increased.

"I should go and attend to my father," Frederick said, in an awkward voice, getting up.

"Oh, they are not in the council chambers anymore," Eunice spoke, drying her tears, "they agreed the prisoners should be interrogated, they have left for the prison rooms."

"Thank you," Frederick said, ducking out of the room quickly.

As he walked through the palace again, he wondered if Halph's familiarity with Eunice meant anything. He remembered how excited he had been at the prospect of his cousin Manual falling for Princess Penalyn. He had felt genuine joy over their coupling, yet those same feelings didn't exist in him now. Frederick wandered the corridors aimlessly, wondering if he was changed at all. He had no intention of visiting the prison rooms. He had seen enough pain and blood and had no desire to watch the prisoners being tortured. He knew it must be so, the Black Knights would not give up any information otherwise, but he had no taste for it. He knew his father wouldn't mind his absence; he would have preferred to shield Frederick from all of this. So, instead he walked in what he thought was the direction of his quarters. He had the idea of writing a letter to Myrbeth. He needed to connect with her by some method. So, once he had located his rooms which turned out to be on the floor above Halph's, he sat down at the writing desk and began to scratch out a letter with quill and ink.

Dearest Myrbeth

By the time this reaches you, you will have received the news that we are safe. It is unclear how long we will be staying here in Arabat.

There is so much still to do, so many dead that must be returned to their homes. I don't like the idea of being away from you for too long but it's important work. I would love your thoughts, I long for your presence, I hope we will be together again soon.

Father said I distinguished myself well in the battle. Father was magnificent, he saved the life of King Valter. The king is hurt badly and is still recovering but says he is eternally grateful to father. I cannot wait to return to you and return to our peaceful planning of better days. We will talk of marriage; wedding plans, perhaps even choose names for our children. That is all I wish to think of....

At this point the door banged opened and Frederick upset the ink bottle.

"Myrbeth is in danger." It was his father speaking in a hurried and distressed voice. Frederick's face blanched as he stared down at the remnants of his ink flooded letter. The happy words he had written now unreadable. "The Black Knights sent one of their number as an assassin to the castle. You must return at once." Frederick let the letter fall to the ground and grabbed his sword, crumpling and breaking the parchment under his fast-moving feet. He followed his father down the palace's many staircases, their feet flying on the steps.

"What did they say?" Frederick asked, wanting to understand this new, unexpected threat.

"Not much more than what I already told you, I'm afraid. At first nothing would make them talk, even enhanced methods which, you know, I generally do not approve of. We were beginning to despair of learning anything until King Leopold mentioned me by name. Then one of the men looked up and spoke for the first time. He was an older man, certainly old enough to have been involved in the first attack as well. I will not repeat the insults he spoke. The words were too disgusting, but it seems they intend to finish their earlier work by killing Myrbeth, as I always feared. They called it a favour, to correct their previous mistake, so I was right, someone is controlling them."

"He confirmed that too?" Frederick asked, as rushed through a long corridor that led to the entrance chamber and outside.

"Unintentionally confirmed it, once he realised what he had said he refused to speak again. That is not important now though, Myrbeth is what matters. She must be kept safe." They raced through the courtyard towards the stables.

"You know I will do everything to protect her, Father," Frederick promised solemnly.

"Of course. I have ordered Sir Thaze and Sir Monkford to travel back with you. I must stay here. These interrogations are too important and there are already too few in favour of them continuing. Also, there are arrangements to be made for Lord Yarrow and the others," Frederick nodded while directing a stable boy to ready his horse. The two knights that were to accompany him were already mounted and ready to leave.

"Did the man offer any clues as to what I should be looking for?" he asked, anxious about the task ahead.

"None, so you must be vigilant, trust only those in the castle who are known to you. Be on your guard for any strangers and make all haste. The assassin will already be there, I do not doubt." Frederick nodded again. The stable boy brought Frederick his horse and Frederick mounted in one smooth motion.

"Father, you must be careful too, now we know that someone amongst us is not to be trusted." His father placed a reassuring hand on Frederick's shoulder for a moment, then removed it and slapped the horse forwards.

Frederick and his companions rode hard all day and all night. They reached Hollthen by the following day, just before dawn. They

had to change horses in Walsea where Frederick was known to the guards, which had delayed them for a short time, but otherwise, they hadn't stopped. For Frederick knew no matter how fast they rode the assassins would be there ahead of them. As soon as they rode through the castle gate, he yelled out orders to the guards to close it.

"Close the gate, close it now!"

"Prince Frederick, is that you? Why, we had not thought to look for you," greeted the surprised guard, Brooke, but Frederick ignored him and carried on with his orders.

"The gate must be closed. No one is to come in or go out of this gate. Ensure that every entrance is locked down and the castle must be searched. Gather the men and search in pairs, arrest anyone who is unknown to you but don't treat them unkindly. I must find the Lady Myrbeth, then I will join you." He jumped down from his borrowed horse and ran into the castle. His escort followed in case there was trouble. They didn't stop running until they reached her chambers. Despite the very early hour of the morning, she was awake, sitting at her dressing table brushing out her long golden-brown hair. Relief flooded Frederick; he hadn't realised until now that he had been terrified of finding her already dead. Myrbeth spotted him in the mirror and her face filled with joy.

"I thought you weren't ...", but she never finished the sentence as Frederick closed the door, rushed toward her and kissed her. As their lips moved gently together it was easy to forget all the events of the last few days, they both felt a moment of blissful peace. Only the current present danger induced Frederick to stop.

"Myrbeth, your life is in danger. Father sent me back to protect you," He babbled out, he had thought of not telling her so as not to frighten her, but Frederick knew she was strong enough to handle the truth.

"In danger, but I don't understand, why?" Frederick briefly outlined to her what they had learned from the Black Knights.

"You mustn't worry too much; I have the guards all searching. I'm sure the assassin will be found, but I should go now to check on their progress." Myrbeth nodded. Frederick could tell she was frightened but doing her best to hide it, just as he knew she would. "I want you to go to Edmund's chambers and hide there, so you can't be found."

"Is that wise, what if they do find me and hurt him too?" Frederick blanched slightly.

"I will send two guards for the door, but I can't spare more so take this with you." He unsheathed a small throwing sword and held it out to her.

"I wouldn't know how to use it," she said, pushing it back towards him.

"You may not have the technique but I'm sure you can grasp it." They both smiled a little at the simple humour of his statement. He held it out to her again.

"I still wouldn't want to use it."

"Nor did I, but it might be necessary, I want you safe. Besides, I told Edmund to keep his sword with him at all times, he will have listened. He also has the knife you brought him." Myrbeth frowned,

"I dislike the idea of Edmund using weapons even more, but, nevertheless, I suppose you are right," she consented to the idea. As the pair parted their eyes were locked on one another for a long moment. Then Frederick left in one direction and Myrbeth another. Frederick joined the search but could not bear to be away from Myrbeth for long. He soon returned to her to ascertain she was safe.

"Did you find anything?" Myrbeth whispered, as Edmund was still asleep.

"Not yet," He whispered back. She beckoned him out into the corridor.

"I didn't want to wake him; he has been working so hard lately."

She explained and Frederick smiled.

"I'm sure you both have been doing wonderfully."

"There hasn't been much to do. The focus was all on the Black Knights return and the battle."

"Of course," Frederick looked away. He had been distracted completely and had forgotten all his after-battle emotions. With this reminder though, he discovered they had not left him, just been suppressed.

"I'm sure I can't begin to understand what it must have been like, but you know I'm here for you," Myrbeth took his hand. Frederick didn't turn around, but he squeezed her hand and spoke.

"I had to kill people …", he stopped, fearful that he sounded childish. "I know they were murderers but …," he stopped again, his words were strained, and he wasn't completely sure what he wanted to say.

"You know that it is different, you know you aren't a murderer. I could go through how you saved lives and protected your people like any good future king, but I think you know that too. Give it time, Frederick, you will find a way to reconcile this." A murderer, did he feel like a murderer? Perhaps that was what made his insides roil, but she didn't think him one.

"Perhaps you're right, but I don't think I will ever forget the sights," he stopped. "So many dead and gone. I saw so much, so much blood." At this he broke down. Myrbeth held him tightly until he mastered himself.

"You will reconcile this," she repeated, but it was a long time before he could answer her.

"I find comfort in knowing I have avenged your family." At this he finally turned back to face her, trying to pull himself together. This was no time to fall apart, she needed him strong and vigilant. "As long as I have you, I will learn to bear anything." He enfolded her in his arms and held her close to his heart. They stayed that way until they heard approaching footsteps.

"Your Grace, we have arrested two men we found in the lower corridors near the kitchen," an approaching guard hailed him. Frederick quickly returned to himself; he must focus on the assassin.

"Good, I will attend to them immediately. Stay here, I will come again soon," he said to Myrbeth, then turning to face the guard again, he responded, "Is the search completed, McDale?"

"Not quite," was the short answer. Frederick moved quickly to leave but as he let go of Myrbeth she wobbled slightly and almost fell back. Frederick gripped her, steadying her in his arms.

"You go, I will be fine," Myrbeth straightened herself. "I'm sure it's just the worry; I will lay down with Edmund for a time."

"Yes, rest, I will handle this," he kissed her hand. Myrbeth gave a half-hearted smile and he watched as she re-entered Edmund's chamber before forcing himself to leave. He would go to the dungeons and if they had found this assassin, he would show no weakness.

CHAPTER 19

Under the main part of the castle a large steep staircase led to the dungeons. It consisted of two levels. The lower level held the long-term cells and the upper levels consisted of short-term cells. Frederick, accompanied by the knight Sir Monkford and his father's secretary, arrived at the upper level of the dungeons in a small antechamber. They were greeted by the head guardsman, Sir Norman Korth.

"Your Grace, we arrested these men as per your orders. They are not known to any of my men and seem suspicious."

"Thank you, Sir Korth, we will question them now, I've brought Modwin to transcribe." Modwin and Sir Korth nodded to the prince to indicate their readiness. Sir Monkford who was there to protect the prince stayed a little way back. "Have they said very much?" Frederick asked.

"Mostly just complaining, Sire." Frederick nodded too, then took a deep breath and tried to look calm and collected. He felt nervous but walked along to the interrogation chamber. This chamber was mostly bare, housing only a small scribe's table and seat and a large cage with nothing but a long bench on which sat two men chained to the floor. Outside was a guard named Kelas, who bowed to the prince before returning to closely watching his charges. The first thing that struck Frederick was how very different the two men were. The first man was just entering old age; his long scruffy blonde hair and beard were blanching to white. He wore three layers of clothes all of which were dirty, patched and riddled with holes. His skin, too, was dirty and his nails were cracked and torn. Frederick wondered if he was living roughly.

The second man was much younger, and he couldn't have looked more dissimilar, dressed in smart, fresh clothes. Though he also had blonde hair it was cut short and was slicked back. There was a faintly floral smell about him. Frederick wasn't sure what he had expected but neither seemed to fit the bill of assassin. He found himself uncertain where to begin but knew he would have to tread carefully if he wanted them to confess. Assuming one was the assassin, of course.

"Forgive us, your Highness, but I don't understand, why have we been brought here?" asked the second man, saving Frederick the trouble of beginning things.

"You were found trespassing in the castle," Sir Korth answered in his sharp voice. Frederick held up his hand to silence him, he needed to prove he could handle this himself.

"We need to know your business within these walls," he asked. Both men remained quiet.

"You must answer the prince," Sir Korth said sternly.

"What will happen to us if we don't?" the first barked back.

"No, that's the wrong question. What will happen to us if we do is more important?" the second man countered. Frederick didn't know how to answer either question.

"You must answer all the prince's questions truthfully and then he will decide what is to be done with you," Sir Korth explained.

Frederick didn't feel confident about sitting in judgement especially since everything was unclear. Was an assassin an assassin if no one was actually killed?

"Oh, is that how this goes?" the second man said sarcastically.

"Too right it is," Sir Korth had not picked up on the second man's tone. Frederick spoke louder trying to add authority to his voice.

"I would like to know why you have visited the castle. I won't hand out punishment if you can explain your presence here satisfactorily. I will be fair to those who are honest but remaining silent will only lengthen your imprisonment." For a moment they were all silent waiting to see who would speak. The two men exchanged a look and then looked at the prince. They were sizing him up no doubt, so he kept his face set and didn't break the silence.

"Alright, the tunnels are warm and sometimes you can sneak food from the kitchens. What does it matter to you?" The first man answered in a blasé tone.

"He is telling the truth," Sir Korth nodded calmly. "My men are always clearing folk out of the tunnels, especially when the weather is bad."

"So some of the kitchen folk might recognise him, if he regularly sneaks food from them," Frederick said happily, proud he had worked that out on his own. He changed his tone back to authoritative; the interrogation was not done. "We shall check on that," Frederick added, and Sir Korth nodded, then turned back to the second man.

"What about you?"

"Hypothetically, of course, I might have a girl in the castle I visit," the second man spoke more tentatively. Frederick thought over these answers. Both were plausible but could easily also be false alibis.

"We will need to know all your movements and who, if anyone, you were visiting?" Frederick insisted.

"It sounds as if we are suspected of something," the second man added. Frederick wasn't sure about answering that question, but he couldn't see a way around it and they had answered him. He told as little of the truth as possible, not wanting to give away everything.

"We are looking for a criminal."

"That's not very specific," the first man growled.

"How can we assist, your Grace, if we don't know what you are looking for? We might have seen something, but how can we know?" The second man added, his voice taking on a smug tone. They had Frederick trapped, even if neither were the assassin it was true they still might be able to provide a useful piece of information. But if Frederick revealed that they were looking for an unknown assassin then it would show how little they knew to possibly guilty suspects. Frederick felt lost and certain that his father would not have been so easily led along. However, his father was not there, and he had no choice but to divulge details.

"There are threats made against the Lady Myrbeth," he offered, still trying to keep information to a minimum.

"Who would want to hurt the girl?" The second man asked quickly in a concerned tone that could have been false.

"Isn't that obvious? It's those so-called Black Knights," the first man sneered and spat.

"Ah yes, everything revolves around them currently," the second man responded. Frederick stayed silent, letting them talk, hoping they would reveal something. "What use would it be to them to harm the girl though? She couldn't know anything."

"Men like that don't care about use. They are all full of pride and pride would demand they finish the job," the first man responded to the second. "We didn't have any weapons, your men searched us," he offered, turning to face the prince again.

"That's true, your Grace, both men carried very little about their persons. Certainly nothing that could be used as a weapon," Sir Korth agreed.

"Well, we wouldn't have been able to get weapons past your gate-guards, would we? No, surely anyone intent on violence would be more subtle and intelligent. Something as crude as a knife, they would be caught," the second man theorised in his smug voice.

"What else would they do?" the first man raised his voice.

"I would consider poison a far simpler method," the second man replied.

"Poison is a coward's weapon," the first man spat again.

"No, it is a clever, careful weapon." Were they turning on each other? Frederick wondered; he wasn't sure. They were talking a lot though, so he and his men stayed quiet waiting to see where this would lead.

"Oh, and how would you poison the girl?" The first man asked, still sounding sceptical.

"There must be all sorts of ways, I can't say."

"Oh, the clever man can't say," the first man mocked.

"If you insist. I understand that it is traditional to put poison in food, though I have no experience of such things," the second man continued to speak smugly.

"Phah," the first man cried loudly. "The whole castle eats food; you would never be able to poison just one person."

"Haven't you ever heard of just poisoning a plate?" The second man snapped.

"Oh, and how will you know which plate? Have her name on it, will it?" The first man laughed. The second man was stumped but only for a moment.

"If these men don't shy away from killing, why worry about the number of bodies?" The second man gave a sigh.

Frederick continued to listen to them argue back and forth and still didn't interrupt. He was getting answers now, in between the theorising it became clear that one or both knew something. If they kept talking, they could even reveal everything. So, when the pair began to descend into a huffy silence Frederick felt the need to encourage them.

"But that can't be the case, otherwise I would have returned to find the castle people all dead. The food can't have contained poison, dinner was served hours ago. It doesn't fit," he offered, but the second man said nothing, and the first man just tutted. So, he tried again, "Killing everyone or drawing a sword would be too obvious, there might be a struggle, but they would get away. But poison could offer a quiet exit if done right, I see your point. Did either of you see anything suspicious that would suggest a poisoner?" Frederick tried.

"But the girl's not dead, is she? So, if there was a poisoner he failed. So why are we here?" The first man bellowed out.

"Or hasn't yet acted," the second man added dramatically.

"Why would you say that?" the first man questioned.

"Because we offered to help the prince. Perhaps the assassin tainted something only the girl would touch."

"Oh yes, please do tell us what?" the first man mocked again.

"I wouldn't know, but a perfume or some such item might work?"

"Guess all you want, it doesn't matter, the girl ain't dead," the first man insisted loudly. The pair lapsed again into silence. This time Frederick decided to let the silence be.

"Thank you for your thoughts. For now, you will be returned to the cells. You will be treated well, and my men will provide you with anything you might need."

"We're not to be released?" The first man asked indignantly.

"Not until all that you have told us can be confirmed and this matter resolved." Frederick took his leave. Sir Kelas swiftly moved to follow Frederick's orders and took the two men back to their cells.

Then prince, knights and secretary returned to the antechamber to discuss what they had heard.

"Very interesting," Modwin commented, reviewing the notes in his hands.

"I've never heard such boastful talk," Sir Korth added.

"Perhaps, but I must admit I don't know what to make of it," Frederick sighed, rubbing his brow, he didn't at all know if these men were involved or not.

"I think it is the old man," Sir Monkford said unexpectedly. "He was the one trying not to talk."

"But that pretty man all but admitted to the crime. Sire, I would like your permission to question him further," Sir Korth asked.

"I'm not certain if either is guilty," Modwin was still perusing his notes. "The details the young man gave were not specific, more speculative. I think it more likely that he saw something and is reluctant to reveal it. I agree, as well, that the elderly man seems suspicious, more questioning could be beneficial."

"I'm not sure of anything," Frederick said, hating to admit feeling out of his depth. "Father will have to decide, I suppose I'm not ready. You can ask them more questions but do so politely. Also get them food, drink and blankets. We have no cause to charge them yet." Sir Korth nodded. Frederick, Monkford and Modwin left the dungeons together.

"I think you handled that very well, your Grace, if you will permit me to say so." Modwin said when they reached the upper levels of the castle again.

"Thank you," Frederick's answer was short. His mind was full of everything that had been said. "Something about their words, it's important but I can't quite put my finger on it." His father would have spotted it he was sure. He was always directing Frederick to listen not only to a person's words but also their meaning.

"Yes, their theories were too well thought out. It is hard to imagine that they just conjured up such information. They must have some knowledge of the assassin. Also, I thought that debate was a little too rehearsed, as if perhaps they had had the same debate previously. Though I suppose that would confirm their guilt." Now Modwin said it, their conversation had seemed rehearsed and that did seem to confirm their guilt. However, even as Frederick thought this, he knew instantly that that wasn't what bothered him. He wasn't surprised at their guilt because they had all but admitted their knowledge of the crime. They had admitted their knowledge, the words hung there in his mind.

"Modwin, I would like you to fetch ...," he paused, "who is left as healer since the court physician is in Arabat?"

"His assistant, Colin. He is young but thorough and dedicated to his work. Do you require his assistance?"

"I might," Frederic said, his mind still working.

"Where should I bring him, Sire?"

"To Prince Edmund's chambers, the Lady Myrbeth is there, and I wish her to be examined, to be safe." The conversation with the prisoners had only heightened his fears for her wellbeing and he felt he needed some measure of reassurance. Modwin gave a small bow and departed in haste.

Frederick went straight to Edmund's chambers on the third floor of the castle. When he arrived, Edmund greeted him happily.

"Frederick," he hugged his brother around the midriff. "I didn't know you had returned." These words sent a cold stone into his stomach.

"Didn't Myrbeth tell you I was back?"

"Does she know? She's asleep right now." Edmund gestured toward his bed. Myrbeth lay on top of the blankets, still. Frederick had not noticed before but her skin looked a strange shade in some places. "She hasn't been doing well since you and father left, I thought she could use the sleep. She has been so sick with worry, I guessed that's why she was here. She didn't want to be alone." While Edmund spoke, Frederick moved towards her still form. At first his touch was gentle just trying to stir her but when she didn't move, he grew more insistent. He began to shake her, growing more and more desperate to wake her.

"Myrbeth," he spoke loudly, "Myrbeth." She still didn't respond or react. "Myrbeth, Myrbeth!" he repeated desperately, shaking her vigorously. She still didn't wake. Her eyes were closed; she was motionless. She had been poisoned he was certain of it. The thought that was nagging at him finally became clear. They had basically confessed because their work was already done. As they had been caught there would be little use denying it. The whole performance was just buying time for the poison to do its deadly work.

The door opened suddenly and Modwin came in followed by a young man with thick, dark brown hair and brown eyes to match. He was carrying two large books and a wooden chest under his arm. The young man quickly registered the distressed situation and moved towards the bed. In the doorway two maid's outlines were now visible, their faces showing shock. Edmund was beginning to panic too, asking constant questions.

"What is happening? Frederick, what's wrong? Why won't she wake? Frederick, I don't understand." Frederick didn't know how to answer. The physician's assistant, Colin, moved him aside and began to examine Myrbeth. He pulled open her eyes and held a small mirror over her mouth. Frederick was torn between wanting to ask what he was doing but also not wanting to interrupt. Thankfully, the young apprentice spoke aloud explaining his work.

"I am checking her responses and her breathing. She is still alive.

I will need privacy to concentrate in order to treat her. Please wait outside, your Graces. I will do everything I can for her. Ladies, I require your assistance." Hisbara, the housemaid, and the younger maid, Madge, moved further into the room and Modwin gently led the dazed and distressed princes out. Frederick wanted to resist but found himself strangely unable. Edmund began to cry, Frederick pulled his brother into his arms and held him tightly. He buried his head into Edmund's dark hair to hide his own tears.

It was a long time later that the door opened again and Hisbara showed them in silently. Myrbeth was still laid out on the bed, but the bed and room around it was heavily dishevelled. She was still unconscious, laying with her arms flat, palms open, still dressed in her thick white lace nightgown. Was she ...? Frederick couldn't bring himself to ask the question.

"Is she alright?" Edmund asked in a trembling voice. Frederick was too afraid to speak.

"Yes, we have revived Lady Myrbeth. I have every faith she will recover in time; however, she is still unconscious as the effects wear off. The poison seems to have been administered through her skin. Which is why the presentation is so severe but yet delayed. Her recovery will be slow, but she will recuperate fully ." Frederick still didn't know what to say. "It's an unusual case," Colin continued, "I might not have thought of it, if it had not been for a slight rash all over her skin."

"Yes, yes, you have done well, and your master will be pleased, but the princes don't need to hear these details. We will give them all a minute with our Lady," Hisbara interrupted and then ushered everyone out into the corridor. She didn't close the door properly, however, and their voices came through the crack crystal clear.

"Who would ever want to harm that sweet girl?" Hisbara asked, her affection clear.

"We have been interrogating two men who are possibly in league with the Black Knights. Prince Frederick came back with news they had sent an assassin for the Lady. They specifically mentioned poison," Modwin explained.

"But how could she have been poisoned, with food?" asked Sir Monkford, who had stayed outside the room as a guard.

"No, no, Cook is always so careful with anything he prepares. He's a perfectionist and tastes his creations at every stage," Hisbara spoke.

"The prisoners said the food was not poisoned, they referred to something specific to Lady Myrbeth," Modwin agreed in a thoughtful tone.

"Indeed, it does fit. The Lady had a rash all over her skin, that means the poison was something she touched," Colin reasoned.

"It isn't right, not right," a new voice spoke, "she is always so kind. People come in here threatening young girls, it isn't right, I say."

"Calm down, Madge, no one is threatening you, or anyone else," Hisbara said, in an exasperated voice.

"Forgive me, but could I look at your hand, Madge?" Colin spoke, it was suddenly all quiet. "This is the same rash."

"See, I am poisoned as well; I am poisoned, I will die for sure!" Madge's voice was becoming hysterical.

"No, it won't be fatal, I can treat you."

"Of course, you won't die, if Lady Myrbeth will recover then you will be perfectly fine." Hisbara tutted disapprovingly at the girl's dramatics.

"I don't see the rash anywhere else but your hands," Colin noted.

"You must have touched the poison as well," Sir Monkford pointed out, "have you waited on Lady Myrbeth at all in the last day or so?"

"I poured her bath last night after dinner. Oh, I remember, the water felt different, and it smelled too," Madge answered.

"That must be it," Colin exclaimed.

"This must be reported to Commander Korth at once. Delbard, go straight to the dungeons and tell him all that has happened," Sir Monkford ordered to a guard.

"That can wait, Lady Myrbeth should be moved to her own chambers and made comfortable," Hisbara insisted. As they re-entered the room Frederick felt himself react. He wasn't completely alert, but his sense of duty was strong and showed him what he must do.

"Sir Monkford is right," his voice came out deadened and empty. "Commander Korth should be told at once. He is questioning the suspects; he will need to know what has happened here. Delbard, make it clear that he may step up the questioning if he deems it necessary. It seems certain they were involved in this now and I want to know all they know; they should be questioned about the Black Knights too. The King wishes to know all about the company, but they must live. Father will want to hear their words himself." The guard took his orders and left swiftly.

"Well, Sir Monkford, I reckon that leaves it to you to move Lady Myrbeth" Hisbara stated.

"No need, I will carry her," Frederick needed to keep her close right now he still couldn't feel any relief though he knew she was no longer in danger. He lifted her from Edmund's bed and carried her out. 'She is alive, she is going to be fine,' he kept repeating in his head. He supposed he was too overwhelmed to feel safe or sure of anything. So much had changed for him, he had suffered and so had Myrbeth. He would be strong for her, like her. He entered her chambers and gently placed her on the bed, stroking her hair back neatly.

"Pardon us, your Grace," Hisbara prompted him. She wanted to redress and tend to her disfigured skin. Frederick slowly backed out of the room, not taking his eyes off Myrbeth. Once he reached the corridor the maid servant Madge approached. She looked at him with a respectful, repentant look as she shut the door on him. He collapsed crying on the floor his emotions just too strong to contain any longer.

CHAPTER 20

Mercy knew as soon as the force of Parvery came down upon them that he had been right. He had been right not to trust the benefactor, right to fear a double cross and here it was in the form of a whole army. Mercy had stood his ground and fought, even though he knew it was hopeless. They couldn't win. He watched as his comrades died one by one. It was not until Finish's throat was slit so deeply that his head nearly came off that the men really started to break and run. He would have stayed if there were any point, but Finish was dead, and this wasn't their war.

He remembered briefly how on his first visit to Parvery, on his first fight with the company, he had been the favourite to flee. The thought made him let out a derisive laugh as he turned his back on the lost battle. Mercy did not run. He moved slowly through the ranks of fighters, tapping the backs of men he knew would come. For some it was not in their nature to retreat, some would prefer to die fighting. Mercy knew this. He knew which men would stay and which would prefer to live to fight another day. To those he would leave behind he gave a subtle salute. This practiced retreat was familiar to every member of the company, though they had never had to use it before. They exited the gully they had been camped in, heading backwards towards the only safe place for them, their ship.

Escaping was difficult as they were outnumbered by the Parvery forces. By the time they reached the deserted village they had cleared, their number was down to only thirteen. They moved faster now as there was a small force pursuing. They stayed together in a close pack and, not having armour, they moved much faster. Now free of any visible pursuit they made it to the coast where Freedom's Price was docked. They saw smoke from the lower coastal houses, thick, deep and grey. It almost made them turn back. Though Mercy had a pit in his stomach, he prayed it did not mean what he feared. But as their feet landed on the sand, they saw the tide was out and Freedom's Price was a burning wreck.

"What now, Mercy?" Whiskey asked, the despair in his voice clear. They were looking to him now. He realised the mantel of command had suddenly passed to him despite his lack of such an ambition.

"We make for the fields, then cross the border." Mercy found himself glad that he had spent all those hours studying the maps of this land. Finish had called it pointless. He said they only had to know where they were going but it hadn't stopped Mercy. He knew that crossing through the fields of Arabat would lead them back to Twickerth where this had all begun. It only felt right. It was also the unexpected move. The border crossing into Pidar was much closer and as a coastal town there were ships leaving all the time. But that would have been expected and they could easily be pursued. Also, the ships weren't headed anywhere other than the other kingdom's of Parvery. It was not much of escape but perhaps Twickerth wasn't either.

"To the border," the men agreed, Mercy had expected to have to justify his choice, not used to the blind obedience they had showed Finish. They were ready to follow him though. They all moved swiftly, still keeping close ranks just in case. It was early evening when they reached the wooden fencing that marked the border. The borders of the nine kingdoms Mercy knew from his map studying were all similarly marked. There were watched border gates for crossing between the kingdoms, but they could not go through those. They travelled to an area where the fences were built higher, but it was nothing to trouble fully grown men. They jumped or clambered over the fencing, depending on whether they were wounded. They found themselves again in the woods of Twickerth.

This is where the maps became of no more use. The wooded area was marked but the pictorial representation didn't capture every tree or what it was like to walk among them. Lost and unfamiliar to the area, Mercy led the remaining men in circles for over a day before they found fresh water. It was a wide and deep river. They stayed there for a time, refreshing themselves and washing their wounds. When they continued forward, they kept near to the riverbed. They could not stop moving as they were sure to be discovered if they did. Mercy led his men through into another kingdom, never stopping long in one place. They could not risk staying in Parvery but had no means of escape. If they tried to buy passage on a ship they would be identified. Without purpose they all became dejected, feeling hunted. Though the pursuit, if there was still a pursuit, never caught up to them. This was fortunate since they weren't moving particularly fast and would be easy to catch. They were footsore, travel worn and uncertain of which way they travelled. Surely any pursuit would have found them by now. Mercy almost wondered if they weren't being tracked after all. It didn't matter though, they had to keep going. Mercy didn't really know where he was heading, he had long since lost any sense of place. Until he reached another border. They had accidently come close to the guarded gate, the crossing sign read Hollthen.

Mercy knew the name instantly, Hollthen was the kingdom on the eastern edge of Parvery and the home of the escaped girl. He had led them here unintentionally. He had studied the maps, remembered which kingdom led to the next and now here they were at his ultimate destination. Why he wanted to see her he couldn't explain but the pull to lay eyes on the child whose life he had spared, was very strong. So, he led the men on towards where he would find her, in the royal capital of Hollthen. However, as soon as he took this road, he knew he would have to offer a reason for their continued presence to the men. After all, leading them to a castle of one of the nine kings would seem like surrender to them. Luckily, an easy excuse came to him.

"Sweets and Doc were sent here on a separate mission; we must check on their progress." He paused, not wanting to explain what that mission had been. He and Finish had kept the girl's survival a secret. Finish had insisted that no others should know about the plot to kill the girl. Mercy didn't find this suspicious; Finish always operated this way. However, Mercy had not had the courage to ask if this secrecy was because Finish suspected that someone of the company had helped the girl. Now Finish was dead, and Mercy never wanted anyone to know how he had betrayed him. It would be his cross to bear silently, for all time.

"We're to head deeper into this place, is that wise?" asked the company advisor, Wisdom.

"Should we all go?" asked a young boy they called Archer.

"No, that would draw too much attention. I will go alone," Mercy's voice was almost insistent, he wanted to do this alone. He wanted to see the girl and he needed to do so privately.

"What do we do?" Archer was again the speaker; he was young, only about twelve or so Mercy remembered. Young and frightened, but he wasn't alone in being fearful of what might come next, none of them knew.

"For now, we need food and safe passage, if it can be found. But no one can know who we are. Those who have gold visit markets and buy what you can but stay in small groups, don't attract attention. Take off your blacks if possible. Trickster, Blade and Green, you all have a likeable air. Visit the docks, see what boats are soon to leave port and to what destinations. Do not discuss our business, you must be careful with every word you speak. The rest of you should set out to forage for what food you can. No one should travel alone. We will meet back here, on that bridge, tomorrow at noon." Mercy didn't know what was stranger, hearing himself give orders or that the orders came so naturally. The feeling did not dissipate when he saw those orders being followed. All in all, it was a relief to get away and be alone.

It was mid-morning by Mercy's reckoning as he travelled along the road by the border. He made his way to the royal capital, the walls of which could be seen from afar. When he finally reached the walls, the gate was open and he walked into the outer village. He could see the castle gate ahead and this was also open, but had guards, two of them, standing watch. They were sure to ask questions if he tried to pass. Still determined he continued to approach the castle when he spotted movement to his right. Built into the wall was an outer building with a small, iron-studded door, out of this door came a guard. Mercy moved close to the door but didn't try to enter straight away. There was an inn, called the Guards Tavern, just a few houses down with a perfect eyeline onto the iron door. He watched the door for the best part of the day, long enough to know each guard had a key: no key, no entrance. That wouldn't be a problem though, the inn was aptly named as it was full of guardsmen.

Lifting a key off a particularly drunk guard was no trouble. Once through the door he found himself in a large and empty cloakroom. Cloaks and liveries decorated with a crest were littered everywhere, some neatly folded next to helms, others hung from wooden pegs, and some just left rumpled on wooden benches. He quickly picked up a set that looked about his size and scooped up a helm to hide his face before carrying on.

The next room was a food hall where a few guards sat eating their evening meal, Mercy had had no real food for days. He and the other remnants of the company had been living off wild berries and the scraps of two rabbits and a squirrel that they had managed to kill, but the meat hadn't stretched far between thirteen. None of the other guards seem to be paying him much attention so he went to the serving table. There was soup, bread, and a rich stew. Mercy chose a table where he could be alone and sat. As he tucked in, he tried to think of what his next step should be. He had gained entry to the castle but was still no closer to discovering what had become of Sweets and Doc.

Mercy and Finish had pondered a long time over who to send on the important assassination duty. The mission would have to be covert if they wanted to prevent sending men to their deaths, so poison was the obvious answer. Where poison was concerned Doc was the clear choice. He was not a true doctor, but he was the closest the company had. He was a learned man who wished to travel in order to study other lands and their medical ways. He had come aboard calling himself a doctor and botanist, but Finish had suspected there was more to him than a simple herbalist. Mercy and Finish had offered to settle the matter of his passage over drinks, which he had accepted. Somewhere around the second bottle of liquor he had confessed that he was on the run. He had been arrested for unnatural experiments on the living and dead but had escaped by killing his jailer with poison. Finish could see the benefit of such a man joining them, so had happily agreed to bring him on board. Finish insisted on him being trained in combat, but he was old and slow and had never been much of fighter. Sweets was a very different kind of man; he was clever and charming. He could convince people to do things with ease and he had a lethal streak when needed. He was new to the company, recruited only a short while before they had sailed for Parvery. He hadn't looked like much but had talked his way into an audition. He had the first man flat on his back in minutes and then knocked over two others. He didn't know much of weapons, he admitted, but he was fast and was stronger than he looked. The two men together made perfect sense Mercy had thought, Sweets could get them in and out and Doc could do the deed. They had seemed the perfect choices, but had they succeeded?

Getting into the castle had been easier than he imagined and now Mercy was sitting, listening. He listened hard to all the noise of the guards around him, trying to ascertain if the deed had been done.

At that moment the door banged open.

"Who is supposed to be relieving Byrne?" the new man asked, in a booming voice and, to his surprise, Mercy recognised him. He was one of the knights who had been present at the battle. He instantly looked down and tried to appear relaxed.

"I don't know, sir," a young guard replied.

"Damn, well you will do, Delbard," the knight replied

"But I'm not finished, Sir, what about him?" the young guard pointed to Mercy who had quickly wolfed down his food. To his horror the knight shrugged and beckoned to him. He had no choice but to get up and follow the knight out of the barracks. Then he pointed to the castle.

"Just head up to the Lady's chambers." 'The Lady' could that mean her? Was he actually being ordered to go right to the very place he wanted to be? Mercy was so surprised it took him a long moment to realise she must be alive then. Mercy tried to move with purpose through the castle, having no idea, of course, where he should be headed. He was beginning to despair and thinking about exiting at the nearest point, when suddenly a page stopped.

"What are you doing?" the young boy asked in a disapproving tone.

"Heading to the Lady's chamber," Mercy said, repeating what he had been told.

"Well, you're on the wrong floor, not to mention heading to the south tower, you must be new. Part of the new security they are hiring, no doubt all because of those no-good Black Knights. Follow me." He followed the boy without question. His arrogance might have bothered Mercy if he hadn't given such useful information. New security and the mention of the company suggested that Sweets and Doc had been discovered.

The young page led him up to the third floor and to a door where another guard stood watch.

"Finally, I'm starving," the guard exclaimed, leaving, and Mercy was soon alone outside the door.

He wasn't sure how long he stood outside the door debating his situation, it could have been one hour or several. He felt ridiculous standing outside that closed door while nothing happened. Even more so because deep down he had not come hoping to discover the fate of his comrades but the fate of the girl. The girl was just inside the room he was guarding. Though he didn't know for sure it was her room, it could be some other lady's. Mercy was just deciding he might as well leave the castle altogether when a door burst open. A middle-aged woman stuck her head around the door.

"Good heavens, the lady has been ill. Come in at once." Mercy did as the fussy woman instructed. There shuddering on the floor, on all fours, was a young girl.

"Well, don't just stand there, help the girl back into bed, while I clean up." Mercy couldn't see her face at first but as he lifted her it came into view. For a moment he flashed back to those woods so many years ago, with the women fleeing in the distance. He knew then this was the girl, the survivor. She looked so like the woman she could only be her daughter. She was alive, she had survived again, it was completely implausible but here she was in front of him.

"Thank you," the girl muttered through chattering teeth. Mercy acted almost reflexively pulling his cloak off and wrapping it around the fragile girl before gently placing her back in the bed. She thanked him again.

"No trouble, Ma'am." But there was nothing but trouble. Clearly the girl had been poisoned, what else could be making her so ill? So, was she dying or recovering? And if she was still alive what had been done with Doc and Sweets?

"Right," the fussy woman said, getting up from the floor too. "I must fetch the physician's lad and the princes, stay with her," she ordered, and Mercy nodded. Once her retreating footsteps could no longer be heard the impulse to run from the room almost overpowered him. However, he stood his ground knowing it would be foolish to draw attention to himself in this way just because he was desperate to escape this girl. A living reminder of his betrayal to his comrades.

"Could you pass me some water?" the girl asked. Mercy poured her a glass and passed it to her.

"Are you alright, now, Ma'am?"

"Yes, thank you, I will be fine," she said taking a sip. "I don't believe we have had the pleasure of being introduced?" She had recognised he wasn't one of her regular guards, Mercy tried to think quickly and not to overreact. For a moment he didn't know what to say. It had been so long since he had used his true name, it felt foreign and false to give it now. So, he decided to invent one. After all this girl was the last person he should trust with such vital information.

"My name is John Mercy, ma'am," he said, giving the first names that came to him.

"A pleasure to meet you, John, I am the Lady Myrbeth." Myrbeth, the name echoed in his mind. He unconsciously reached to touch the hidden pocket he had long ago sown into his undershirt which contained an old, faded family book. He had studied it a lot lately; he had always known there was a chance it belonged to the fleeing woman but had never had confirmation, until now.

"Myrbeth, a lovely name, no doubt a name from your mother?" The fleeing woman who he now knew had been called Myra Rivers.

"My mother chose it, yes. Though I don't know if it was her name, too, if that is what you meant," her voice grew quieter. So, the fleeing woman called Myra hadn't lived after all. She'd lived long enough to save her daughter and name her but not long enough to tell anyone who she was.

"Forgive me, my Lady, I should have known better, given your history," Mercy said, covering his lapse, a true resident of Hollthen would know she had never known her mother, would know all the details of her life.

"It's quite alright; my name is the only thing I have of her, so I cherish it. Yours is quite unusual, Mercy, I don't think I have ever heard of a Mercy?" Another slip up.

"Perhaps not, but it is a name that suits me all the same." The name suited him more than Finish, or even Mercy himself, could have imagined. It was because of his mercy, however misguided, that this girl was even alive. A sudden wave of some deep emotion overtook him,

"It's an admirable quality," the girl said and Mercy lost his senses. The words came from him without thought.

"Mercy is a varied and fickle quality do you not think? It can mean more than one thing and is often difficult to recognise but even more difficult to deliver. Sometimes what is meant as a merciful deed goes astray, or an ill-intended act can have merciful consequences." His jaw clamped shut with an audible snap as he forced himself to stop speaking.

There were many things he wanted to tell her, all that he knew, all that he had done. He wanted to let her know that he had let her mother flee. He wanted to let her know he was the reason she was alive, but mostly he wanted to tell her that her mother had given the lady her appearance as well as her name. That she was her mother's spitting image as far as he could tell. In thinking this he began to wonder if there was nothing of her father in her. However, the realisation that he or another member of his group had killed her father made him feel sick. Guilt and regret hit him like a stone wall. It was doubled when the girl gave a deep cough and then sipped at the water with bloody lips. He had nearly allowed her to be killed again and for what, nothing more than the bidding of a rich and cruel unknown noble.

"I think mercy is a fine quality," Lady Myrbeth replied, once she had recovered.

"Yes, my Lady, a fine quality and hopefully not rare." Mercy was grateful when his guilt-driven babbling was cut off by the arrival of two finely dressed princes. Mercy greeted them, then backed respectfully and slowly out. He closed the door behind himself and left. He made his way back through the castle to the guard's barracks, abandoning his stolen clothes there. It was the dead of night now and no one was around to see him exit, first the barracks, then the outer village back onto the road. As he walked under the stars, he thought about how all the people he had killed had been someone's family. A mother, a father, a child. How hard it must have been for that girl to start over in life. He knew what that difficult and painful road was like. Yet he had caused that for another child and how many others. He had still saved her life, though, surely that had been a good act. His true act of mercy. A new sense of purpose filled him, a new direction opening for him to do penance for all he had done.

CHAPTER 21

Trevard returned to the castle almost a week later. His first act was to rush to Myrbeth's chambers. She was standing shakily, supported by two maids, each holding her firmly by the arms.

"My dear daughter," he announced his presence as he went straight to her side. Myrbeth moved to embrace him, falling into his arms.

"Father, your Grace, you are home," Myrbeth exclaimed.

"You are shivering." Despite the thick deep purple nightgown she wore it seemed she was still cold. "You should rest, please. What your body has gone through is no small matter." He led her back to the bed and tucked her in. Trevard then dismissed the maids, wanting time alone with Myrbeth. "How are you?" he asked once they had left.

"I am still very sickly, as you can see. I can't eat much, I'm feverish, and I occasionally expel blood and bile. The young physician's apprentice, Colin, says it is normal, my body's cleansing the poison, but it is not at all pleasant," she grimaced.

"I'm sure, Myrbeth. I am so relieved you were returned to us;

I could not bear to lose you, too." Myrbeth blushed, a single tear trickled down her cheek. Trevard moved to wipe it away and caress her face. "Frederick wrote that the men have been caught which is good, have they been executed?" he asked, changing the subject. She hesitated at this.

"No, not yet. They are still imprisoned and have been questioned and charged but they await your sentence. Please don't be disappointed in Frederick, I just don't think he could bring himself to preside over their execution."

"I assure you, I am not at all disappointed. I wouldn't mind a chance to hear their confession for myself. I quite understand Frederick's forbearance, he has seen so much death," Trevard sighed. "How is he bearing it?"

"He is shaken and still worried over my health," she confessed, sounding concerned.

"I was the same after my first battle, but my father sustained me, and I will support Frederick. I know you will do the same, but you must allow yourself to heal. That is of paramount importance." She nodded but looked pensive, Trevard waited for her to say what was on her mind.

"I hope you won't mind," she began hesitantly, "I hope you will understand, Frederick has often been sleeping with me." Her voice changed from tentative to hurried. "Merely for comfort, Edmund is often with us also. I think it is the only way we all feel easy enough to sleep." Trevard smiled, his first one in days.

"If it helps you all to bear it, I cannot blame any of you." Indeed, Trevard also longed for someone to share his cares and bed with. He thought of Citria for a time, imagining how they would have talked. How she would have held her sons tight, how she wouldn't have left Myrbeth's side. There was pain in the thoughts but also some small measure of comfort. "I'm afraid I must attend to other affairs now, and you should rest." He got up to leave but paused and turned back to her. "I cannot properly express how good it feels to be home safe with you all again."

"Nor I, Father." The words rang and resonated in both their hearts. "I'm so glad you are both home safe, I was so worried," she continued in a choked voice, "you were victorious as well; I'm pleased for you."

"Yes, in most ways our mission was successful, but not in all," Trevard said no more, this was not the time. He could tell her everything when she was well again.

Myrbeth's full strength began to return. After more than a week of bedrest she was encouraged to take short walks. Every step was stiff, heavy and awkward. At first, she couldn't manage more than a few shaky steps before she felt faint. After a while though, her movements became easier and she travelled further. Which is how Trevard came to find her at the castle steps one day.

"Myrbeth, should you be walking unaided?" She was often accompanied on these walks as they still tired her greatly and she often needed help returning to bed, but as the king approached the guard Delbard melted away.

"It was such a nice day," she offered by way of an explanation.

"I suppose you are right; it is lovely. I will escort you." Trevard offered her his arm and took her to the beach.

"Lord March's memorial went well I assume?" Myrbeth asked.

"It's such a shame, he was Lord of Birchlyn for over 40 years. At least he is at peace. He was very ill towards the end but, still, I will miss working with him. I shall be additionally busy now, with two of my lords lost," Trevard said, sighing. They walked in silence for a while, Trevard so lost in his own thoughts he didn't notice Myrbeth was lagging behind.

"This cloak is fraying, you should let me mend it," Myrbeth offered, interrupting Trevard's pensiveness. He was again dressed in the long, black, traditional memorial cloak.

"Oh yes, I suppose it is not surprising, I have worn this too much of late. But you are tired why don't we sit on the sand for a moment?" They sat and stared at the ocean. "How are you feeling?"

"Truthfully, tired of it all. This slow recovery is becoming very irritating," she answered, giving a little frown.

"I can imagine that is true," Trevard said, smiling, she was usually always so patient it was an unexpected answer. "Though that was not quite the question I was asking. I know Frederick is managing well with recent events and Edmund is back to his old self, but I'm not certain how things are faring with you?" There was a pause before Myrbeth responded.

"I have been thinking a great deal, but I fear my thoughts are perhaps too morbid to share."

"Try me, please, as you know I do love to think." Myrbeth looked at Trevard a long time before answering.

"I have been thinking about what happens after we die," was all she said at first, hesitantly. Trevard understood why she had been reluctant to speak; this was not a subject often discussed in Parvery. Trevard even knew that some of the common folk believed that to discuss death invited it's presence. It was very superstitious in Trevard's opinion.

"I understand, that is only natural after facing death yourself, and I'm sure it won't surprise you that it's a topic I have often considered as well," he assured her. This seemed to put her more at ease.

"Truly, well I have been trying not to fuss over it too much, but, well, I just wondered if we continue on somehow."

"What do you mean, more specifically?" Trevard asked.

"I'm not certain, but I would like to think our consciousness," she stopped, uncertain how to explain. "I just wondered if we could still be aware, still live some sort of life."

"Yes, I have thought the same, perhaps we could still be alive in a different plane of existence or perhaps we could be re-born, starting from scratch." Trevard had often thought on the idea of being with Citria after his death or whether perhaps he would receive a clean slate, a new life.

"I'm not certain I can like this idea. When I thought on the concept, I thought could I be reunited with my parents? Would I see Queen Citria again? Of course, I am grateful I survived; I did not wish to die, but still, I would hate to think we simply cease to exist in any form." Myrbeth outlined in a cautious voice.

"I have often thought the same thing, but the problem is, there is no way to know. So I agree that we should not dwell on it too much, but I am happy to discuss it. I'm sure your parents have been much on your mind. I am sorry we were able to learn so little from the Black Knights, I don't doubt you wanted to learn the reason for their deaths."

"Actually, I think it is for the best. The reason would have most likely been shallow and full of greed, nothing justifiable. I would rather not know; it won't ease anything." Her voice grew hoarse and she stopped speaking. Trevard could see she was tired and he had much work to attend to.

"I think we should get you back to the castle." She nodded and Trevard assisted her back to her chambers.

"You should eat something before you sleep again, I will order you some food straight away," Trevard said, having helped her back to bed. He moved to leave but turned to check on her when he reached the door, he noticed she had already drifted back to sleep.

It was high summer by the time Myrbeth's health recovered fully and she could return to her normal routine, including family breakfast.

"I was thinking of visiting the village today."

"Alone? Is that safe," Frederick asked, still concerned for her. Trevard thought he and Frederick had been very busy of late and there had been little time for much else.

"I also do not like the idea of you travelling alone. Perhaps you should all go."

"Truly, Father?" Edmund asked.

"Absolutely, you all deserve a little fun," he pronounced, and his children all gave happy cries and began discussing the trip. "Ah, good, the post," Trevard remarked, as a servant brought him a small stack of letters.

In Parvery the kingdoms could keep in touch in three ways; the kings regularly communicated monthly about the business of their respective kingdoms in reports sent by royal couriers. Scribes or guards were sometimes sent out with special messages of an important nature, especially if the messages required an urgent response. Finally, for personal correspondence there was the post. The post was handled by a small group of men who lived very nomadic existences in wagons, travelling constantly. They carried letters from kingdom to kingdom charging a small fee for each letter to provide themselves with a livelihood. This method was sporadic and unpredictable but also provided a pleasant surprise when a delivery occurred. Trevard began opening letters and reading.

"Oh, I have some wonderful news," he announced, holding up one of the letters. "This is a wedding invitation; it seems Prince Manual is to marry Princess Penalyn." They all let out joyful cries.

"I've never attended a royal wedding before. It will be so exciting and wonderful," Myrbeth exclaimed. Trevard said nothing, pleased that the invitation had been left ambiguous. He suspected people would not be pleased by Myrbeth's attendance, but he had no intention of dashing her hopes again. "We shall all have to order new clothes," she continued happily.

"Will there be time?" Edmund asked.

"Oh, plenty, the wedding is not to be for some months it seems." Weddings could often be quite quickly arranged with a royal staff to assist with every detail. However, Trevard suspected that marriage contract negotiations were the cause of the delay, both King Rollin and Tunora were very particular.

"That will be Penalyn, I'm sure she had plans for a very large and extravagant wedding," Myrbeth said, offering a different theory. Trevard went back to the post as the others continued to discuss the pending wedding.

"You have a letter as well, Frederick." Trevard handed it to him. Frederick opened and read the letter, taking some time.

"It's from Princess Gisella, I wrote to her shortly after her father's death. I must admit it was a short letter, I mostly rambled, unsure of what I wanted to say. But she has written back, a very long letter, I never knew she was capable of it."

"She chooses when to use her words, but she was clearly grateful for your concern. It seems she has warmed to you," Trevard suggested, briefly wondering if there was hope for a match between them after all.

"She says she has been in Twickerth for some time. It seems she is to be engaged to Prince Davond once things settle." Trevard gave up that hope as quickly as he had let it grow.

Frederick and Myrbeth were growing closer every day. Trevard had watched what he had not seen before, their deep affection present and growing daily. He had become increasingly worried about what was to happen between them.

"Your Highness, we have an unexpected guest." Trevard looked up from the last of the post to his secretary. "Prince Wexlar Pedcott of Twickerth has arrived." They all exchanged a look of surprise.

"I will come to my parlour straight away, please show him there." the king said, in a bemused voice. Surprise visits were unusual, as word could easily be sent ahead of any plans. It was interesting that this prince had chosen to come without notice.

"He is awaiting you in the throne room, Sire," Modwin said.

"Why?" Trevard asked, confused. A young pageboy behind Modwin cleared his throat, his voice was nervous and weak.

"Forgive me, your Grace, but he insisted. I told him you were not there but ..."

"He insisted. I quite understand, I will only be a minute," he spoke in a reassuring voice. Trevard stood up. "The prince wants a formal audience," he explained, and his family nodded, understanding. Trevard made a quick visit to his chambers first to change into more elaborate garb and collect his crown. Trevard was not surprised by this want for formality, some of the royals insisted on these airs. Personally, Trevard thought they were unnecessary unless part of a state ceremony, especially between the royal families. After all they were all on equal footing.

The throne room in Hollthen castle was also only used for court and ceremonial purposes. It was a small room but cavernous, with large columns that held stone beams supporting a painted celling. The design was a detailed map of the kingdom. The walls were covered in tapestries and the only furniture in the room were three holly wood thrones. One each for king, queen and crown prince. When Trevard entered Prince Wexlar was seated in the throne which was usually reserved for Frederick. He was looking around the throne room studying its features with a disapproving look. Trevard could guess his thoughts, the room might be considered plain by most royal standards, and he knew it wasn't as grand as the Twickerth throne room. When Wexlar spotted the king, he jumped up and gave a slight bow.

"King Trevard, I am Prince Wexlar Pedcott of Twickerth. You met me and my brothers in Arabat before the battle, my father, King

Ivan Pedcott, introduced us," Prince Wexlar bowed again. The king, in truth, barely remembered him and they had never spoken so he supposed this overly formal greeting wasn't unnecessary.

"Of course, Prince Wexlar, welcome to Hollthen, and I am sorry for your recent loss," Trevard replied politely.

"Urvant, my brother, yes," was all Wexlar said, which seemed unusually reserved, but Trevard supposed they hadn't been close. He could not judge him too harshly, after all, he was no closer with his sister Tunora. Though he was sure if she were to die Trevard would be distressed.

"Do you have some message or request from your father?" the king asked, seeing this as the logical reason for the visit, he could not imagine another.

"No," Wexlar replied curtly, with a dry smile, as if such a task would be beneath him. "I have come of my own volition. I know our meeting was brief, but I admired you and your kingdom." Trevard just inclined his head, uncertain of the purpose for this flattery. The boy didn't seem to need any encouragement to continue. "I have a proposition for you, King Trevard. I believe it could be very beneficial for us both, and to your profit." Trevard's uncertainty only increased. Unwilling to let the prince continue to steer the conversation he chose try to discover his purpose by a different method.

"Is your father aware you are here?" he asked.

"No," Wexlar's answer was again curt, "I am certain he would approve though."

"How can you be so certain?" Trevard asked politely, suspecting he was lying.

"He always encourages us to be independent and take opportunities, to stand on our own feet. Father taught us that, just because we are royal, we shouldn't expect to easily inherit everything." Trevard supposed the lesson was a sound one, similar to the one he taught his own sons but there were subtle differences.

"A sound principle," Trevard replied all the same.

"Yes, but a difficult one to follow," Wexlar's voice was disgruntled but brightened quickly. "However, I believe I might have found a way. I know that you have two newly vacant lordships; I wish to take up a lord's seat, either will do."

"You want me to name you a lord?" Trevard had taken a moment to respond due to his deep surprise at the audacity of such a request.

"Yes, a prince must have some employment," he smiled.

"Well, as a matter of fact, I only have one vacant lordship. Lord Yarrow has a young son who will be inheriting his seat."

"I had not heard. I thought Lord Yarrow was a casualty of the battle over a month ago, surely his son would have already been raised to the lordship?" Wexlar seemed annoyed that his information had been inaccurate.

"The ceremony is set for a week from now. In Hollthen it is traditional to honour the passing of a lord by leaving his seat empty for a period of two months of mourning," Trevard explained.

"How quaint," Wexlar's tone made it clear he thought the opposite. "Well, one lord's seat is much like another, as I said, I would be happy with either seat." Trevard tried not to seem irritated by these words and the boy's cold, confident manner.

"And there is no position for you at home?" The prince's request was highly irregular, it was a king's responsibility to find either a position or match for his sons.

"Even with my brother Urvant's death in the battle I have an older brother ahead of me in the line of succession. Davond and I do not see eye to eye often. He has always preferred my younger brother Nathaniel. Besides I will never succeed to a lordship in my own kingdom, none are vacant. So, I must make my own way." Wexlar spoke so prosaically, Trevard liked the prince even less. He felt the young man had missed the point of his father's lesson entirely.

"You spoke of a proposition?" Trevard asked, wishing to bring the conversation to a close.

"Yes, in return for you granting me the lordship I will marry your ward Myrbeth. I know you are eager to find her a match, the wife of a prominent lord would be a good position for her."

"You wish to marry Myrbeth? I didn't think you had ever met her?" Trevard was even more surprised.

"I haven't. My brothers and I were absent from her ball." Trevard remembered the response he had received to their invitation; it had been particularly offensive. Those words had been King Ivan's, however, not that of this prince.

"Yet you wish her to be your wife?" Trevard didn't understand. Wexlar's request grew stranger and stranger. He clearly didn't care for Myrbeth and expected to be handed the lordship. Trevard hoped by questioning the boy he could make him see the ludicrousness of his request.

"She is not unpretty I hear, obedient and knows her place. I am slightly older than her, I turned nineteen recently but I'm sure our marriage could be perfectly satisfactory," Wexlar didn't smile, every word was calm and clear, not at all registering Trevard's incredulity. So Trevard tried a different tack.

"Birchlyn is a fishing village primarily and since Twickerth is a landlocked kingdom I can't imagine that you are very familiar with how a port village runs," Trevard said, still trying to poke holes in Wexlar's confidence.

"Perhaps not, but I'm sure I would learn. I'm quite intelligent and I'm sure you could assist me with any finer points," was Prince Wexlar's only response, so Trevard decided to be more direct.

"Prince Wexlar, my lords must act as my agents, and I must trust them to do so. It would be unethical of me to put a stranger in such a post, and it would be equally unethical to marry my daughter to the same stranger. I'm afraid I cannot grant you this request." Trevard spoke in a firm voice. However, this did not put an end to Wexlar's designs.

"You're a wise and cautious king, I see your point." The words were meant to be flattering but came out as patronising. "As the lordship is currently unavailable, I will endeavour to earn your trust during my stay." This was a twist Trevard had not anticipated, but it seemed discourteous to refuse him something as simple as to stay in the castle. He could only hope the visit would be short.

"I will have a room prepared for you. However, I will caution you, I rarely change my mind." The prince just bowed in response.

After the audience, Trevard sent servants to help settle the visitor and requested that both Frederick and Myrbeth be brought directly to his parlour. He only hoped they hadn't yet left for the village. When Frederick and Myrbeth arrived, thankfully they had not gone further than the castle gate, they were holding hands. Trevard saw this as bad sign.

"Father, is there more trouble?" Frederick asked, both of them were clearly concerned.

"Not exactly, please take a seat, I have a shock for both of you. First, I must explain I am not disposed to grant the requests that were just made of me. I must tell you that as not to alarm you, but I'm getting ahead of myself and must explain." Trevard outlined the conversation he had just had with the visiting prince.

"He wants to marry me?" Myrbeth asked, in nonplussed tone.

"Absolutely not," Frederick insisted, getting to his feet. Trevard had expected this reaction and he could not blame Frederick.

"I am inclined not to grant his request as I have said. I have little faith in his sincerity and don't appreciate his audacity," Trevard chose his words carefully.

"Then why is he staying?" Frederick asked loudly.

"Having good relations between the kingdoms is highly important right now. I do not wish to cause offence if it can be avoided." Though if he were being honest there was another reason. He had meant his refusal and didn't expect to change his mind, but it seemed foolish to instantly dismiss a prospect for Myrbeth. It was possible his first impression of the prince could be proved false with time, though he doubted it. "Prince Wexlar does not strike me as the type to make a great effort or to persevere under adversity. I'm certain that after a few days without success he will go back home, affronted but resigned." This was true as well and he didn't wish to explain his other motive to Frederick or Myrbeth. So he said no more.

"You wish me to entertain him?" Myrbeth's tone was uncertain.

"Yes. I do not expect you to encourage him in any capacity, but he has come here to court you. So you must play the host." the king spoke clearly so they would hear the command in his words.

"But he isn't the right fit, even you said so," Frederick complained. Trevard sighed.

"No, I don't believe he is but still we must be respectful." It was the king's voice that spoke, and Frederick fell silent.

"Of course, your Grace. I will make Prince Wexlar feel welcome," Myrbeth replied dutifully.

"Not too welcome, I don't wish to give him a false impression of success," Trevard replied.

"What is your plan with regards to the lordship?" Frederick asked, perhaps a little too directly.

"That's not an easy question to answer. With no clear candidate I will have to find a lord that the fisherfolk will respect. If Edmund were older, I could name him to the seat and the men would accept that. However, he is much too young. So, I must search for someone else. I highly doubt Prince Wexlar will do. The men would never accept him. He is too much the outsider and has no knowledge of the water or those who live their lives by it." Trevard also thought the prince's proposal had been a little opportunistic, he was taking advantage of the difficulties of finding a match for Myrbeth and hoping to leverage that for a position he technically had no right to expect. He didn't like the attempt to back him into a corner. Trevard however had a stronger will than the prince seemed to estimate.

"I don't trust him; this isn't just bold, its disrespectful and more," Frederick said, echoing his father's unspoken thoughts.

"It's certainly an odd move I cannot fathom his thinking. I don't approve and will make no secret of it to him. There is another important point I wish to make." Trevard said, changing the subject. "Prince Wexlar cannot discover your feelings for one another. He could damage you both if he chose to expose you. I cannot stress this enough; you have lapsed of late, but you are protected within these walls. Outside I fear matters would be much worse. He cannot suspect anything, not your preference and not even jealousy." Myrbeth and Frederick looked at one another for a long moment before finally letting go of one another and giving an acknowledging nod.

"Of course, your Grace." Myrbeth said.

"I will keep my distance," Frederick promised in a reluctant tone.

"From both Myrbeth and the prince?" Trevard meant it as an order, but he felt badly so it came out more as a question. Frederick nodded again.

"I suppose the village trip will have to wait," Myrbeth spoke glumly. "But what shall I do?"

"Take your cue from Frederick's time as host. The prince is in the guest quarters, I will take you now and introduce you." He stood and came round to her, trying not to notice his son's pained look. As he escorted her, Trevard remembered his earlier concern about separating Frederick and Myrbeth, but now such an opportunity had presented itself, he felt regret. The king wasn't certain that he didn't prefer them happy together.

CHAPTER 22

As Myrbeth walked behind the king she tried not to dwell too much on Frederick. She had hated leaving him alone in the king's parlour but knew there had been no alternative and no way to comfort him. She didn't truly manage to stop thinking of him though until she realised that they were outside her chambers not the guest quarters. She looked up at Trevard questioningly.

"I think you ought to change, the prince should see you at your best." She remembered the prince's insistence of an audience in the throne room, and she then noticed the king's garb and understood.

"Thank you, I won't be long." She was very grateful. The simple, unadorned blue dress she was wearing would never do for this prince. Instead, she chose a pink gown of a light airy material that was lined with pearls and a pearl hairnet to match. Suddenly as she dressed, she felt very nervous about her reception. She remembered the attitude from those of royal status towards her at the ball and was certain she was about to receive a similar reception. As promised, though, she was quick and soon re-joined the king. He gave a nod of approval before leading her silently to their guest's room.

Her first meeting with the prince only confirmed her fears.

"Prince Wexlar, may I introduce the Lady Myrbeth," The king made the introductions, the prince bowed and Myrbeth curtsied in return. The prince had dull brown hair, small grey eyes, a sharp nose, chubby cheeks, one of which showed a recently healed scar, and a dimple in his chin. He was not unpleasant in his appearance, but he had no handsome features like Frederick, she decided.

"Lady Myrbeth, well met." Then he quickly spoke to the king instead of to her. "Thank you for bringing her to me."

"Lady Myrbeth will give you a tour of the castle," Trevard's voice sounded stiff to her but she wasn't surprised.

"Not yourself?" the prince spoke, clearly surprised and unhappy.

"I'm afraid I am far too busy, and I thought the two of you should get to know one another."

"Of course," was the prince's only response. Trevard left and Myrbeth directed the prince around the castle. She took the king's advice and copied Fredrick's tour, but it was awkward since the prince never said a word the entire time. She described the great rulers of Hollthen as they passed their pictures in the portrait gallery and showed him round all the castle, inside and out, but still he was silent.

Prince Wexlar joined them for dinner that evening and was introduced to the rest of the family. He ignored Frederick and Edmund, who ignored him likewise. To the king Wexlar was full of flattery. In comparison he said little to Myrbeth, only enough to be civil. Myrbeth recognised this sort of politeness, it was sweet enough but entirely false. So she was mostly silent as well.

"I was very interested to hear of your ancestors today. King Terrance, your father, seemed particularly distinguished." Showing that the prince had at least been listening during Myrbeth's tour.

"I thank you, he was a good man, no doubt that is what you found so interesting." Trevard responded clearly not impressed. Prince Wexlar ignored this though and changed the subject.

"Perhaps the lady would take me tomorrow to your lovely village, hopefully my village to be?" His tone was casual and his smile wide. Myrbeth noticed that he didn't speak to her directly if he could avoid it. Often looking to the king to answer on her behalf. She also noticed that despite his gentle words he wasn't asking. Frederick swallowed hard and bit his tongue. Trevard opened his mouth to respond but Myrbeth spoke first.

"Of course, your Grace." Wexlar smiled in acknowledgement, but still didn't look at her.

"That will be perfect." He addressed the king who frowned in return.

The following morning Myrbeth met the prince at the royal stables. This was the first time she had been riding since her poisoning. She was unsteady mounting and gripped the reins tighter than usual, feeling slightly insecure. She could see the prince sneering at her. But her horse, Perrotta, was a gentle creature and Myrbeth soon felt soothed by her. Two guards, Byrne and Delbard, were to join them.

"We are in need of an escort?" the prince asked unimpressed.

"Forgive me, but I have been unwell lately. I am recovered but I would hate to risk your Grace having to help me back home," she explained. She had correctly predicted the prince's distaste to her infirmity. He quickly changed his attitude to the guards, thanking them for their time. The four of them rode out of the courtyard, through the village and out of the River Gate. They were silent as they rode over the canal bridge and down the River Road that followed the bright water straight to the ocean. Myrbeth realised after some time that the responsibility for making conversation would fall to her.

"Are you enjoying the scenery, Prince Wexlar?" she asked, beginning pleasantries. The road was a short distance from the water and along its banks grew, willows and a variety of wildflowers. Myrbeth recognised a few of the plants, Lady Grouse had been teaching her, and Myrbeth enjoyed going out to gather specimens with her friend. She saw wild geraniums, phlox, lobelia and wild columbine plants. However, when the prince merely glanced over at the beautiful sights and then looked away again, she tried again. "Do you have anything like this in your home?" This time it worked, he answered.

"No, we have forests thick with trees. We do have the Rivers Tyiver and Twland and there are some flowers, I suppose" His response was basic but not disrespectful. She was pleased with the start and carried on.

"I have only visited Twickerth twice. Though I was a baby the first time when the memorial was erected. The queen and I went back to see it again some years later. We didn't visit much more of the kingdom. Perhaps you could tell me about it?"

"Twickerth has its charms. I've never seen the memorial but I'm sure your visit was pleasant," Prince Wexlar replied in a bored tone. "Our palace is something more to see, the rooms are vast and lavishly decorated. Though I doubt you will ever have the occasion to visit."

"No, I don't suppose so." She knew what was meant. Her presence would never be allowed, even if she were to marry this prince. "I'm sure your home is lovely, which makes me surprised you would want to leave it." The king had suggested to Myrbeth that if the prince could be gently led to the conclusion that his scheme was a poor one, he might decide on his own to abandon his plan.

"It is necessary." His tone was curt again, obviously not wanting to explain his actions, but Myrbeth didn't feel like giving up.

"Ah yes, the need for employment, still are you certain that you will be happy settling in Hollthen? It will be quite different from what you are accustomed to." He was quiet for a while, as if the question was difficult to answer.

"I am not attached to Twickerth or my family. I believe I could settle here." Wexlar's basic answers were getting her nowhere, so Myrbeth let the subject drop. To her surprise though he continued the conversation.

"You are aware that I have asked for your hand, my lady?" Wexlar's question sounded more like an announcement of fact.

"Yes, I am aware you have asked, but the matter is not settled."

"It will be shortly; the king and I will arrange things satisfactorily," he spoke with complete confidence and Myrbeth was uncertain what to say next. They continued down the road in silence for some time before the prince spoke again.

"I noticed that King Trevard refers to you as his daughter," it was clear he disapproved. "At least you do not return the familiarity."

"Not in a formal setting," Myrbeth couldn't help feeling a little provoked by this.

"It was an odd decision, to make you his ward. I suppose he explained his reasoning to you?" The direct question was quite rude and Myrbeth was sure if she answered it, he would ask her more personal questions.

"That is between us, I'm sure you can respect that, and I don't think you would agree with his logic," she answered brusquely, but this didn't deter the prince.

"Father has often spoken about your survival and your rise to being the king's ward. It baffled us all. My father is quite a shrewd man and he couldn't understand it at all." His statement didn't seem to require an answer, so Myrbeth let them lapse back into silence.

"I don't think it should have taken place." The prince also returned to silence now had given his decide opinion on her status.

Birchlyn was a small village with a large docking berth for fishing boats. The river now became separated from the road by a tall stone wall and took them right into the heart of the village. The houses were tidy, pebbledashed buildings that were built far back from the dock and the sea beyond. The village centre housed the school, fish market and a few other local buildings. The prince looked around the village critically.

"These hovels, this is it?" his disappointment was clear.

"The houses," Myrbeth emphasised the words, "are homes to the fishermen and their families. The town is designed specifically to serve that purpose." She found herself strangely protective over the folk of Hollthen since she had been spending time with them. Wexlar continued to survey his surroundings; he spotted a large structure in the distance not far from the fish market.

"Is that the lord's manor?" he asked more expectantly.

"No, that is the Fishermen's Hall. It is a feasting hall, and the upper quarters provide beds for fisherfolk without a home," Myrbeth explained.

"There are homeless here?" the prince quickly blustered out.

"Not in the traditional sense, but fishermen spend days at a time out at sea, often longer. Not all of them find a permanent residence necessary. King Titus, whose portrait I showed you, commissioned the hall to be built at the request of the men some many years ago. It provides temporary safe lodging which is much needed." Prince Wexlar nodded.

"Oh yes, I remember him. You said he built many of the Hollthen towns."

"He restructured what was already present to better suit his people's need. He was a great king and King Trevard admires him highly." Again he nodded then changed the subject.

"Where is the manor house then?" Myrbeth led him a short distance to another building that was similar in appearance to the village houses, only slightly larger, with an accompanying garden and stables.

"But this is nothing, it's nothing," he complained, in an incredulous voice.

"I don't think Lord March saw things that way. His father was one of the fisherfolk himself. They relied on him in a crisis and he became a great lord. Lord March grew up in the port and around the men, so they treated him just as they did his father, as one of their own."

"A commoner was named lord?" Wexlar exclaimed, repeating the only part he had heard.

"Yes, it is not so uncommon here since a lord must represent his people. If there was one among their number now that the fishermen rallied around, then the king would have done the same, elevated one of their number." Wexlar was quiet for a time trying to master his reactions.

"An interesting choice," Wexlar finally said, unconvincingly.

"These men live a certain type of life, take risks and depend on one another. They respect men who understand that. Their lord needs to understand the fisherfolk in order to guide them." Wexlar said nothing, but Myrbeth was sure that he had not taken the point at all.

"Well, let's go see the manor," Wexlar said, his voice souring. The party travelled to the front of the manor and stopped outside the low stone wall. Wexlar dismounted his horse.

"Forgive me, your Grace, but this is as far as we can go."

"Whatever do you mean? I wish to inspect the hall." Wexlar clearly did not appreciate Myrbeth telling him what to do so she was careful with her response.

"We have a tradition in Hollthen, that when a nobleman dies his position and holdings are left empty except for direct family, as a sign of respect."

"Yes, yes, the king explained this sentiment, but I fail to see...," The frustration and anger in the prince's voice led Myrbeth to babble the rest of the explanation in haste.

"That house is empty and must remain so. It would be seen as a great insult by the people of this village were you to enter. If you hope to lead these people, then you must start by respecting their traditions. It is the least the king would expect." Wexlar paused and considered this for some time before remounting his horse. Myrbeth expected him to say nothing but instead he turned to her and said, quite calmly.

"I thank you for the advice, perhaps it would be best if we leave."

"Let's ride along the docks before returning," Myrbeth suggested. The prince just nodded.

For the rest of journey he behaved like a polite observer. He occasionally asked questions and listened respectfully to the answers. However, it wasn't until they returned to the castle and were alone that he spoke of his plan again. They were heading back to their separate quarters to wash and dress before dinner, when the prince spoke in a much gentler voice than previously.

"I wish to thank you for your company today, it showed me you would be useful to me as my lady wife." Myrbeth could tell he meant it as a compliment, so she tried to take it as one.

"Thank you, your Grace" She curtsied and left, pleased to have a moment to herself. The evening meal was awkward, just as the previous meal had been. The king was absent, as he was busy with state matters, so it was only the four of them.

"Will you be attending the ceremony tomorrow, Myrbeth?" Edmund asked.

"Yes, the prince has requested to see the event. I know you have been helping the king, but I hope you are still keeping up with your studies?"

"I have done some work but helping father is more interesting." Myrbeth smiled at him, in a motherly fashion.

"You educate your brother?" Wexlar asked, his tone almost

amused. "Is this another tradition?" Frederick supressed a grimace and faked a grin.

"It was Myrbeth's choice," he said through gritted teeth.

"Yes, it was, and I very much enjoy it," she agreed. She was surprised by how patient Frederick was being, but she couldn't blame him for being frustrated.

"Interesting," was the prince's only response.

"What will you be doing together? Tomorrow there is the ceremony and then what else?" Edmund asked.

"I was thinking of taking Prince Wexlar to the market at Royal Holly, to enjoy some local scenes."

"Oh, could I come too?" Edmund asked. "I would like to meet your village friends. You did promise to introduce me? And the prince too, of course," Edmund continued excitedly. Myrbeth had intended to avoid doing just this, certain the prince would be rude to her friends but now Edmund had raised the idea she wasn't sure what to say. Wexlar spoke before Myrbeth could answer.

"You have villager friends?" he asked not disappointing by being his sneering self.

"Yes," Myrbeth responded simply. She did not want to force her friends to meet this rude man, so she made an excuse. "They will be busy with the ceremony. I wouldn't want to pull them away from the festivities, I will introduce you another time, Edmund."

"You know the commoners personally?" Wexlar asked incredulously.

"Yes, she does, I've met them, they are fine people," Frederick said in her support. Myrbeth hoped Wexlar would read this as Frederick defending his people not her. They had to be careful. Myrbeth would have to remind Frederick again, Wexlar couldn't suspect there was anything between them.

"Perhaps that is not so unusual given your humble beginnings. Still perhaps it is not especially wise. I must admit I didn't expect our kingdom's traditions to be so different." Myrbeth wondered over these words long after the meal was completed. She was not surprised that the kingdoms were different places, that was only to be expected. The doctrine might outline traditions and basic rights of the kingdoms but one of those rights was the king's discretion of sovereignty. In fact, Parvery's nine kingdoms had been created just for that purpose. To allow each set of people their own unique land and way of living. However, what stuck with Myrbeth from Wexlar's words was that Twickerth was very different from Hollthen. Twickerth, the kingdom of her birth, was different, believed in different traditions and levels of respect. She again asked herself what living there would have been like?

The following morning, very early, there was a knock on Myrbeth's chamber door. She had not long woken, but the summer sun was already bright and blinding. She was still dressed in her night clothes so peered a little around the door before opening it. It was the king, with tired eyes and a haggard expression.

"Oh, Father, you weren't up all night, were you?" Myrbeth asked, worried.

"No, no, don't be concerned, I will be fine. After all the ceremony is today, Lord Yarrow's son's confirmation as lord, that will simplify matters," he explained.

"Yes, the prince wants to attend, I do hope you don't mind."

"I feared as much but it shouldn't be a trouble. The prince is who I wished to discuss." Myrbeth had expected this but had no clue what she could tell the king. He surely wanted her to make the best of what could be an advantageous opportunity to marry well.

"You would like to know how it's stands between us?" she assumed, but Trevard shook his head.

"I am well aware of how it stands; I am aware of all the goings on in my castle."

"Did Frederick or Edmund tell you?" Myrbeth asked, she wasn't annoyed. She was perhaps even a little relieved.

"Both have mentioned concerns, but would it surprise you to learn that the servants and guards have also come forward?" She was shocked but she could guess why.

"The incident at the lord's manor? He just didn't fully understand, once I explained to him, he did come away," she explained.

"I am surprised to hear you defending him, given the other reports I have received." Myrbeth sighed.

"It's all true, but you asked me to try with him, so I am."

"Yes, you have done as I asked. I am grateful for this, I know it has not been easy. However, no more. I think the prince has made it more than clear that he is not suited to be the kind of lord I require or, for that matter, the kind of husband I wish for you." Myrbeth went over and hugged her father, deeply relieved.

"What will you do? He won't be easily told such things."

"Not by me, but I have already taken a necessary step that I believe will resolve matters. When the prince arrived, I sent an urgent message to his father."

"You did?" Myrbeth was surprised.

"Yes, I deemed it only what the king was due. Even if matters had gone well, I could hardly make his son a lord or allow the two of you to marry without consulting him. That would be very wrong and highly discourteous. I know I would be vastly displeased if another king took such actions with Edmund without informing me. I truly do not know what the prince expected in coming here." Trevard shook his head.

"I don't think he put much thought into it," Myrbeth agreed.

"Well, I, or more likely the prince himself, should receive a response in a day or so I would imagine. Until then we must continue this pointless exercise, but I did not want you to worry any further." Myrbeth thanked him again and Trevard left her alone to dress for the day. Now in a much more joyful mood than previously, she put away the formal black dress she had been planning to wear and choose a lovely deep green one instead. She rushed but still arrived late to breakfast.

The formal swearing in ceremony took place in the throne room with only a few in attendance. King Trevard, Frederick and Edmund, all in their finest garb, sat upon the three thrones. Myrbeth and Prince Wexlar stood in the hall with the lords-to-be's family. There was his mother, the dowager Lady Yarrow, still dressed in black mourning clothes. His new wife, who had married the lord-to-be almost a year ago, and his younger brother, Oscar Yarrow, who was only a little older than Edmund. Olivard Yarrow stood in front of the three thrones, tall and also finely dressed, with a proud look upon his face. It began with Frederick formally reading from the Doctrine of Kings. He read a passage that outlined the role of a lord and his responsibilities to his king and kingdom. Oaths and promises were then made to the king and by the king. Finally, Trevard descended and Olivard Yarrow knelt. Edmund handed the king his sword and Trevard dubbed Olivard Yarrow Lord of Royal Holly. Once these private formalities were completed the party left the throne room to travel to Royal Holly Hall for a large feast. This was a formal gesture of the king honouring his new lord. As they rode out the people of Royal Holly and other parts of Hollthen had lined the road to cheer and celebrate their new lord. They clapped and threw flowers while the new Lord Olivard rode at the front of the column waving to the people.

Myrbeth was surprised by how quiet Prince Wexlar was through the whole day, she had expected more comments or questions, but he seemed intent on studying every detail of the ceremony. This left her free to watch Frederick. The king had not said whether he had told him, or planned to tell him, the good news and she was eager to know what Frederick would think. They were not free to talk until they were alone, so Myrbeth tried to discern by his manner or looks if he knew but this had little success. He was too focused on the ceremony. She supposed this was only right, still her longing to know was making her impatient. However, when she and the prince formed up to ride at the back of the column, she saw Frederick look back. He looked wistful and unhappy and by this Myrbeth was certain he did not yet know that her supposed courtship was at an end.

Myrbeth bided her time until the feast was well under way, and everyone was mingling. A feast of this sort was never a traditional, seated affair, rather it was held on the land of the lord's hall in the open, with tables heaving with food for all. The people were welcome to come and greet their new lord and many had come to do just that, creating much noise and commotion. Myrbeth left Prince Wexlar talking the ceremony over in detail with King Trevard to find Frederick. She gestured for him to follow her discreetly. She left the lord's compound and stole over to the empty schoolhouse. Frederick approached her, clearly pleased but surprised.

"Is this wise, we could be seen?" he asked.

"It is true, we cannot risk being affectionate which is a shame, since I very much want to kiss you."

"I have missed you too but ...," she interrupted him feeling like she might burst with happiness.

"It isn't just that, Frederick, the king has released me from any obligation towards Prince Wexlar. He has written to the king of Twickerth and expects him to recall his son any day now. We are free." Frederick rushed to take her in his arms.

"We are free to wed?" he asked, also bursting with joy.

"Oh no," she said, suddenly contrite, she could see how her words had misled his thinking. "No, Frederick, I only meant I don't have to marry Prince Wexlar."

"That's still great news." Frederick recovered from his disappoint-ment quickly. "I'm very glad, I couldn't have borne you being mar-ried to him; he is just awful."

"Yes, I agree. I am very pleased and grateful to the king."

"I was sure he wouldn't force you into such an unhappy situation." It was clear he meant the words but still Frederick didn't seem as happy as she had expected. "Shall I escort you back? We will be missed," he offered his arm and she took it, but the moment had not at all been what she had imagined. She had been so thrilled at the news, not because she had believed that the king would ask her to marry unhappily, but she, like Frederick, had had faith in their fa-ther. However, she did still expect the king to ask her and Frederick to marry others despite their love. She supposed she should have seen this coming; she could not share Frederick's faith that the king would allow them to wed, so was more prepared to be matched with another whom she did not love, and she was resigned to this. For Frederick though, only Myrbeth would do.

CHAPTER 23

The expected response to Trevard's letter arrived two days later, in the form of two Twickerth guards come to escort the prince home. Trevard was informed of their arrival, upon which he invited the prince to his parlour to greet them.

"What are these guards doing here? How could my father possibly have discovered where I am?" the prince asked. Trevard thought he seemed worried, and he chose not to answer his questions just yet. When they entered the parlour, the guards stood straight and bowed to their prince. Wexlar did not acknowledge them in the slightest; one of them handed him a letter which he snatched. Trevard offered his guests refreshments which they refused. Then took his seat, preparing himself for the prince's no doubt angry response.

"My father has ordered me to return home. You wrote to him?" The prince said angrily, not disappointing the king's expectations.

"It became necessary," Trevard replied, remaining calm. "I've tried to suggest that you would be unsuited for the position you seek but you have refused to hear it. I am not your king and therefore have little authority over you, but I agree it is time you returned home," Trevard spoke firmly.

"This letter doesn't speak to the lordship. It only outlines my plan to marry Myrbeth." Wexlar continued disrespectfully, clearly not in command of himself. This only strengthened Trevard's conviction, plainly Wexlar was not at all suitable to lead others. He barely had control of himself.

"I can assure you I did mention both, but I'm not surprised that your father found that news the more shocking. I remember vividly his views on Myrbeth." Trevard still remained calm which only seemed to annoy the prince further.

"What can you expect, she is nothing but a commoner, some wood-cutter's daughter most like, but not yours," Wexlar goaded. Trevard stood, finally enraged despite his usually even temperament.

"Let me assure you that she is my child. She may not be of my blood, but this is her home and we are her family. I will not stand to have her insulted within these walls. You have made your opinions quite clear. I would never force my daughter to marry you or trust you with my people." He spoke so forcefully that for a moment Prince Wexlar did seem diminished, but he continued to speak.

"You never had any intention of allowing me to succeed in my goals," he accused in a petulant manner.

"I will admit I was reluctant, but I did consider it. You gave me little reason to accept your proposition, however. You have shown no respect for my rule, my daughter, our traditions, or my people," Trevard remained on his feet but forced his voice to be calm again.

"Perhaps I am not a perfect fit, but I have nowhere else to go. Do I not deserve a lordship position?" Wexlar's voice was almost whining now.

"You treated this like a game, expecting me to hand you a prize just because you asked reasonably politely. You have behaved like a child, in short, I do not believe you are ready for the responsibility of being a lord." At these words Wexlar stamped his foot and gave in to a childlike tantrum, spitting out his words in a hurried and indignant manner.

"You are fool," he spat, "a complete fool, treating HER like an equal, expecting others to accept her, calling her your child." He gave a hysterical laugh, "you will never find a match for her. No one else understands why you care for her. No one will have her." He finished with another foot stamp.

"You have made your point. Now I suggest you leave my castle before I have you removed." Trevard's voice was thick and dangerous, he towered over the boy menacingly. Prince Wexlar turned and left the room without another word. His guards who had remained entirely silent throughout the exchange followed him out. Within the hour they were gone from the castle, without saying farewell.

The king pondered a great deal on all that had happened that afternoon. He decided not to tell his family about Wexlar's outburst and kept his musings private. Frederick's mood was light and cheery as they got back to focusing on their work. Edmund had returned to his studies with Myrbeth, so they were alone and Frederick freely expressed his thoughts.

"I'm glad she didn't have to marry him; I'm glad it's all over. I never liked him, she deserves someone better."

"Yes, she does," Trevard replied, automatically at first. Yet even through his preoccupation he could sense what Frederick was hoping for. Trevard realised there was something he needed to say. "I owe you an apology, Son. I promised I would consider your desire to marry Myrbeth, but recent events have distracted me too much. I will admit I have not thought on it a great deal since our first discussion."

"I understand," Frederick smiled, still feeling cheerful. "But you will consider it, won't you?" Trevard could hear doubt in his son's voice, did he worry that Trevard considered the problem a forgone conclusion? Did he believe that Trevard was simply waiting for some likely match to appear and the matter to solve itself? He couldn't blame him if he did, mostly because he wasn't certain he wasn't guilty of doing just that.

"Though my concerns have not altered I will take the time to think on the arguments you made." Trevard took a short pause and made a quick decision. If he was going to truly prove to Frederick and himself that he had seriously considered his request, then there was only one action he could take. "I wanted to tell you this before I leave tomorrow."

"Leave? You are leaving, but we're so busy. Where are you going?" Frederick asked.

"To Walsea, to visit King Emil." Trevard kept his response short and sharp so Frederick wouldn't question him further. His son knew him well enough to know he often visited Walsea when he had a complicated matter to consider.

"Would you enquire into how Halph is healing? I haven't heard much from him; he is a terrible correspondent. I'm sure he is fine, but I would like news of him," Frederick asked instead.

"Of course, I should only be a day or two and I could use a small break. Things should be simpler here now Lord Yarrow has been sworn in, I sure you will manage." Trevard nodded and Frederick agreed. That night Trevard had too much on his mind.

He should have been tired, but he couldn't stop his thoughts. So, he left early in the morning, wishing to settle the matter of matches and marriages.

"Dear friend Trevard, you are always welcome. To what do we owe this surprise visit?" King Emil boomed, greeting his friend on the palace steps. King Emil Yenton was a large red-faced man who smiled and laughed easily. He wore his long hair slicked back into a ponytail and had bright eyes that sparkled when he laughed.

"Forgive me, Emil, but I find myself in need of a consult."

"Then my friend we shall consult just as we used to do as boys." He led Trevard to the nearby orchard for a walk between the fruit trees for which the kingdom of Walsea was famous for. "Trevard, it must be a serious matter that brings you here, but then you always were so serious. Debating all those practice scenarios, preparing us to become kings. Did we ever think we would have so much to worry about?" Emil sighed and then laughed a little.

"Indeed, how is Halph recovering?" Trevard asked, understanding his comment. He had also never imagined he would have to take his son to war so soon, or at all.

"He is back on his feet, though still recovering." He sighed again but then he smiled, nothing kept Emil down for long. "How can I help you?" he asked, changing the subject.

"I knew as a king, as a father, I would face hurdles, but I didn't expect marriage to be one of them," Trevard began, agreeing with Emil's previous point.

"Ah, so now the danger has passed we return to the everyday troubles. I presume it is Myrbeth's marriage to which you refer?"

"And Frederick's. I'm afraid I must rely on your discretion, my friend." Despite this request Trevard already knew he could rely on Emil; they had been friends since they were small children.

"Of course, of course." Despite his trust of Emil, Trevard still was uncertain how much to discuss with him. So he began with the simpler elements and outlined the recent visit by Prince Wexlar.

"I see and you are naturally concerned that he is correct in his prediction that no one else will want to marry Myrbeth," Emil summarised.

"I am more concerned that he had the correct idea; that the best way to match Myrbeth is to offer a lordship as an incentive. It would be selling her by another name, I want more for her. Yet more seems to be out of reach." Trevard felt a little uncomfortable lying to his friend, but it was necessary. He wanted Emil's objective opinion on Myrbeth's chances first before he revealed more.

"That is only natural, and I hate to say it, but your concerns are not unfounded," was Emil's only response. Trevard hesitated, unsure of his next move.

"I thought perhaps Judan might consider a match?" he added hesitantly, uncertain of his choice. Judan was not Emil's heir, being his second son, but still it was much to ask. By agreeing to the match Emil would be setting himself and his son against the other kings and inviting their prejudice. Emil did not seem upset or offended though.

"Ah, how most unfortunate," Emil exclaimed dramatically. "I'm sure he would have considered it; he has always spoken well of Myrbeth. But I'm currently in a negotiation for a match already." This news quickly dashed Trevard's hopes and did more still. It seemed all of the royal children of eligible age were fast matching with one another, leaving Frederick and Myrbeth on the outside. He supposed he should not be surprised, matching always went this way.

"Oh, I see, might I ask with whom?"

"Well, isn't that a story, I will be brief though, in light of your distressed state. In short, we were some time in Arabat while Halph recovered. He became quite fond of the Princess Eunice, so much so that he was very unwilling to leave her. Upon his return he insisted that he would marry her. Well, it's a good match so I reached out to King Leopold, and we began to settle the details. However, almost from my first overture, Queen Barilsa demanded that both her daughters be married to my boys. I wasn't certain at first since Princess Odette is a few years younger than Judan. She is perhaps even a little too young to be wed at all, but Judan is open to the match, so it seems I might soon have a double wedding to plan." The king laughed with joy.

"Congratulations, I'm glad for you and your sons." Trevard said, breaking into an honest smile.

"Indeed, indeed, there is joy all around. Though I want to ask, since you are here, you know the princesses well? I must admit I don't remember them particularly. Is there some reason Barilsa would be so eager to dispose of both her daughters so fast?"

"Oh, it won't be anything unscrupulous. Barilsa is very assertive when she wants something. It will be just what you said, a practical, quick way to marry them both. Citria often remarked that her methods and perseverance in pursuing King Leopold bordered on the mercenary. Odette is a sweet girl, very beautiful, like her sister, I'm sure Judan won't regret the match." Trevard sighed, fed up with matching.

"Ah well, marriage is a tricky business. At least we are lucky to have a few years before we must go through this again. Me with my girls and you with Edmund. I'm sorry to still leave you in this predicament." He truly did seem sorry and Trevard decided it was time to tell the whole truth.

"Well, there is one other option which has presented itself. Truthfully, this is the actual matter on which I need your advice."

"And the discretion for which you asked. I might not have your brains, old friend, but I have enough intelligence to know that you are not afraid I would carry tales of a spoiled young boy or a disappointed young girl." Trevard smiled again.

"You know me well," he agreed, and then paused briefly trying to find the right words. "Frederick has asked to marry Myrbeth, they have fallen in love." King Emil threw back his head and laughed.

"Here you are bemoaning a problem with no solution, when the perfect solution is in front of you." Emil laughed hard for several minutes. "Trevard, why are you not happy, this would make her truly your daughter. If they are in love what obstacle could there be?" This reaction astounded Trevard so much it took him a moment to answer.

"Of course, in principle I have no objections. They are both so happy when they are together." Trevard hesitated, conflicted about the decision in front of him. "Yet, the way people treat her, Emil. I have never seen such cruelty; they have no mercy or compassion for Myrbeth. My fear is that the treatment will only worsen if she became queen and what of Frederick's ability to rule if the other kingdoms do not respect him. It could complicate relations for years."

Emil stopped walking and, though he still smiled, his face became more serious as he took in his friend's problem.

"I have two rather lengthy points to make, so bear with me as it is my turn to lecture you. Come sit with me, come sit." He led Trevard to a small stone bench under the shade of a particularly big apple tree. He gave a few huffing breaths then began his lecture. "Firstly, I will not deny that a wave of confusion and gossip circled Parvery when you took in Myrbeth. Your actions went above and beyond the norm. Few would have done the same for a village girl for whom they had no responsibility. I think you know this so I will not dwell on the details. That feeling did not dissipate with the years but your affection for Myrbeth was clear, so most of the questioning stopped." He took a long breath then continued. "When you began seeking a match for her many saw that as you asking someone else to repeat that action. It brought out the worst in people I will not deny, and we all found ourselves incapable of following your lead. I regret Myrbeth has not found more acceptance but perhaps I am no different." He stopped once more and seemed to leave this point behind. "However, it is my belief that the action of marrying your son to Myrbeth will seem almost the natural continuation of events. There may, again, be some rumbles but on the whole I do not think it will cause the problems you expect. It will be keeping the responsibility in the family. Forgive me if I seem unfeeling, I do not mean to be. I will be more than happy to celebrate their wedding and to see Myrbeth's happiness, which she most justly deserves."

"They both do. I won't deny this has been eating at me. I know that love, I had it with Citria. How can I deny them the same joys that I was blessed with. Yet duty before all is one of the principles of being king and I cannot betray it." Trevard interrupted Emil during another of his long breaths and finally showed his distress.

"Which brings me to my second lesson," Emil continued, regardless. "Trevard, you think too much and always have. Your mind is brilliant, a true gift, but you use it too often. You should rely more on your heart and your instincts, both of which are also good. You are always trying to find the perfect solution to every dilemma, just as you did when we were boys. But we are no longer children and there are rarely perfect solutions. I cannot promise that there will not be backlash from such a match, but I believe that this is the perfect example of your clever mind getting in the way of what you know to be right." Trevard took in the advice, processing it for several minutes. Then he got up and began to walk again. His friend followed, taking in the scenery in silence.

"The irony is that in order to consider the possibility that I think too much I must think it over," Trevard jested after a while. Both men laughed heartily, Emil relieved he had not caused offence. "I will consider all that you have said, and I am grateful for all that you have given me to think about."

"What you need is a puzzle to solve, a real problem to task your mind with." Emil tapped his head and gave Trevard another wide smile.

"A thinking problem you say, hm," Trevard mused.

"Yes, keep your mind engaged so you don't lapse into over thinking."

"Yes," Trevard repeated a glint now in his eyes. "I might have just the puzzle." The mystery identity of the shadow entity behind the Black Knights still weighed on him. The villain, whoever he was, had shown great intelligence in keeping his identity a secret. Indeed, most people had not even picked up on the fact that someone had been controlling the knights. Perhaps Trevard had just enough intelligence to match this person and defeat him. If he could first discover him.

"That is good, that is good," Emil interrupted his contemplations. "Though if I could add one final plea?" Now Emil's voice had a hesitance that Trevard had never heard before, it did not suit him. "A marriage made from duty is not a pleasant thing. You have seen perhaps too much of this with your sister I know. But let me assure you, especially if there is an alternative, it is not a burden you would want to place on your children. I'm still reluctant to ask it of my son but Judan has no great love to set aside so perhaps it will go easier for him." This advice spoke of a personal experience which surprised Trevard.

"But Emil, I always believed that you and Queen Oonella were happy?"

"And so we are, but it is a weak, pale sort of happiness. A fleeting imitation of the real thing, it does not compare to what you had with Citria." He paused but did not elaborate. "I'm not surprised that Frederick and Myrbeth have found true love as the stories say. He will do as you ask, but do not ask him to set her aside. It will be your deepest regret and the lifelong pain of all involved."

"Thank you, Emil, you are a true friend." Trevard said politely not asking more questions, he could sense Emil felt uncomfortable admitting what he had. Emil nodded.

"Think on it all, dear friend, but now we should go inside, I have had enough of walking," he said, becoming jolly again.

Trevard stayed overnight in Walsea and headed for home the next day. He still did not reveal the reason for his trip to anyone and was grateful when they did not pry. The advice had been clear, and Emil had truly moved him. Trevard felt compelled to follow it, but he would wait for the right time to reveal this. He wanted his conviction to be complete before he gave his permission because only then could his joy be equally complete.

That night he again had trouble sleeping so in the dead of night, when he was sure the castle was asleep, Trevard rose. His mind now free of matching, his focus has turned to his new puzzle. Who could the traitor in Parvery be? He had already fathomed that he was not searching for a low ranking noble or Lord. They did not fit. They were too overseen and didn't have the necessary power. No, instinct told him he was looking for a fellow king. Emil had told him to trust his instincts. He took a fresh sheet of parchment and on it he wrote the names of his fellow kings. King Rollin Boutiner of Sandoz, King Edrick Prester of Merchden, King Emil Yenton of Walsea, King Ivan Pedcott of Twickerth, King Valter Lavington of Pidar, King Jonathan Navara of Sedgebarrow, King Isaiah Hennen of Valance and finally King Leopold Haughton of Arabat. He sat back in his chair and considered the eight names, each in turn by the light of his small candle.

First, he crossed off the names of King Edrick and King Valter. Edrick was too young, only aged ten at the time of the first village attack. King Valter, though older, had not yet been crowned, so was also unlikely to be involved. His quill hovered over King Jonathan's name, surely his death in battle meant he could not have been in cahoots with the Black Knights. He did not cross out the name though, he couldn't be certain he wasn't guilty. Next, he considered King Emil, his long-time childhood friend. The man he knew would never be capable of such evil and yet without proof, he decided, no one could be eliminated. Six kings remained and any one of them could be this shadow king, Trevard sensed a long and difficult hunt ahead of him.

CHAPTER 24

U pon his return the king was quiet and pensive. Frederick recognised this thinking mood all too well and knew it was best to disturb him as little as possible. Frederick was pleased, knowing his father was thinking over his marriage to Myrbeth. He only hoped his father would decide to favour the match. He could tell Myrbeth had very little confidence that they would get to be happy together and he too, at times, found himself despairing. He longed to know what had happened in Walsea. The visit had been a short one and Frederick couldn't decide whether that was a good or bad sign. He wished his father would consult him so Frederick could at least know his thoughts and try to persuade him further. But the only matters his father wanted to discuss were the possible candidates for the Birchlyn lordship as the position needed to be filled soon and they were still without a choice for lord.

The day after his father had returned from his visit, they received a surprise visitor of their own. Frederick and Trevard had moved into the long hall as they had so much paperwork to lay out regarding the lordship, but before they could start two young pages came to announce that King Valter Lavington of Pidar had arrived and was requesting an audience.

"Of course, Frederick help Modwin tidy these away and I will see him here," Trevard replied.

"King Valter, didn't you save his life during the battle?" Frederick remembered, wondering why he was here. His father just nodded, no doubt pondering the same thing. The king was shown in. Valter was a tall man with thick blonde curls and sharp handsome features. He was dressed in dark riding clothes, a small golden band as crown his only adornment.

"Your Grace, it is a pleasure to see you again," Valter said, exultantly as he entered. He had a thick unctuous voice that had a warm quality to it.

"King Valter, it is an honour to receive you. You've recovered from your wounds?" Trevard stood, smiled and the two kings exchanged bows.

"Completely, I am quite well. I wished to come sooner, but my wife wanted to keep me home until we could be sure the journey would not be too much for me. She is a wonderful woman, truly," he praised, grinning widely. "Hello to you as well, your Grace," he said, noticing Frederick's attentive presence, and bowing. Fredrick bowed back. He did not know this particular king well, but both his first and second impressions only made him want to know him better.

"To what do I owe the honour?" Trevard asked, curious.

"Well, in truth, I was hoping to receive the hospitality of your castle for a few days. Perhaps my man and I could freshen up before we speak further? It has been a long journey," the king asked pleasantly. Pidar, which was Valter's Kingdom, was around 100 miles away from Hollthen.

"Naturally, you are most welcome to our home. I will have the servants show you to our guest wing. I will have a private supper prepared, you and I may talk in confidence over food and wine."

"That will be most pleasant. I am grateful, but I would have no objection if your son were to join us." Frederick grinned and thanked the king, wondering if he had sensed Frederick's curiosity. For dinner Frederick and King Trevard had changed into formal clothes and added crowns of their own. The three men took seats around the compass table in the private dining chamber and Trevard spoke.

"How may I assist you, King Valter? I assume your journey here is not just for leisure. Though, of course, you would be welcome to explore our kingdom anytime should you wish."

"You are most gracious, King Trevard, and clever too. For I do have a matter I wish to put before you. Though first I feel I must apologise for not sending word of my visit. I am not a man who enjoys surprises so I hope you will forgive me for surprising you. I was not certain how else to put this matter in front of you other than in person. Any note would have only raised questions, so I thought it best just to come."

"It is truly no trouble, please speak to me of this matter," Trevard invited. Frederick felt his curiosity only rise.

"Perhaps 'matter' is the wrong word, it makes it seem like a difficult topic. I should say I am here to put a proposition in front of you." Frederick and his father exchanged a look that did not go unnoticed. "No need to look so worried," King Valter said in his warm, thick voice, smiling. "I have been dwelling on a way to repay you for saving my life."

"I have told you that's not necessary," Trevard said, interrupting Valter.

"Yes, so you keep saying. That made me think about the type of man who does good deeds but requires no reward. That is a man of true honour. I can see your son agrees." Frederick had been unconsciously nodding his head but stopped at this. Deciding to intrude less on the conversation he focused on his food but still listened.

"Well, it just so happens I am hunting for these qualities," King Valter continued explaining.

"Hunting?" Trevard asked, it was an odd word, Frederick thought so too.

"Forgive me, perhaps I am not explaining myself very well. Let me begin again. I have been blessed with four lovely daughters, but no sons. My queen, Carlotta, is now of an age that it is not likely she will provide me with any more children. I love her and our family but as a fellow king I'm sure you can understand my concern."

"You have no direct heir," Trevard replied, nodding.

"Indeed, my eldest daughter will one day be queen and whomever she marries will become the future king. Naturally I am uneasy about leaving my kingdom to some unknown person. I know I need not say why, I'm sure you comprehend my concerns. So instead, a thought came to me. If I could betroth my daughter while she is still young, I could know my successor."

"Betrothals are unusual in Parvery," Trevard remarked.

"True, but can you fault my conclusions?" Valter asked, with an expansive hand gesture.

"No, I can see the logic. It's a well-founded plan."

"Thank you," Valter made another gesture. "Having decided upon this course of action I thought about the type of man I would want to marry my daughter and rule my kingdom. I will not deny it was hard to identify the qualities that I would prize. I became stuck on how I would find any individual that would suit. But now I think I have found him, through you."

"I don't understand?" Trevard uttered, Frederick was equally lost, what could King Valter be suggesting?

"A man of honour would raise a son in his image, to be every bit the good man that his father is. You have a young son I believe, Edmund, who would be around the same age as my Theolotta?"

"You want Edmund to be your successor?" Trevard interjected in surprise.

"Wow," Frederick said, forgetting his decision to be quiet in his surprise. Edmund, a king, it was incredible.

"I would like to consider him, if you have no objections," Valter asked smiling, clearly pleased with the shock he had caused.

"Of course not, I am deeply honoured and would be pleased to explore such a match," his father said, recovering more quickly than Frederick who was still in shock. "Did you have some idea on how you would wish to proceed?"

"I thought I might bring my daughter here for a visit if you were amenable. If the children become friendly then perhaps, we could arrange regular visits. I would hope that Edmund would consent to visit Pidar so that he might become familiar with the kingdom. Once the children are of age, if they do not care for the match, we can end the agreement but hopefully they will grow fond of one another."

"That seems to be a fair arrangement." Frederick couldn't understand how his father could seem so calm. That a chance encounter, a moment in a battle could led to such good fortune was exhilarating. Any king could have saved Valter's life, Frederick was sure they would have, but it had been his father, and now his brother could become a king.

"Do I detect reservations?" King Valter asked, as there was a pause in conversation.

"No, of course not, rather bewilderment. What you are offering is no small reward," Trevard explained.

"I'm glad you see it as a gift. I feel as if you gave me a gift, I place a high value on life, and you saved mine. Besides we will both benefit, that is how a proposition should work."

"Well, in that case, would you like to come and meet my son?" Trevard offered, giving a rare grin.

The kings agreed that, for now, the reason for Valter's visit should be kept between themselves so as not to pressure the children. King Trevard led King Valter to the drawing room where Myrbeth and Edmund often spent their evenings. Myrbeth was sitting with her needlework at one table and Edmund at another one with a book, ink, a quill pen, a sheet of parchment and a bored expression. Trevard introduced their guest to the room, Myrbeth and Edmund stood to bow, and the king bowed back to both. He then went straight over to Edmund, Trevard following, leaving Frederick free to sit with Myrbeth.

"What is it you are learning?" King Valter asked.

"Mathematics, your Grace," Edmund replied.

"And do you enjoy mathematics, Edmund?"

"No, it's very difficult," Edmund had never been shy. Everyone laughed, but no one harder than King Valter.

"My daughters are the same, I am always testing them, and they never care for it. Here though let's see if we can add some fun," he said, taking Edmund's sheet and rewriting the problems.

"King Valter seems very friendly," Myrbeth remarked quietly to Frederick. He turned to see if she disapproved of this adaptation to her lessons.

"Yes, I must say I think highly of him," Frederick said, and then, because he couldn't read her expression, he asked. "He isn't disturbing Edmund's learning? Because I'm sure the king would understand." She shook her head.

"It isn't that," she sighed heavily. "I think I have reached the limit of how far I can go with Edmund. I love to teach him, but I believe he needs a more formal education." She looked unhappy but Frederick thought she was right. He didn't say anything, for if this scheme were to go ahead then Edmund's education, indeed his whole life, would change very rapidly. "So, what brings the king to Hollthen?" Myrbeth asked, changing the subject. Frederick didn't know what to say, he looked across to where his father sat and caught his eye. He smiled and gave the smallest of unnoticeable nods. Frederick smiled and leaned closer to Myrbeth to whisper the truth of the situation.

"Edmund as king? Well, that's wonderful," she exclaimed in hushed tones, "and he is to return for another visit? This time with his family?" Myrbeth asked.

"Yes, he is to bring his daughters and Queen Carlotta soon." Myrbeth gave a deep sigh.

"Oh, I can't wait to meet her." Frederick knew just who she meant, and he had to admit he was interested to meet the girl, Theolotta, as well. "I have no doubt he will make us proud."

"Yes, he will be a great king."

"Just like his brother."

"What are you two whispering about?" Edmund interrupted them.

"Nothing important," Frederick said quickly. "We are discussing the vacant lordship," he lied, and Myrbeth nodded. Trevard distracted Edmund again and Frederick was relieved at how quickly he had thought of that excuse. Myrbeth engaged him again,

"Actually, I have been wanting to discuss the lordship with you? Are you still struggling?" Frederick nodded.

"Yes, very much," he confirmed.

"I might be able to help; I have a possible candidate," she spoke very nervously. It was clear she was still not sure of her ability to manage the intricacies of political matters.

"Whom are we missing?" Frederick asked.

"Are you familiar with a Bartholomew Huntington?" she asked.

"Huntington? As in Lord Huntington, he is a relation?"

"Yes, Bartholomew was a younger son of the late Lord Oswin Huntington. Bartholomew sold fish at the market. He created strong relationships with the fishermen themselves by transporting and selling their catch. He was always fair to the men, insuring they got a cut. When Bartholomew passed his son-in-law took over the business, Thomas Monroe. He used to be a fisherman before his marriage and comes from a fishing family. He would have the level of respect from the men that you are looking for, I believe; they would trust him. I'm not sure his connection to the nobility is strong enough but I thought he might suit."

"Nobility might not matter; Lord March's father was not of noble blood, he was simply as you described, a man that the fisherfolk trusted. I'm sure father would at least consider it. How do you know all of this?"

"He is married to Lady Grouse's eldest daughter," she explained, and Frederick instantly understood. He knew why Myrbeth had told him and not father, she didn't want to seem forward by advising the king, but Fredrick saw it as proof she would make a great queen. He tried to explain to her.

"Knowledge of the people gives you an advantage, don't be afraid to connect with them, it will only help you. Thank you, Myrbeth." Frederick longed to kiss her, he longed to tell her the true reason for his father's visit to Walsea. He desperately wanted to promise her that his father was considering their match, but he was afraid of raising her hopes.

It was late into the next day when the king and Frederick finally returned to the subject of the lordship. Frederick instantly took the opportunity of suggesting the new candidate. His father smiled and asked,

"This was Myrbeth's suggestion, wasn't it?" Frederick was pleased that his father had guessed the truth. He had wanted him to know but, like Myrbeth, Frederick was hesitant to come forward.

"Yes, she thought I should tell you," Frederick explained, knowing his father would understand the meaning behind his words.

"Son, please follow me." Frederick did just that and Trevard led him from his parlour to his chambers and closed the door behind them.

"Is something the matter?" Frederick asked.

"No, there will be time for lengthy discussions and explanations later but for now I have something to give you." Trevard held out the small box he had retrieved from a locked chest. Frederick took the box full of curiosity and opened it. Inside lay a ring. At the centre were two ruby hearts that were decorated either side by emeralds and diamonds on a silver band. Frederick recognised the ring at once as the ancestral ring of the kingdom. His mother had worn that ring, as had every queen of Hollthen.

"Father?" Frederick's voice quavered so much that the word came out as a question.

"For Myrbeth, give her the ring. She has made up my mind in the matter. She will make an excellent queen." Frederick took the ring out and held it tightly, examining it soundlessly.

"I can marry her. You are happy for me to marry her?" His voice was disbelieving, Frederick realised then that perhaps Myrbeth had not been the only one too cautious to hope. His father so rarely changed his mind, especially when it came to matters of duty, that deep down Frederick had thought Trevard's first refusal wouldn't change.

"Yes, Son, and I wish you every happiness," Trevard said, smiling widely and Frederick began smiling too as it started to sink in.

"But I haven't planned a proposal." Frederick wanted it to be perfect, but he wasn't yet sure how he should go about making it so.

"It won't matter as long as it's from the heart," his father advised. "I remember vividly the day I gave this ring to your mother." He reached forward and gently took the ring from Frederick. Trevard rang a single finger over the design. "I promise you it's a moment you will treasure forever. Frederick, when you give Myrbeth the ring she will want to come thank me. She is always so humble but assure her it can wait. This should be your day to celebrate." With that Trevard put the ring back in the box and again pressed the box into Frederick's hand. This time Frederick smiled, gripped the box tightly and patted his father on the back before leaving with the ring.

Frederick went straight to Myrbeth's chambers.

"Come for a walk with me?" he insisted breathlessly.

"But aren't you busy? And King Valter ought to be attended on." Frederick moved forward and scooped her up into his arms ignoring her objections.

"Trust me," was all he said as he carried her outside. He took her out to his mother's tree, the white flowers looked shockingly beautiful against the blue sky but they were starting to fade.

"What is this about?" she asked confused. "You seem happy, is there more good news?"

"Yes, I needed to give you this." Frederick went down on one knee and held open the ring box. His mother's ring glittered in the setting sun. Myrbeth collapsed slightly, also falling to her knees.

"How?" she asked in a shaking voice, trying not to cry.

"Father gave it to me with his blessing." Frederick took the ring out of the box and held it out to her.

"Truly?" she asked, still clearly full of disbelief.

"I swear he is happy for us," Frederick explained nodding. Myrbeth didn't take the ring instead she hesitantly stretched out a finger and stroked the ruby hearts. Frederick watched her, feeling blissfully happy, understanding her hesitation, he had been the same way at first. It was a while before she said anything.

"I remember playing with this. I was fascinated with it when I was a small child. The queen would hold out her fingers to me and I would try to grab the glittering stones. It's still one of my favourite memories of her," she paused again. "I never thought I would wear it," she said, withdrawing her fingers quickly as if she felt she ruined her chances by expressing her desire out loud.

"I believe somehow she would have wanted you to have it," Frederick said encouragingly, wiping a tear from her cheek with his free hand. The other still held tightly to the ring.

"We can really be married?" Myrbeth asked, showing her shock and disbelief.

"Of course, at last, forever." Frederick's jubilation spilled out and he kissed her heartily. When they broke apart, he said, "though technically you haven't answered me yet."

"Technically, you haven't asked." Frederick smiled.

"Myrbeth, will you marry me?"

"Yes, with all my heart, yes." They kissed again. Frederick slipped the Holly Ring on to her finger.

"Just where it belongs," he whispered lovingly.

CHAPTER 25

Mercy had done a lot of thinking that fateful night after meeting Myrbeth. Not having to meet his comrades until the next day, he was in no rush. So, he had camped out in an old barn he found. Mercy was used to sleeping rough outside and he fell asleep almost instantly. He had been quickly awakened by a horrible nightmare, he had been in that first village again, blood everywhere, only the faces of the dead were all of the girl. Myrbeth lay mangled and dead in a hundred ways. He hadn't managed to sleep the rest of the night. Such nightmares of the dead were not a new experience to him, but he had not had one since he was a child. It bothered him, that this girl had had such an effect on him.

He had taken out the old family book again and studied the pages once more. He looked at the page for Myrbeth's father first, Kenneth Shepard. Underneath the name was his profession, wood foreman and then a description of his appearance, tall, light blonde hair, blue eyes. Myrbeth had had blue eyes too, he remembered. He flicked to her mother's page, Myra Rivers, she had had blue eyes too, the book said, with brown hair. She had been a seamstress. Rivers, Mercy repeated, Rivers; he checked the book, they were married at the age of eighteen, the year D593 scratched in the at beginning of the line entry. He supposed women didn't take their husbands' names here but retained their own family names instead, an odd custom. Myrbeth's page was next, but it only held her name Myrbeth Shepard the rest was left blank. Mercy was struck by a strong urge to fling it from him and leave it behind. This urge had filled him many times before though and never once had he actually disposed of the book. Instead, once it had passed, he decided on a different course of action.

When morning came, he travelled into the nearest village and found himself on the outskirts of a market square. Mercy didn't have much gold on his person but enough, he reasoned. He had told the others to buy supplies, so he should too. First, he found a small shop near what appeared to be a school. He bought a quill pen, ink and a string woven bag. None of these items were particularly dear, just as he had hoped. He left the store and headed back to the square. It was still early; the stalls were just setting out their goods. Mercy surveyed the tables and made some shrewd judgements. He judged not only the items on sale but also the sellers themselves. He picked out likely targets open to haggling over price. Mercy knew how to bargain well and in such a pleasant way the sellers often didn't mind a jot. Such sellers open to bartering over price were easy enough to spot, they were the chatty ones.

"Good morning," they would hail one another. They would discuss their goods in an offhand manner.

"Good day for selling salt."

"You're always saying that, Halbert."

"Maurice be careful with those bottles, wouldn't want to break any."

"How's your veg growing, Gregor?" and they would also exchange local news and gossip.

"They say the prince has returned from the battle."

"Wounded, was he?"

"Nah, there is trouble up at the castle though, so many guards running this way and that."

"It's the lady, I heard."

"Not that sweet girl, who knows what's next." Mercy felt a lurching sensation of guilt at this and stopped listening.

Instead, he began to approach a few of the quieter folk, those who perhaps didn't feel the need to talk in the early light of the sun. First looking at their goods in detail until they offered him one item or another. At which he would politely refuse and then move on. He was setting himself up as a discerning customer, this would make people trip over themselves to get him to buy, he knew. It sounded strange but sellers are always hungry for a sale and even more hungry to sell to someone who didn't want to buy. It made them feel like they had achieved something. Mercy knew all this from his youth. It had proven a useful skill in the company too, so he was well practised. His first true target was the bread stall. There were loaves in all shapes and sizes, all still warm. The cheaper fares were the grain and brown loaves, but Mercy had his eye on the rich loaves filled with raisins and seeds.

"How can I help you, sir" the bread seller asked in a polite, friendly voice, clearly eager to engage him.

"How much bread would you recommend to share between thirteen?" Mercy began, wanting to get him talking.

"Thirteen at home, hey? What a number. You would need more than half as many loaves, I reckon."

"So, seven or so, that could add up fast."

"Well, if you want to really fill them up with not too much outlaid, then you can't go wrong with my date rolls. One each ought to do the trick and won't cost too much."

"Fruit rolls, you say. Yes, perhaps, and they would be very good for your health, I suppose."

"Oh yes, the finest, perfect for making you strong."

"Well, six or so of those, I think, and a couple of the seeded loaves, how much would that be?" Mercy had already decided to pay whatever price he was quoted. He had to whet the other's appetite. If he could be seen being talked into a purchase, then the others would all come at him. Besides it wasn't as if he hadn't worked the man down some. He had given the number thirteen to make him think he would be getting a nice big fat order. He also played on his sympathy by allowing the seller to think Mercy was a man with a large young family to feed. He never had any intention of buying for all thirteen men though. They knew how to share food and he wouldn't be the only one buying supplies.

The baker though had tried his best to sell him as much as he could, and Mercy had played along. In the end he bought no more than what he had always intended to buy. Next, he chose a stall with a woman selling fruit jams.

"So many choices," Mercy said in a complimentary tone. "I can only buy two jars, though, however will I decide?" The bit about only going to buy two jars was true. Such things were best carried safely in pockets, not squashed in with the rest of his wares. Two pockets - two jars, but he was lying about the choice being hard, he knew exactly which jars he would choose but he wasn't going to give that away.

"My peach and pear are my favourites. Just the right amount of sweet and quite difficult to make, if I say so myself," the women offered in her sugary voice.

"I'm sure it's divine and you must be very skilled, but it's just too rich for me," this was true in a way. They were the most expensive of the jams and Mercy couldn't afford to blow so much of his gold all at once.

"Well how about something humbler then, my blackberry and apple is very popular?"

"Yes, yes, you are right, that will be expected as a standard." Mercy replied, pleased, she had picked one of his choices.

"A large jar then?" she offered, already picking up one such jar.

"Oh, I'm not sure I could stretch to that," Mercy said, ready to begin the haggle dance.

"Well, to be neighbourly I could sell it to you at the regular price if you don't shout about it to anyone," she whispered, and Mercy was shocked at this easy win. He supposed he shouldn't be so surprised; she was probably just happy to be selling anything at all. Jams were something of a luxury item for most. He knew that none of the rest of the company were likely to pick up anything like this. Mercy also thought that jam was good for filling up a person. His mother had taught him that, with growing boys to fill she had always kept a little jam in the house. The jam could be eaten on its own and if used sparingly would last. His final reason was that he was commander now and a commander had to been seen to treat his men. Jam might seem like an odd reward, but it was rich and good for a man's health. Men who had spent most of their lives struggling, poor and starving understood that. To the men of the company, his company now, it was a rare luxury indeed.

He thanked the jam seller for her quickly won offer.

"That would be generous, thank you so much. I will splurge a little and get another large one of the strawberry, it's always been my favourite," and, just as he had hoped, the gullible women, so sweetened by his kind attitude. She threw that one in at the regular price too. A small compliment or gem of personal information could be highly valuable in haggling. The cheese seller he visited next was not nearly so simple. He clearly enjoyed bargaining just as much as Mercy and was unable to stop himself from countering Mercy's every offer. By the time he reached his next stall he was starting to run low on funds.

"Don't you have any real meat?" he asked.

"Course, at my shop just down the street there." the butcher pointed. "But I only bring the dried stuff out here to my stall."

"Perhaps dried would be better," Mercy said, making a show of displaying only a few coins, as if they were his last. His strategy worked like a charm and when Mercy was done he walked away, his string bag bursting.

Finally, he bought a small bottle of nettle wine. This was a luxury, too, but he had a taste for it. Also, the others were bound to buy bottles of the strong, cheap grain liquor that was easy to purchase. He wanted something a bit finer. Mercy smiled to himself and returned to the idea behind his very first purchase of the day, the ink and quill pen. He left the now busy market and found a nearby bench down one of the cobbled streets. There he sat and filled in Myrbeth's page in her family book as the morning slipped by. He wrote of her blue eyes and fine brown hair but mostly he wrote about how she was a well-respected lady now in a castle. That was as much as Mercy had been able to tell, she was happy and loved.

He sat on the bench in the sunshine too long. It made him slightly late for the meeting with the remnants of the company. He had to rush back down the road to that same bridge near the border. It was easy to find again, he just followed the road along the water until it came into sight. They were all there waiting for him.

"Where have you been?" the boy, Archer, asked anxiously.

"You said noon, but you weren't here at noon," Boot stated the obvious.

"Yes, we were just thinking of leaving you," Bloodlust added in a drawl.

"Where are Doc and Sweets?" Green asked.

"Dead," was the only response Mercy gave to all these questions. Technically he realised he didn't actually know this, but they must be. He knew they had been caught and what else could be the penalty for poisoning the king's ward but death. "We must flee this place now," he said, and the men, his men now, asked no more questions. They all began to move out, back towards the border. Mercy took one last look at the far-off castle before he followed. They walked for the rest of the day, Mercy took the lead and led them into the far fruit fields of a kingdom he now remembered was called Walsea.

At nightfall Mercy and his twelve men sat around a fire. They were some distance from any dwelling so the risk of the flames drawing attention was low. They shared out the food that had been bought and foraged. Mercy ate little as he had already been fed recently, unlike his men. They talked about basic matters at first; the search for a ship had gone badly, no boat was headed away from the nine kingdoms at this current time; how they had successfully found or bought what was now being consumed; how they would need to ration what they had.

The company's despair was becoming stronger, except for Mercy's. His thoughts on the road had all been for the dead of Parvery, all those they had killed for no purpose. But then his thoughts had taken a change in direction, it wasn't for no purpose. It just had not been their purpose. Knowing that he could not act alone he had decided he would have to tell the others enough of the truth. He would have to be careful though. Mercy would have to explain his thoughts in a manner they could relate to and more importantly agree with.

"My friends, I wish to share with you a secret. A secret about why we came here."

"We came here to work, no mystery there," Bloodlust shrugged, as did some of the others, but not all.

"Yes, we came to work. Some of you may have wondered, though, how we came to be paid for the ugly work of killing a whole village?" No one said anything, Mercy knew he had their attention. "Well, I will tell you; we have done this work before, here in this very land, as some of you know. Finish revealed to me that these particular jobs were done at the behest of a benefactor."

"He was the one paying us then?" Green remarked in a drawling voice.

"Clever leap," Trickster joked, and many of the men laughed. Mercy waited until the laugher was done, then carried on.

"Yes, I don't know his identity, but I do know he holds some high office here. A lord, or even a king, perhaps."

"But aren't they the ones that just came down on us?" Liquor exclaimed, sloshing the liquid in his flask.

"Betrayal," cried many of the men as one.

"I agree, we were sold out," Mercy paused, deciding whether or not he should tell them that he had suspected this would happen. That he had even warned Finish about it, but no, to do so seemed like dishonouring him only days after his death. He was keeping so many secrets and telling only this one. Perhaps that was part of being in command. After all Finish had kept secrets, but his had gotten him killed. Mercy pushed that thought away. "So, we have a choice in front us. We can leave these shores never to return, find work and live our lives. Or we could stay."

"Stay, for what purpose?" Archer asked.

"For vengeance, that would be our purpose. Twice this man has used us to do his dirty work. Then he tried to dispatch us when we were no longer of use. Hunting him will not be easy but if we don't hunt him no one else will."

"Aye, we must, we owe this to Finish and the others," Boot said, nodding.

"Aye, Aye, Aye," the others all chanted.

"We shall be the company of Thirteen," Trickster cried out.

"The Black Thirteen," Bloodlust corrected.

"Well then, that is decided," Mercy pulled out the bottle of nettle wine he had bought and poured them each a generous measure. "Tonight, we drink to honour those we have lost but tomorrow we begin our hunt."

"To the hunt," they all toasted.

CHAPTER 26

"Are you ready?" Trevard asked, as he came to collect the bride. As Myrbeth turned to face him the long draping, gold dress she was wearing swirled around her elegant frame. Her hair was braided with the last blossoms from Citria's tree and though she wore little other finery she shone with happiness. The warm months were nearly at an end, but the day had perfect weather for a wedding.

"Yes, I think so," Myrbeth said, with a shaky smile, Trevard surveyed her.

"One thing is missing," he pronounced, bringing forth a box and opening it. Inside the box was nestled a small, bright tiara. It was very lightly decorated with small teardrop shaped diamonds hanging from an intricate frame. Myrbeth took it gently in both of her hands.

"It's a blossom tree," she exclaimed in surprise and delight.

"Yes, this was Citria's. It was a present from her parents, I believe. She wore it to the ball on the night we first met. It was always her favourite and years later it inspired me to plant the tree in her honour. She loved you very much. I'm sure she would want you to have it."

"It's beautiful," she hesitated, "but is it appropriate?"

"It couldn't be more appropriate, and after today you must never ask that question again." He smiled at her. "Today it will become official, you will be royal, and you need no longer be humble. You are a part of this family as you always have been and my daughter in truth at last." With this Trevard placed the tiara on her head, "let's not keep the guests waiting."

As they walked out towards the guests seated for the ceremony many voices drifted to them.

"I'm sure I always suspected about them," Trevard recognised the voice of Lady Delilah Prester who was talking to her sister Lady Rachel Prester. He could just about make them out, Lady Delilah was holding her brother's young daughter in one arm, supporting the small girl against her body. Her arm was outstretched holding the hand of Edrick's son, his eldest child and heir. He was seated in between Delilah and his mother Queen Parnella who was stroking her large, swollen belly in a soothing manner.

"Try gentle pats to stop the kicking, Parnella," Lady Rachel offered, before replying, "heavens I'm sure I never knew anything about them until Trevard's letter and invitation arrived. It was shocking."

"Enough, both of you. Parnella, you will be fine in a moment, I'm sure." King Edrick said, trying to silence the gossip. Trevard wasn't surprised when it didn't work. Frederick's and Myrbeth's wedding had indeed caused a stir among the nobles, but not the one Trevard had expected. Just as Emil had predicted.

"I only recently met Prince Frederick and the Lady Myrbeth, but the love was very clear to me from the start," King Valter joined in. He was seated behind the sisters. His wife and daughters occupied the seats next to him. Except for the Princess Theolotta who was sitting at the front happily chatting with Prince Edmund. Trevard smiled at this, reason to be hopeful he thought.

"We always thought Frederick was sweet on Myrbeth but never that it was so serious, right Halph?" Judan had leaned across the aisle to join the discussion. Halph just nodded briefly.

"Leave your brother be, I'm still not sure you are strong enough for this," King Emil insisted on fretting over his eldest son.

"I'm not missing this," Halph added determinedly.

"I don't know what all this fuss is over, does it matter who knew what," Queen Tunora uttered loftily from the back row causing Trevard to roll his eyes. They had nearly reached the guests now.

"Oh, but it's all so romantic," Princess Penalyn replied in a dreamy voice.

"It all seems to be. I hope they will be as happy as us, darling," Prince Manual was very besotted with his soon to be wife.

"I see Queen Barilsa was not invited," Queen Carlotta leaned across her husband, King Valter, to address Barilsa's sisters.

"Heavens no, not after the fuss she made after the ball invitations," Lady Rachel turned in her seat.

"The whole family is still in mourning, I'm sure Trevard just wanted to be respectful," Lady Rachel's husband; Lord Cavil of Merchedge spoke firmly. This was only half true, Trevard had sent a notification to the Arabat palace but had received no response. For which Trevard was grateful but he had no doubt that when Barilsa awoke from her grief she would have her say.

"More likely King Trevard didn't wish to hear more of her animosity until the occasion was completed. She is sure to have her say though, she always does," Lady Delilah echoed his thoughts.

"Enough, it's about to begin. Now let's all be quiet and just be happy for them," Edrick spoke loudly and ended the chatter. He had spotted them and Trevard gave him a nod of thanks. Trevard turned to Myrbeth to see how she had taken all of this but she was smiling widely, clearly undisturbed. Trevard smiled back and led her down the aisle to all the happiness she deserved. Normally having so many eyes on her would have made Myrbeth blush, but not today Trevard noted. Today she only radiated a delighted glow of joy, he looked forward to his son and seeing a similar glow radiating from him.

The ceremony itself was intimate and took place under Citria's blossom tree. It was the custom of Hollthen to marry under holly trees, but this was far more fitting. The tree was at last shedding its flowers, it had been an unusually long bloom. The petals fluttered down over the scene. Almost as if the queen herself was crying and blessing the event. Trevard led Myrbeth to Frederick's side. It began with the wedding song, a piece of joyous music as old as the Doctrine itself, being played on wooden flutes and pipes. Once completed Trevard, as father and king, gave a speech about the importance of marriage. How it was sacred, ancient and vital to the prosperity of the Kingdom. Then, as was the custom, the bride and groom married themselves, with an exchange of vows. The words of commitment and the promises that were spoken at all royal weddings had been created in the Doctrine of Kings itself.

"I pledge myself to this kingdom and this match.

I will uphold the integrity of my high office and honour my wife/ husband.

I promise to protect my people and promote their welfare.

I will endeavour to be kind and wise in all doings,

To be a true friend to my comrade kings and keep this realm at peace.

We will love, honour and cherish one another,

And forever be faithful, until my last day, to crown, kingdom and spouse."

The words were spoken by both in a solemn and reverent tone. Myrbeth and Frederick beamed at each other as they expressed the feelings in their hearts. Then finally the couple's hands were tied together by King Trevard to complete the bonding.

After the ceremony, a huge feast and festival was held in the royal courtyard outside the castle. The celebrations were an open affair and almost all of Hollthen came out to greet the newlyweds. Myrbeth and Frederick were seated at a grand table in the centre where guests could approach to offer congratulations and best wishes to the happy couple. Trevard sat nearby quietly, the day had been very moving. He found himself immersed in memories of his own wedding over twenty years ago. Trevard soon found himself tired; he moved closer to Myrbeth and Frederick to apologise before retiring. They were speaking with Lord Huntington, so he waited.

"Well, my congratulations again prince and princess," Lord Huntington bowed and retreated. Trevard moved to approach but the pair began to talk.

"Princess Myrbeth, I don't think I shall ever get used to it," Myrbeth said, touching her flushed cheeks.

"It will be Queen Myrbeth in years to come," Frederick smiled and kissed her hand.

"I don't want to think about that. It's all so unbelievable."

"Personally, I rather like it. Princess Myrbeth Bardeves, it suits you." Normally tradition dictated that the family name did not alter upon marriage. However, Myrbeth had never known her family or any other name but that given her by her mother.

"While it feels strange, I suppose it also feels right, like finally coming home." Frederick kissed her again and Trevard decided to leave them in their wedded bliss.